M000211174

RAVE REVIEWS FOR
HEIDI BETTS'S *ROSE* TRILOGY

"[*Almost A Lady*] is just too excellent for words! . . . An exciting read that will most certainly hit the bestseller lists!"
—*Huntress Book Reviews*

"*Cinnamon and Roses* is an engaging and fast-paced tale . . . a well-crafted debut novel that will leave readers eager for Ms. Betts's next one. Excellent!
—*Rendezvous*

"Books like *Cinnamon and Roses* are few and far between. The story will tug at your heartstrings and tickle your funny bone . . . . *Cinnamon and Roses* is a keeper."
—*Reader to Reader*

"A delightful romance that enthralled and enchanted me from the beginning. An outstanding read."
—*Rendezvous* on *A Promise of Roses*

"Snappy dialogue makes this a quick read."
—*Romantic Times* on *A Promise of Roses*

"The dialogue is dynamic, the writing superb! Ms. Betts is an absolutely wonderful writer . . . . Don't miss any of [the *Rose* trilogy]! FANTASTIC! 5 BELLS!"
—*Bell Book & Candle* on *A Promise of Roses*

"Ms. Betts's *Rose* trilogy is well worth reading."
—*Old Book Barn Gazette*

ALMOST A MARRIAGE

Brandt shifted on the cushioned seat. "It will be interesting during this little adventure to see how well we share a bedroom . . . and a bed, don't you think?"

What little oxygen the tight corset allowed froze in her lungs. Swallowing hard, she forced herself to look him in the eye. His lips were crooked in a sexy, suggestive grin, but she steeled herself against his charm. "We'll share accommodations by necessity, not by choice. And I'm trusting you to keep your hands—as well as your lascivious thoughts—to yourself," she added with what she hoped was a firm hands-off glare. "I don't let personal issues muddle the clear lines of an investigation."

The cocky grin remained while his eyes drifted over her face, her shoulders, down to the swell of her breasts. "Usually," he said softly.

She raised a brow. "Excuse me?"

"Usually," he repeated. "You don't *usually* let personal issues conflict with professional ones." His gaze held hers, his hazel eyes burning like hot coals. "You're a woman. I'm a man. It's obvious we're attracted to one another. It's going to be hard to ignore that attraction while sharing a chamber, a bed, a marriage—however fraudulent."

"It may be difficult," Willow said, "but I do hope you'll try." Because God knew, she didn't have the strength to resist him alone.

Heidi Betts

ALMOST A Lady

LEISURE BOOKS   B   NEW YORK CITY

A LEISURE BOOK®

January 2001

Published by

Dorchester Publishing Co., Inc.
276 Fifth Avenue
New York, NY 10001

ISBN 0-8439-4817-5

Printed in the United States of America.

Visit us on the web at www.dorchesterpub.com.

To Sandra Hill—for everything. For all the years of critique and conferences; for pushing me into my first agent/editor appointments and teaching me everything I need to know about promotion; for being such a great friend and mentor. And most of all, for saying you think this is my best book yet.

ACKNOWLEDGMENTS

A very special thank you to Harvey Turner and Tim Hartman of the Union Pacific Corporation in Bethlehem, Pennsylvania. Years ago, you took the time to talk to a budding author about the history of the Union Pacific Railroad, and to answer my many questions. There's only one thing I've never figured out for sure: Would Brandt and Willow sleep on the top or bottom berth of a Union Pacific sleeper car?

ALMOST A Lady

Prologue

His eyes darted up and down the dock. Other than a few drunken sailors and painted prostitutes, the dark, fog-shrouded wharf of the Lower East Side was nearly deserted.

Perfect, he thought. Perfect.

He tapped the roof of the carriage with his cane, giving instructions to the driver—also his valet and trusted companion. He chuckled wickedly. Outram would never speak a word of what he witnessed to anyone, of that he could be certain. Poor Outram had lost his tongue at the age of fifteen to an abusive father.

The shiny black carriage slowed, pulling up beside a petite young woman. Strands of dirty black hair fell from the loose coil atop her head. A well-worn, dark blue shawl covered shoulders left bare by her camisole. Which, along with a heavy, too-short woolen skirt was all she wore.

He pushed open the door, beckoning her into the car-

15

riage. She glanced warily inside, hesitating. He extended a hand, giving her a comforting smile. "It's all right, my dear. No harm will come to you."

Her delicate fingers shook as she took his proffered hand. She climbed in, perching nervously on the burgundy cushion opposite him. Two quick taps to the roof signaled the vehicle once more into motion.

"Don't mean to seem so jumpy," she said with a mottled accent common to immigrants new to America. "It's just that we're all kind o' skittish lately. The last body was found not a mile from here."

"Body?" he asked, his tone flat, showing no concern whatsoever.

"Two of 'em now. Some bastard's been cuttin' up us workin' girls and dumpin' the bodies near the East River." She shifted uneasily. "That's why I didn't hop in your buggy right off. Have to be careful these days."

"Indeed you do."

"So where are we headed?" she asked, straining her neck to see through the small space between the fluttering curtain and the window.

"Not far," he answered. "Don't worry, my dear, I'll return you to the wharf soon enough."

Chapter One

Jefferson City, Missouri, 1886

"Care to try that again?" She bobbed to the right, bouncing on the balls of her feet, waiting for Sammy to take another drunken swing. "Come on, Sammy, give it up," she coaxed.

"Who are you, mister?" he asked, a moment before striking out with a weak right hook.

The punch grazed her shoulder. She stumbled back a step before regaining her footing and landing a solid punch to his midsection. He dropped to the ground with a heavy thump.

With the sky turning to dusk, few people were out, but her eyes darted to either end of the darkened alley, assuring herself that their conversation was still a private one. "Now, are you going to come willingly, or do I have to do a little more convincing?"

"No, no." Sammy raised his hands in surrender. "I won't give you any more trouble."

"Good." She pulled a pearl-handled Smith & Wesson revolver from the waistband of her pants. "Get up."

Sammy stumbled to his feet, his eyes blotched red from too much drink.

"Turn around." She flattened his hands against the side of the building, smoothing hers down his body from shoulders to ankles to check for weapons. "Fancy that, Sammy. You haven't been this clean since the day you were born."

"I didn't do nothin'," he protested.

"You squealed on your best friend for a bottle of whiskey and a train ticket out of town."

He whirled around. His beady eyeballs nearly popped the sockets of his long, narrow face. "H-how'd you know about th-that?"

Her free hand slipped inside the pocket of her over-sized coat for a set of heavy metal handcuffs. "It's my job to know these things, Sammy," she replied easily, motioning him back toward the wall.

The hairs on the back of her neck rose as she sensed a change in her surroundings. Her head swung around a second before she heard the deep male voice.

"Hey! What are you doing?"

The stranger stepped closer, into the shadows of the alley, until all she could make out clearly was the broad expanse of his shoulders.

The barrel of her gun pressed more deeply into Sammy's back as she replaced the cuffs in her pocket, readying herself to deal with this newest threat. "This ain't none of your concern," she told him, making her voice unnaturally rough. "Mind your business and get the hell out of here."

"I don't think so," he said evenly.

"You gotta help me, mister," Sammy whined.

"Shut up, Sammy," she growled.

But Sammy didn't heed the warning. He edged forward a step. "I told him I ain't got no money on me, but he don't believe it. You gotta help me," he pleaded with the stranger. " 'Fore he shoots me in the back."

The last thing she needed was some good Samaritan poking his nose where it didn't belong. With any luck, he'd back off and she wouldn't have to shoot him.

The stranger took another step forward.

So much for that, she thought.

"I'd hate to waste a bullet killing an innocent man," she said, changing the direction of her aim.

He stared down the barrel of the revolver. "I'd hate to die," he replied smoothly.

"Then just turn around and walk away."

"I can't do that."

Suddenly Sammy broke free, racing for the street.

"Sammy!" She aimed for his thigh, intending to hobble, not kill him.

But before she could get off a shot, the stranger barreled into her, knocking her to her back on the hard ground. The air rushed out of her lungs as the revolver spun across the ground, out of reach.

She kicked, but the man pinned her legs. She tried to wriggle away, but strong hands pressed into her shoulders, keeping her flat.

"Give it up," he ordered.

Her struggles ceased. She forced herself to relax, letting her muscles go slack.

"Good," the man said.

She watched him carefully, waiting for his guard to drop.

He sat up on his haunches, straddling her hips. "Christ, for such a scrawny fellow, you sure can hold your own," he said, wiping the palms of his hands on his thighs as he got to his feet. "We both know the odds are against you, mister. Get up." He extended an arm in her direction.

She watched him carefully. "You taking me to jail?" she asked.

"You did try to rob that man," was his only answer.

Letting out a breath, she lowered her eyes in defeat. With great reluctance, she put her hand in his. He gave a tug and pulled her to her feet.

"Let's go," he said, beginning to turn, as though he expected her to follow.

Lightning-quick, she struck out with the heel of her hand, catching him on the side of the face, just below the eye. He gave a yelp of pain. She knocked him off balance, propelling him into the nearest building, while in the same motion drawing a pearl-handled stiletto from inside her boot.

Her fingers curled around the collar of his shirt. "For such a big man, you sure don't have much brains," she said.

Brandt's eyes narrowed. There was something not quite right about this whole scenario. How had a man of such small stature gotten the drop on him—all six feet three inches of him? And why would this fellow be robbing a man with clothes more tattered than his own?

He looked more closely at his captor's face. Even in the muted evening light he took in long, thick lashes, high cheekbones, and smooth skin without a hint of beard stubble. And bright eyes the color of . . . amethyst.

His own eyes widened. His assailant was no man. "You're a—"

"Shut up. Unless you want to explain a new medical condition to your wife."

For a minute he didn't know what she meant. Then he felt the cool steel of a knife at his groin. His gaze darted downward in surprise a second before a grin spread across his face. This woman might be the most able-bodied female he'd ever had the misfortune to run across, but there was no way she'd actually do as she threatened.

"Listen, you're not really going to do anything with that knife," he said.

"Oh, yeah?" The sharp point of the blade pressed against his inner thigh.

He winced. Maybe she did intend to use it. But even if she didn't, accidents happened. She might slip. And he might end up a eunuch.

"I'm going to be real sweet and give you two choices. You can either walk away and never look back, or you can become uncommonly intimate with the blade of my knife." She moved the stiletto a little to the left, cutting into the sensitive flesh of his manhood. "Which is it going to be?" she asked.

"I think I'd like to keep everything right where it is," he said.

She slid the knife from between his legs, slowly. "Then I suggest you start walking."

He cleared his throat, tugging at the front of his trousers to make sure everything was intact.

"It's still there," she told him. "But it won't be for long if you don't get moving."

The silver blade glittered in the pale lamplight. As she palmed the weapon, Brandt noticed a uniquely intricate design carved into the pearl handle. It looked like two forms standing beneath the bowed branches of a large tree.

He raised his head, taking in her loose trousers, baggy black jacket, and knit cap tugged down about her ears.

21

But a heart-shaped face and sparkling eyes belied the masculine ensemble.

And no mere woman was going to get the drop on him.

His hand shot out, grabbing her wrist in a vicelike grip. With a harsh yank, he turned her away from him, twisting her arm behind her back. "Drop the knife," he hissed.

For a moment, she struggled against him, knuckles white on the hilt of the blade. Then her grip loosened. The weapon fell to the dirt with a thud.

He let go of her wrist, sliding an arm seductively about her waist. He couldn't decipher any feminine curves, but that did not dispel his belief in her gender.

"So tell me what a woman is doing out at this time of night," he whispered above her ear. "Dressed like a man."

He didn't feel her movement until the heel of her boot made contact with his shin. Shards of razor-sharp pain splintered up his leg. At the same time, she drove her elbow into his stomach. He doubled over, cursing a rainbow of colorful language.

The woman grabbed up her knife and revolver and took off down the alley without a backward glance.

Brandt limped after her for several paces, then stopped at the corner of the building to soothe his bruised and battered body. A favor to a friend had brought him to this godforsaken town, and he was none too happy about it. But he would take tracking down a simple songbird looking for her missing brother over following *that* woman any day.

And, suddenly, going after Willow Hastings didn't seem like such a trial after all.

Chapter Two

A knock sounded on the door. "Ten minutes, Willow," a woman's voice warned.

Grunting, Willow pushed herself the rest of the way through the window, hitting the floor with a solid clunk. "Coming," she managed to call out.

Ten minutes.

She pulled off her cap, shaking the curl back into her long hair. She'd have been back and ready in plenty of time if that brainless Neanderthal hadn't interfered with her plans.

The heavy black coat, boots, and trousers joined the cap in a pile in the corner. Now she was unprepared to go on stage *and* she'd lost Sammy the Snake. Robert would not be happy about that.

With more force than necessary, she tugged her favorite royal blue show dress over her head. It took some doing, but the stiff fabric finally molded itself to her body. The tight, tapered waist left little to the imagination, and only a few well-placed black ruffles kept her bosom from being completely exposed by the off-the-shoulder gown.

She gave herself a quick once-over in the full-length mirror. If she didn't hit the high notes tonight, at least she knew the audience—entirely male—would enjoy the view.

She grabbed a pair of pale silk stockings from the bureau, hurriedly sliding them on. Royal blue garters, the same color as her dress, held them in place. Removing the stiletto scabbard from her boot, she slipped it through the garter on the inside of her thigh. She never went anywhere without at least one weapon.

"Five minutes." Beverly, the house's madam, tapped rapid-fire on the door.

"Coming," she yelled again. With a quick twist, she fixed the hair atop her head, leaving a fall of brownish-red curls to cascade down her back.

Francis and Robert, her Pinkerton supervisors, would both kill her if they knew she was singing in a saloon/whorehouse, she thought. The Agency motto might be, "We Never Sleep," but personally, Willow liked "We Get the Job Done" better. What did it matter how she solved a case, as long as she solved it?

She headed for the door, then stopped abruptly. "Shoes." Her eyes scanned the room. No shoes. "Where are they?" she mumbled, throwing open the closet door. When she didn't find them there, either, she got down on her hands and knees and started rooting around under the bed.

"Shoes, shoes, shoes . . ." They had to be somewhere. She'd worn the dark blue slippers just last week.

She heard the door open behind her and let out a long-suffering sigh. If her singing didn't draw such a crowd, Beverly wouldn't have cared less if Willow was on stage on time or not. But the men who came to see the show ultimately stuck around to spend money on Bev's girls.

"I'm coming," she said. "Give me a minute."

"Take your time."

At the deep male voice, Willow swung around, cracking her head none too gently on the wooden bed frame. "Son of a bitch," she swore, rubbing what was sure to be a good-sized goose egg in the morning.

Then her eyes widened as she recognized the man standing just inside her room. The brainless Neanderthal. Six-plus feet of pure masculinity. In the well-lit room, she noticed how truly handsome he was, with dancing green eyes fringed by sharp, defining russet brows. Tight doeskin breeches encased his muscular legs. The white of his shirt peeked through the vee of a buttoned, dark brown jacket. Clean-cut from his short chestnut hair to his spit-shined black boots. A high-class dandy if ever she'd seen one.

The sight of his yellowish, red-tinged cheekbone made her flinch inwardly. She rarely saw the results of her defense methods.

It's a coincidence that he's here, she thought. *He can't possibly know I'm the person from the alley. Stay calm.*

She smiled. "Can I help you with something, honey?" she asked in her best brothel voice.

"They told me this is Willow Hastings's room. You must be Willow."

Panic squeezed through her chest. *How does he know who I am? And why is he here?* "That's right," she answered. "And who might you be?"

"The name's Brandt Donovan. I'm a friend of Lucas and Megan McCain."

The tension poured out of her body in a wave of relief. "Lucas and Megan," she said. Her brow creased with sudden dread. "Is something wrong? Oh, please tell me Megan and the baby are all right."

Brandt watched Willow closely. She seemed truly concerned. He couldn't help but see the irony of the situation. Lucas and Megan were sitting home, frantic over this woman's safety, and here she was, fearing for them.

"They're all fine." He saw the lines of worry in her face ease. "Megan's stomach still enters a room ten minutes before the rest of her, but everyone's doing well. They're awfully concerned about you, though."

"Me?" she asked, perplexed. "Whatever for?"

"They haven't heard from you in a while, and Megan's gotten it into her head that you're in trouble."

"Oh, how sweet," she said. "Tell them I'm fine and that I'll write to them soon. I promise." She moved toward the door, obviously expecting him to step aside.

"I'm afraid it's not that simple, Miss Hastings. Lucas and Megan asked me to make sure you're all right. I can't assure them of your safety until I'm sure myself."

Her face held an odd expression, as though no one had concerned themselves with her welfare in a very long time.

"Willow, get moving!" a woman shouted from the hall.

Willow kept her eyes locked with his a moment longer. Then she seemed to shake off whatever emotion kept her silent. "I appreciate the trouble you went through to find me, Mr. . . . Donovan, did you say?"

He nodded.

"Well, Mr. Donovan, I do thank you. But if you want any more assurance of my safety, you'll have to wait until later. I've got a show to do."

"Show?"

"Yes, a show. You don't think I'm wearing this getup

to attract customers, do you?" she asked, tilting a hip seductively.

One side of Brandt's mouth quirked up in a lascivious grin. His gaze raked down her body. With all the hills and valleys cinched into that tight little dress, that's exactly what he'd thought. Her mouth looked infinitely kissable. Pink and pouting, just begging for a man's attention.

Although his tastes usually slanted toward blondes, there was something about this curvy brunette that made him want to give up a month's pay to spend one hour in her bed.

"Yeah," he admitted. "I guess I did."

"Tut-tut, Mr. Donovan," she chastised, walking past him to open the door. "Assumption of a woman's low morals is not an attractive trait in a man." She stepped into the hall, then stopped and turned back to him. A smile curved her full, rosy lips. "You might want to remember that."

One brow winged upward as Brandt watched her saunter down the long hall. His gaze slid from the wavy curls of her reddish-brown hair to the narrow nip of her waist, to the exaggerated sway of her hips. For his benefit, no doubt.

"Hey, Dora," he heard her call to one of the girls loitering in a paneled doorway. "Those are my shoes." He glanced toward the floor as Willow bent to retrieve a pair of sapphire slippers from the other woman's feet.

He couldn't contain a chuckle at the sight of her stockinged toes peeking out from beneath the hem of her gown. Would she really have gone on stage in her bare feet?

Probably.

He pushed away from the doorjamb, ambling down the hall in the direction in which Willow had gone. He

27

wanted to make sure everything was okay before reporting back to Lucas and Megan. Plus, he grinned ruefully, he'd be damned if he was going to forego the show.

Brandt took a seat at one of the tables closest to the wide plank platform. He didn't want to miss a note, not an inhaled breath or fluttered eyelash of the woman about to take the stage.

Voices hummed through the room. Men clustered around the tables, bar, and doorway, filling the Silver Spur near to overflowing. To Brandt's surprise, no women speckled the crowd. Not one feminine form mulled about in an establishment known for its hard liquor and easy women. And, strangest of all, no one seemed to mind.

Raucous hoots filled the air when a busty woman with wide hips and jet-black hair sauntered onto the stage. Her purple gown clashed brutally against the blood-red curtains that hid the rest of the performance area.

"All right, all right," she called over the noise. But her smile said she didn't mind the ruckus a bit. "Hush up, you randy bastards," she shouted. "Do you want to see the show or not?"

More catcalls and wild applause greeted her question.

"All right, then. Here she is, our very own songbird . . . Willow." She walked off the platform as the curtains parted.

The piano man tapped out the first tinging notes of an old Missouri favorite, "Flat River Girl," and a hush fell over the audience.

Willow stood in the center of the stage, in all her regal splendor. The sapphire blue of her dress shone in the bright luminescence of the chandelier overhead. Auburn highlights streaked through her otherwise light brown hair.

Brandt watched the rise of her breasts as she took a deep breath and began her song.

"Come, all you fine young fellows with hearts so warm and true,
Oh, never believe in a woman, you're lost, boys, if you do;
But if you ever see one with long brown chestnut curls,
Just think of Big Jack Haggerty and his Flat River Girl."

Brandt sat back, in awe of the effect she seemed to have on the audience. A rougher, tougher, more deviant crowd he'd never seen, and yet the gentle caress of her voice lulled them into an almost frightening calm. He would expect this sort of respectful silence from those who frequented the higher-class theaters and opera houses in Boston, New York, or even St. Louis. But in a cowtown like Jefferson City, Missouri? In a brothel by the name of the Silver Spur?

The song drew to a close, but the room remained cloaked in appreciative quiet. It was obvious they knew there was more to come.

"I met her on the mountain, and there I took her life," Willow sang sorrowfully, accompanied by the tinny notes of the off-key piano. *"I met her on the mountain, and stabbed her with my knife."*

Brandt noticed that her bottom lip trembled just a bit as she began the chorus.

The tune that followed "Tom Dooley" was another ballad sad enough to tear at even the hardest of hearts.

Heidi Betts

"He was just a lonely cowboy
With a heart so brave and true,
And he learned to love a maiden
With eyes of heaven's blue.

They learned to love each other
And named their wedding day,
When a quarrel came between them
And Jack, he rode away."

She strode across the stage, smiling wistfully at the audience, making eye contact with those she could see, treating each man like he was the only one in the room.

Brandt couldn't believe it. When the song ended with Jack's lady on her deathbed, pledging her love to him, Brandt actually thought he saw a few of the men around him dabbing at their eyes. A quick shake of his head failed to dispel the image. He'd have bet a thousand dollars that nothing short of a visit from the devil himself could wrench a tear from these hardened men.

Suddenly Willow slapped her leg and let out a wild whoop. Two dozen girls, all dressed alike in gaudy, thigh-high red- and white-striped outfits, danced onto the stage behind her. Linked arm in arm, they skittered across the wooden platform, yipping and yawing and singing along—though not always in key—to a loud, lively rendition of "Old Dan Tucker."

Half an hour later, singing the foot-stomping ditty for the third time in a row, the candy canes—as Brandt had come to think of them—skipped their way off the stage and into the melee of eager cowboys. He watched them for a few minutes, then turned his head back to where Willow stood.

Or where she'd been standing. He got to his feet,

straining his neck for any glimpse of sapphire blue. But all he saw was an empty stage.

"Damn," he swore, bumping his way through the crowd, searching for Willow Hastings. But it was no use.

She was gone.

Chapter Three

Dearest Papa,

Please don't be angry with me, but I've lost Grandfather's gold pocket watch. I know how much the watch meant to you and would do anything to retrieve it. I do believe someone must have interfered with its placement.

I will continue to search for the watch as I await word from you.

Your loving daughter,
Willow

Willow quickly scrawled her name across the bottom of the page. Sealing it with a smear of melted wax, she tucked the letter beneath a corner of the mattress until she could see it safely posted.

That done, she gave a calming sigh and moved across the room. She stripped out of her confining show clothes and hung the blue dress in the wardrobe, tossing the matching slippers in after it.

"Ahh," she sighed, wiggling her pinched toes. She strode to the bed, tying the sash of her red oriental robe, a seething golden dragon surrounded by exotic flora emblazoned on the back. The robe had been a gift from Robert after one of his many trips overseas.

Balancing one foot on the high mattress, she slipped the scabbard from her garter. Without concentrating, without even taking aim, she hurtled the knife at the far wall. The dagger hit its mark—a notch left in the rough wood from a time when Willow had been bored enough to practice her marksmanship while hanging upside down over the side of the bed.

Willow sighed and flung the leather sheath toward her pile of earlier discarded clothes. She slid the dark blue garter past her knee and down the rest of her leg. Then she began rolling the soft silk stocking over the same path.

As she lifted her other foot to the bed, the red satin of her robe fell away, revealing the length of her leg from ankle to hip.

"Lovely."

Willow raised her head, not the least bit surprised to find someone in the doorway of her room. There were no locks on the doors, and Beverly's girls were always popping in to borrow this or that—which was why she hid anything she didn't want them accidentally "discovering."

What did surprise her was seeing Brandt Donovan standing just inside her room, looking for all the world like he belonged there. She'd forgotten about him during her performance, assuming he would take one of the girls upstairs after the show like the other men did.

She began to suspect that Brandt Donovan was not at all like other men.

"I do have impeccable timing," he said, closing the door behind him. A wolfish gleam shone in his eyes as he stared unabashedly at the ample view of her leg.

Willow knew he meant to intimidate her with his lustful glare. And if she ever made a habit of anything, it was not backing down.

She hooked a finger under the tight lace of her garter, dragging it slowly, seductively down her thigh. It caught on the angle of her knee and she leaned forward to help it along, knowing that when she did so, the front of her robe would fall open to reveal a risqué amount of lush flesh. She'd worn no frilly undergarments earlier with her male clothing and hadn't had time to put any on before dressing for her performance. There was nothing beneath the robe that God hadn't given her. She wondered if Brandt could tell.

The garter fell to her ankle and she slipped it carefully over her foot. "Like what you see, Mr. Donovan?"

She couldn't help but notice that his gaze had shifted to her bosom. It took him a full minute to respond to her question.

He cleared his throat, forcing his eyes to her face. "Excuse me?"

Willow lowered her head, a secret smile playing on her lips. "I asked if you like what you see." She snapped the garter at him, hoping to catch him off guard.

The lace band landed against his chest. He caught it with one hand before it could fall to the floor. "Let's just say I have no complaints."

"I'm glad to hear it." She rolled the stocking down her calf, letting it fall in a silken heap on the bedspread. No longer having an excuse to tempt him with her bare flesh, she lowered her foot and adjusted the sash at her waist.

"Was there something you needed?" she asked, well aware of the double entendre in her words.

He didn't take the bait.

"I told you I wasn't leaving until I made sure you're all right."

She put her hands on her hips, throwing back her shoulders so that her breasts pressed firmly against the front of the robe. "Don't I look all right to you, Mr. Donovan?"

His eyes raked down her body. An amused grin curved his lips. "You look like a woman who could get herself into a boatload of trouble."

She chuckled. "I admit to stirring things up once in a while, but I assure you, sir, I am in no danger whatsoever."

"And what am I supposed to tell Megan and Lucas?"

"Tell them I'm fine. Tell them you saw me with your own two eyes and that I looked perfectly healthy. Better yet," she offered, an idea dawning on her, "I'll write a quick note for you to deliver to them. That ought to put their minds at ease." She moved to the bureau, pulling a sheet of paper out of the top drawer.

"*Dear Megan and Lucas,*" she wrote, speaking aloud for Brandt's benefit. "*Your friend . . .* How do you spell your name?" she asked.

"B-r-a-n-d-t."

"How original." She quickly scrawled his name on the page. "*Your friend, Brandt Donovan, is hovering over me as I write this at the Silver Spur in Jefferson City, Missouri.* I like to let them know where I am," she said, casting a glance in his direction. "*I'm sorry I didn't write sooner, but please rest assured that I am fine and in no danger. I simply got sidetracked and forgot to answer your last letter. I feel terrible that I worried you so.*

"Still no word from Jeremy, and no new information about his whereabouts. I will write again as soon as I can. Until then, please know that I am safe.

"Megan, please take care of yourself, and let me know when the baby arrives. Love to all. There." She signed it and handed the letter to Brandt. "Does that meet with your approval?"

His eyes scanned the note. "Who's Jeremy?"

"My brother," she told him, avoiding eye contact by busying herself with straightening the pile of stationery in the dresser drawer.

"The one who's missing?"

"I only have one brother, Mr. Donovan. And, yes, he's been missing for several years now."

"Maybe he doesn't want to be found."

She turned to meet his gaze. "Perhaps. But I don't intend to stop looking."

When he spoke again, his tone was soft. "There's always a chance that he met up with something he couldn't handle."

"What you mean to say is that there's a chance he's dead—has been all along."

Brandt looked away. "It's a possibility."

"Don't you think I've considered that?" she asked quietly. "But even if it's true, I at least want to find out what happened. I have a right to know."

"Then I wish you luck."

"Thank you."

"But I'm not returning to Leavenworth," Brandt said, handing the letter back to her. "I'm moving on to Boston. I was supposed to telegraph Lucas and Megan when I found you."

"Well, then," she said, stuffing the paper into an envelope. "You can tell them in your telegram that I'm fine, and that they should be getting a letter from me soon." She waved the sealed letter in front of him. "You saw me write it, after all. And I promise to post it first thing in the morning."

Brandt shrugged. "Fair enough."

"Now, I've written to Lucas and Meg, you're going to telegraph them in the morning, and you've seen for yourself that I am in perfect health. I think that takes care of just about all your concerns."

"Guess so," he said, but made no move to leave.

"Then why are you still here?" she asked bluntly.

He took a step forward. And then another, backing her up against the edge of the bed. His arm snaked around her waist, pulling her flush with his tall form. "I was thinking, as long as I'm here, that we might see just how healthy you really are."

"That's a lovely offer," she said, ignoring the heat that seemed to envelop her body at his nearness. "But I really must decline."

A thick, dark eyebrow quirked upwards. "Why is that?"

She ran a slim finger over his swollen cheekbone. The skin, beginning to bruise, was now tinged a sickly shade of purplish-blue. "Because it looks like you've already tangled with one wildcat tonight." She pressed her lips softly to his and whispered, "I'd hate to do you any more damage."

Brandt leaned back in the stiffly uncomfortable train seat. He punched at his rolled-up jacket, hoping to transform it into some type of makeshift pillow. Cursing under his breath, shifting position, he admitted that his discomfort had less than nothing to do with his jacket, the train seat, or the woman snoring noisily across the aisle from him.

No, his mood didn't hinge on any of these small annoyances. It was due much more to the fact that his body had yet to cool down after such close contact with one Willow Hastings.

And he couldn't believe he'd walked out of her room.

Not after smelling the rose scent of her sweet perfume, touching the velvety softness of her lips.

Not after being close enough to feel her breasts against his chest, her taut nipples burning his skin. Hearing her breathy whisper. *Looks like you've already tangled with one wildcat tonight. I'd hate to do you any more damage.* He could just imagine the kind of wildcat she'd be in bed. All sharp claws and purring moans.

Not after feeling her hair brush over his arm more softly than the satin of that blasted red robe. And he was damned sure she hadn't been wearing anything underneath. The thought of red satin brushing seductively over Willow's slim, lithe form sent another bolt of desire through him. Christ, he had to find himself a willing woman—and soon!

Two weeks later

Willow hurried back from the post office, the letter from Robert tucked securely within the folds of her blouse so no one would see it. She hurried through the empty saloon and upstairs to her room.

With her thumb, she broke the seal on the envelope and with careful fingers she removed the folded paper.

My dearest daughter, Willow,

I am very upset to hear that you lost Grandfather's pocket watch. You know how much the piece was worth and how much it meant to me. I think it would be best if you returned home now. Send word

*as to when you will be arriving so that I may meet
you at the railroad station.*

Signed,
Your loving father

Uh-oh; Robert was not happy. She could always tell
when he was upset, even in his letters. The order for her
to return home rather than track down Sammy the Snake
meant that Robert was practically livid.

Willow moved to the wardrobe to change clothes. She
put on a burgundy taffeta traveling gown and comfortable button-up boots, then opened her faded carpet bag
and began searching every nook and cranny of the room
for her belongings.

An hour later, she was on a train bound for New York
City.

Chapter Four

Willow smoothed a pair of black satin gloves over her fingers and readjusted the long pin in her bonnet as the Union Pacific pulled into Grand Central Station. She was back in New York City, and back to dressing like a lady rather than a dance hall girl. The part came easily to her, as did all of her different guises. Sometimes she wondered how anybody could live with only one personality when role playing was oh-so-much fun.

The car lurched to a stop, disturbing the feathered black hat she had just pinned in place. As she stood to stretch her legs and neck, a familiar face near the vestibule area caught her attention. She narrowed her eyes, trying to make out the man's features through a crowd bustling to collect their things and depart the train.

The man closed the door between carriage cars and moved closer. She noticed that he seemed distracted, perhaps even nervous, glancing over his shoulder every other step.

"Charlie?" she called quietly as he passed.

He stopped in his tracks, looking at her with wide eyes.

"Charlie Barker, I thought that was you."

"Willow." It was a breath of relief. He shifted his position so that he stood next to her, facing the direction from which he'd just come. "How've you been?" he asked, fingers fumbling in his coat pocket.

"Fine. And you?" Something was wrong. It didn't take a professional sleuth to figure that out. Charlie was more nervous than a long-tailed cat in a room full of rockers. And in their line of business, nervousness spelled trouble. Big trouble.

"What is it, Charlie?" She put her hand on his arm and felt the skin jump.

"Nothing," he said, almost too quickly. Then he smiled, a gesture meant to reassure her. "It's nothing. Just a case I've been working on. Great seeing you again," he said distractedly as he moved away.

She opened her mouth to stop him, but he'd already headed down the aisle, and as she took a step after him, her taffeta skirts caught on the corner of the cushioned seat. She yanked the burgundy material free, but when she turned back, Charlie was gone. Muttering under her breath about mule-headed men and company secrets, she gathered her things.

With carpetbag in one hand and burgundy-and-black, fringed parasol in the other, she took her place in the slow-moving line of departing passengers.

Her eyes scanned the dusty windowpanes, hoping to find Robert waiting for her on the platform outside. He was meeting her at the station—no doubt to chew her out for fouling up with Sammy.

She thought she saw him and raised a hand to tap the glass when a woman's scream rent the air. Followed by

41

another and another, until the train filled with the shrill wails of female hysterics.

Willow dropped her bag and parasol, pushing her way to the front of the crowd.

She spotted him immediately, lying on the floor of the passenger car in a pool of blood. His hands clutched at his side, where red ooze poured from his body.

"Charlie!" she cried, sinking to her knees beside him. She gathered the thick folds of her skirt and pressed them to his wound, hoping to staunch the flow of blood. Her eyes darted around for some sign of the culprit. A suspicious passenger, a depraved lunatic standing in the foreground watching the results of his task. But no one stood out.

"Someone find a doctor. Hurry!" she screamed at the people behind her. "Hold on, Charlie. Help is on the way." But she didn't know if it was, and the color was leaving his face faster than steam from a boiling teapot.

She pressed more firmly on her skirts. He winced. Then his hand came up to grasp her arm, his fingers ice cold against her skin. He shoved a small square of paper into her hand.

"He's . . . the one." The words were garbled, loud enough for only Willow to hear. A fit of coughing overtook him and blood bubbled at the corner of his mouth. "Careful. Be . . . careful." His eyes shone hard as steel for the flicker of a moment before his body went limp, his head lolling to the side.

"No. Charlie, wake up." She pounded on his chest, trying to revive him by sheer force of will. "Dammit, Charlie, you can't die on me."

Someone stepped forward from behind her, coming to one knee beside Charlie Barker's prone form to check for a pulse. "I'm sorry, miss, but he's gone."

Tears stung the backs of her eyes as she shook her

head in denial. She hadn't watched anyone die since her mother, and that had been more than ten years before. Thankfully, her father had simply walked away one day. And, not surprisingly, in a matter of weeks he had been found lying dead in a gutter with a broken neck, stinking to high heaven of rotgut whiskey and unwashed flesh.

"Blast and damn," Willow heard from somewhere over her left shoulder. She swung around to see Robert Pinkerton, dressed in a fine gray wool Mackintosh overcoat and black galoshes, standing not three feet behind her. He cocked back the rim of his bowler hat with one finger.

"That's Charles Barker, isn't it?"

Willow nodded, then launched herself into his arms. He held her close, patting her back with brotherly concern.

"Did you see who did it?" he asked.

She lifted her head, embarrassed by her rare show of female waterworks. But it did give her an opportunity to hide the paper Charlie had given her. From her sleeve, she pulled a white lace handkerchief—at the same time stuffing the square of paper far enough into her cuff that it wouldn't accidentally fall out—and dabbed at her eyes.

It wasn't that she didn't trust Robert with whatever information the note held. Quite the opposite, actually; she trusted Robert with her life. But the idea of turning over evidence, perhaps a piece of crucial information, before she herself had a chance to look it over didn't appeal to her. Not in the least.

And if it turned out to be nothing, or if she didn't understand whatever clues rested within the folds of that paper, then she would give it to Robert and claim that in the confusion of the moment she had forgotten all about it.

"Sequester everyone still on this car," Robert told the nearest conductor, showing the man his identification and Pinkerton badge. "And don't let anyone near the crime scene until the police arrive."

"Yes, sir, Mr. Pinkerton."

Robert retrieved Willow's valise and parasol, then put his arm around her shoulders to guide her to the nearest exit.

"With respect, sir," the conductor began, inclining his head in Willow's direction, "this young lady was a passenger on the car as well."

"She is also a close acquaintance of mine. Though I'm sure she had nothing to do with this, I'll question her myself. And she'll be at my office should the police wish to talk to her. The Pinkerton Agency always cooperates with the authorities," Robert informed him. "When they show up, allow them to do their job without interference. Just be sure to request that my people be allowed to look things over before anyone leaves."

The conductor nodded, then turned to give orders to another railroad employee, while blocking the front exit with his body so panicked passengers couldn't escape.

Just as Robert and Willow stepped down from the train, two uniformed police officers came into view, racing along the platform toward the crowded railroad car. Robert stopped them before they could board the train.

Again he showed his identification as he filled the officers in on what had happened. "The victim is one of my men," he said, a thread of anger and pain evident in his voice. "Though this young lady was present during the incident, she also works for me, and I'd like to get her back to my office, so I'm turning the investigation over to you. I'll want to be closely involved, mind you, and should you need to speak with her"—he inclined his head in Willow's direction—"contact my office and she'll make herself available. I'd also like to send my people to question the passengers and search for evidence, if you don't mind."

Brandt flexed his fingers about the handle of the valise in his hand. Grand Central Station bustled all around him, the crowd shuffling past and bumping into him more than once. He forced a smile and acknowledged such collisions with no more than a polite nod.

He didn't particularly like this city. Too many people in too much of a hurry. He preferred the slower, more relaxed pace of Boston, where the Union Pacific kept their headquarters. Luckily, he had taken care of the piece of business that had brought him to New York and was now on the way back home to Boston.

Rounding another support post in the center of the station platform, Brandt lifted his bag over the head of a little girl whose gaze was fastened on a spot other than the path ahead. The train to his right was letting off passengers. One of them, a tall, bald gentleman, nearly knocked him down in his hurry to depart the station. Brandt muttered a curse and doubled his efforts to reach his train before he was overrun by the throng of people.

The first scream sounded natural enough, like some young lady happy to see a relative after a long separation. The second scream didn't sound quite so common. Even though he ran the risk of being trampled, Brandt stopped, cocking his ear to listen more closely.

Like a row of dominoes, the entire train burst into a panic. He crouched down, trying to see through the small, smudged windows lining the passenger car. All he could make out was a gathering of people crammed together near the front of the compartment.

In one long stride, he pulled himself onto the back of the car, but try as he might, he couldn't get through the crowd or make sense of the conversations buzzing around his head. After several minutes of trying to understand the situation, he settled, instead, for leaning over the railing and looking around the other side of the cab.

He recognized her immediately. With her head tucked against the shoulder of a well-dressed gentleman, Willow Hastings made her way across the platform, away from Brandt. Even dressed to the nines, Brandt knew it was the same woman he'd encountered at the Silver Spur in Missouri.

But what was she doing in New York?

He called her name, but she either didn't hear or chose to ignore him, for she never slowed her pace. Planning to follow her, he turned around, but curious onlookers had piled on behind him, blocking his only exit.

"Damn!" he swore, pounding a fist on the metal rail.

What was Willow doing here, he wondered, when she'd seemed so adamant about staying in Jefferson City until she found her brother?

News filtered back through the crowd and one word caught Brandt's attention. *Murder.*

Someone had been murdered on a Union Pacific train. And Willow had been right in the thick of things. Why didn't that surprise him?

If a murder had occurred on a Union Pacific train, a UP officer would have to investigate. And as he was Head of Security and already at the scene of the crime, he was obligated to take the case whether he wanted it or not.

He let out a tortured sigh and made his way slowly back to the platform. It didn't look like he'd be leaving for Boston after all.

Chapter Five

With Robert's arm around her stooped shoulders, they moved quickly through crowded Grand Central Station, hailing a hackney cab to take them to his office at 66 Exchange Place.

As Willow passed beneath the Pinkerton symbol, an unblinking eye and the words WE NEVER SLEEP, she thought of Allan Pinkerton, the company's founder. She had known him briefly, before his death in July of 1884. In that short time, she had decided that he was one of the greatest men ever to walk the earth.

It was because of the elder Pinkerton that she now had a job with the Agency. Allan had taken her under his wing, convincing his son to train her and put her to work for the Agency's New York branch.

But she would be the first to admit that her job was in danger. Since Allan's death, the number of female detectives in the company had dwindled. Many supervisors didn't want women working for them, didn't trust a woman to do the job of a man. And so, slowly but surely, female operatives were being pushed out.

Willow had been lucky thus far. And she knew it was primarily because of Robert. Like his father, he had taken a special interest in her, assigning her simple tasks, guiding her through more difficult ones, until she was ready to go it alone.

He had taught her to dress and act like a man so she could disguise herself. To fight so that she could protect herself against even the most fearsome enemy. She smiled, remembering the moment student had surpassed teacher—and the limp Robert had suffered for more than a week.

But even Robert couldn't protect her position with the Agency if his superiors decided to fire her—or assign her so few cases that she would have no choice but to quit. He might be Allan Pinkerton's son, in charge of the eastern and southern sections of the United States, but he answered to Superintendent Warner the same as she.

And losing Sammy the Snake did not bode well for her. It wasn't a life-threatening case, or even one that particularly mattered in the scheme of things. But it would be a blemish in her otherwise flawless career file. An easy excuse to have her terminated.

They stopped to speak to Robert's personal secretary, a pleasant, vibrant older woman, who helped to keep the busy Agency organized.

"Mrs. Girard, Charlie Barker was killed this afternoon." Robert broke the news in a matter-of-fact voice.

The woman gasped.

Robert nodded solemnly and went on to give her a list of tasks. "Please find five available agents and send them to Grand Central. Then have an arrangement of flowers sent with our condolences tomorrow afternoon.

After I talk to Willow, I'll pay a visit to his wife to break the news, if the police haven't already. She needs to know we will do all we can to support and help her."

They passed into the privacy of his office. He set Willow's valise aside, took her wrap, and hung it on a row of hooks behind the door. His overcoat soon followed.

"Have a seat," he said, rounding the large, mahogany desk.

Not the least worried about her appearance in front of her old friend, she plopped down on the nearest chair, sinking into its cushioned depths.

"I see you've gotten yourself into another fine pickle," Robert observed.

"I wouldn't call it a pickle, really," Willow answered. "I'd say it's more of a full-blown cucumber."

He threw her a quelling glance. "I'm in no mood for your wit, Willow. This is serious."

"How well I know." She looked down at the stiff, stained folds of her skirt. Blood. Charlie's blood. Soaked through to her shift, no doubt. It took all of her willpower not to rip the clothes from her body just to rid herself of the metallic smell, the sticky feel of it.

"Are you all right?" he asked, brows drawn, regarding her closely.

"I'm fine," she said. She wasn't really, but it would do no one—including Charlie—any good for her to break down. She took a deep breath to steel her nerves. "Why do you ask?"

"Because a man died in your arms today, Willow. It's all right to show sorrow over that. It's all right to be afraid and to cry."

Willow noticed the slight shake in Robert's hands and realized he was far from unaffected himself. "I'll be fine, Robert. Truly. Please don't worry about me. I'd rather you put your energies into finding the man who murdered Charlie."

"Oh, we will, don't worry about that," he vowed, seemingly letting the topic of her well-being drop. But Willow knew better. He would keep an eye on her for a while to see that she really was holding up as well as she claimed.

"I suppose that's one of ours," Robert stated, looking pointedly at the hem of her dress.

Willow looked down at her marred gown and recognized Robert's attempt to change the subject. Talking about the high cost of fashion was a far sight better than thinking about the sight of Charlie's body, lying supine on the floor of that railroad car, and Willow was more than willing to play along. "Bought for the express purpose of infiltrating St. Louis high society," she told him.

"Cost a pretty penny, too, I'm sure." He relaxed into the soft black leather of his chair. "The Agency will replace the gown," he said. "Damned women operatives cost us an arm and a leg."

"I caught the bad guys, didn't I? And regained ten thousand dollars worth of stolen jewels, to boot."

He harrumphed, knowing it was the truth but too blasted stubborn to admit she'd done a damn fine job.

"I still want to know what the hell happened out in Missouri," he said, "but for now I'll settle for finding out what happened on the train."

"I don't know what happened," Willow answered honestly. "When Charlie stopped to talk to me, he seemed nervous. He kept looking over his shoulder, watching everyone around him."

"Did he tell you what was wrong?"

She shook her head. "I asked, but he said it was just a case." She met Robert's shadowed brown eyes. "What was he working on?"

"I can't tell you, you know that, Willow. A client's privacy—"

"I know, I know," she said, waving off the much-used line. " 'No operative may be privy to the information of a case in which he is not directly involved.' Well, Bobby, me boy," she said, switching to the brogue of his Scottish heritage, "I'd say I've been caught right in the thick of things." She stood to pace, eating up the length of the office with long, agitated strides.

Robert watched her for several long minutes, letting her burn off a good amount of energy and anger. Then he cut to the quick of the matter. "Did you see anything?"

"No." She stopped in front of his desk, resorting to the impatient tapping of one leather-clad foot. "He didn't seem to want to take the time to talk, and I didn't want to disturb his cover. Then some woman started screaming. The only thing I saw was Charlie lying in a pool of blood."

"Did you check the crowd?"

"For what? A man standing there with a bloody knife? My bet is, the murderer was gone before Charlie hit the floor. But, yes, I checked the crowd. As best I could without knowing what in blue blazes I was supposed to be looking for." She fixed Robert with a glare that conveyed her feelings in no uncertain terms. If he would only tell her what Charlie had been working on, she could answer his questions with more detail.

Willow noticed a strange light in Robert's eyes, a light that told her his mind was racing miles ahead of hers. "What?" she asked skeptically.

"How do you know the murderer used a knife?"

She rolled her eyes. "Because I didn't hear a shot, and the hole in Charlie's gut was leaking blood faster than Niagara Falls leaks water. When are you going to stop

51

testing me with these paltry schoolgirl questions?" she asked.

"When you no longer mess up on simple assignments like the one in Missouri."

Her mouth fell open. "Oh, now that's cruel, Robert Allan Pinkerton. You know darn good and well this is the first and only time I have lost a suspect. Ever."

"Then let's hope this isn't the start of a new propensity for you."

"It isn't," she told him.

"Good. Care to explain how you lost Samuel E. Triton?" he asked, flipping open a file on his desk.

"Let's just say that Sammy the Snake slithered out of my grasp." She didn't bother explaining about Brandt Donovan's interference. Robert would only see it as an excuse. And she knew that if there was one thing Robert Pinkerton hated more than fouled cases, it was excuses for fouling up to begin with.

"Let's not," Robert ordered sternly. "Details, Willow. I want them now, and then I want to see them in your written report."

"I had Sammy cornered in an alley. Someone saw us, and Sammy got away."

"That's all?"

"That's all. I looked for him the next day, and every day after that until I heard from you, but he was long gone. I'll be happy to go back and finish the case," she offered hopefully.

"No."

"But—"

"No." Robert's voice softened. "You know what's going on around here, Willow. Because you're a woman, and because my father is no longer alive to fight for you, your position with the Agency is in jeopardy. I'm doing my best to keep them from inventing an excuse to let you go," he said, referring to his higher-ups, "but it isn't easy. And this latest job isn't going to help matters. An incomplete case in your file will draw them like a pack of hungry wolves."

She swallowed, returning to her seat. "I know," she said quietly. "Robert, you know how much this job means to me. How much I need it."

"I know. And I'm going to do my best to keep you with us." He tapped the Triton file against the desktop. "So from now on, you're going to be extra careful. About what you say, what you do, with whom you associate. Understood?"

"Yes."

"Also, from this moment on, you're being taken off active duty."

"What?" Willow couldn't believe her ears. Not Robert. Robert would never do this to her. Investigation was her life, her livelihood. He couldn't take that away from her.

"I'm sorry, Willow. Believe me, I am. But if I assign you another case now, everyone will be salivating, just waiting for you to foul up. I think it's best if we let things simmer down a bit before putting you back in the game.

"Don't worry," he continued. "You'll still be on full salary. We'll find something for you to do in the office."

"I suppose you want me to assist Mrs. Girard? Perhaps I could bring you another draught of coffee, Mr. Pinkerton, sir?"

"Willow . . ."

"This isn't fair, Robert. I have a sterling reputation, a flawless history with this company. And you know damned well that I'm a better detective than half of the men you have on the payroll."

"I would never argue that point, Willow."

"Then why are you putting me on the shelf?"

"I'm not putting you on the shelf. I'm taking you out of the field—temporarily. Until the Triton case isn't an issue."

Stalking to the door, she put on her wrap and grabbed up her carpetbag. Her parasol popped open in a flurry of whispering black fringe, and she fought to close it without setting down her valise.

"I'll be at the Astor House." She had given up her old apartment before going West and knew the company would cover the hotel bill until she could find a new place to stay. And she wanted to hurt the Pinkerton Agency, if only in its bank account.

"Let me know when you decide where I might be most valuable as a mere office clerk." She turned to the door, then stopped. "And Robert . . . I'll have to send the receipt over later, but . . . add fifty dollars to my expense account."

Robert's eyes narrowed. "For what?"

She threw him an engaging smile, lifting the hem of her gown. "Why, for a new dress, of course. This one is positively ruined."

Chapter Six

Willow checked into the Astor House around supper-time, asking for the most luxurious—and most expen-sive—room available. She ordered dinner and a bath, and prepared herself for an enormous dose of relaxation.

But foremost, she had to see what was in that note. When the bellboy left her alone, she quickly removed the bodice of her gown, separate from the skirt. For the first time, she noticed smears of blood on the page, dark red now that they'd had time to dry. The thought of Charlie lying in her arms almost made her drop the note. She took a deep breath and steeled herself not only to touch the bloodstained paper, but to read whatever in-formation rested inside.

She unfolded the square. Then stared blankly at the one word written there. *Gideon.*

"Gideon?" she said aloud. What did it mean?

She finished undressing, tucking the paper into the toe of her boot for safekeeping, and got into the bath. While

she soaked, she thought about the word *Gideon.* And
what it might have to do with Charlie's murder.

Was it a last name? She could think of no families by
the name of Gideon in New York. But then, her investigating radius wasn't necessarily confined only to the
city.

Or was it a first name? The first name of the man who
stabbed Charlie and left him for dead? Perhaps Charlie
had suspected that he would be harmed and wrote the
name as a clue to his killer's identity.

What if it wasn't a name at all, but a place—a town
or theater or club of some kind?

She stepped out of the tub, about to change for bed,
when a knock sounded at the outer sitting room door.
Still wet, she grabbed up her red oriental robe to cover
herself.

Expecting the hotel staff with her dinner, she pulled
open the door. Only to find Robert standing there, a dark
scowl on his face.

"Robert. Come in." She stepped back to allow him
entrance. "What's wrong?"

"Nothing," he said shortly. He took off his bowler cap
and overcoat, tossing them onto a nearby chair while he
folded his long frame onto the settee.

"Don't lead me on a merry chase, Robert," she said,
clutching the folds of robe at her neck to ward off the
chill on her damp skin. "Something is bothering you,
now what is it?"

"Nothing," Robert said again. "Our agents and the police both went over every inch of that railway car and
came up with nothing. None of the passengers heard or
saw a thing."

Willow bit her lip, wanting to tell him about the note
but still possessing the insane desire to keep that tiny

piece of evidence to herself. Especially now that she had been put on inactive duty.

And yet she didn't feel right keeping something— something as vital as this might turn out to be—from him. If he would open up to her, then she would be more than willing to share her knowledge with him.

Folding one leg under her, she sat down beside him. Her hand rested on his knee. "Will you tell me now what Charlie Barker was working on?"

He closed his eyes on a sigh. "I can't. It's Agency policy. Unless you're involved in the case, I cannot give you information from the case file."

"Then let me work on this case."

His head snapped up. "What? No. It's too dangerous."

"It's my job, Robert. I'm a detective. If you're not going to let me investigate, then I might as well hang up my derringer and call it a day. I know you're disappointed that I messed up with Sammy Triton. Let me prove myself. Let me show you that I'm still a good operative, worthy enough to carry a Pinkerton badge."

He looked at her for a minute. When he spoke, it was in a soft, serious tone. "I trust you, Willow. Maybe more than any other agent under my supervision. And I know you can handle any case I assign to you. But I'm not talking about your job being in danger, Willow. I'm talking about your life."

She shook off the involuntary shudder that coursed through her body. "I've taken on dangerous cases before. Or are you forgetting the time I was kidnapped and held hostage by a band of renegade army deserters?"

His brow wrinkled. "I'm not forgetting anything."

"Then put me on this case. Let me catch the bastard who killed Charlie."

* * *

He turned her down. Flat.

Two days later, she was still fuming over Robert's dismissal of her request. So she decided to give him one more chance at redemption. She dressed in her best day gown, a peach and white vertical-striped concoction she'd picked up on her last trip to Indianapolis. The jacket fit her form snugly, leaving a vee open at the neck for the lace of her snow-white blouse. The long, straight skirt pulled into a large bustle in back. She slipped on a pair of peach satin slippers with two-inch heels and topped off the outfit with a tall, extravagant bird nest bonnet, a dozen orange and white plumes fluttering in every direction. A few tiny ring curls framed her face, intentionally left out of the tightly coiled braid atop her head.

With an air of optimism, parasol balanced elegantly on one shoulder, she left the hotel and marched her way down Fifth Avenue toward the Pinkerton National Detective Agency.

Mrs. Girard greeted her with a pleasant hello when Willow requested an audience with Robert.

"He's in a conference with Mr. Warner just now, Miss Hastings. If you'd care to wait in Mr. Pinkerton's office, I'm sure he wouldn't mind. I'll let him know you're here just as soon as he's available."

"Thank you." Willow sauntered into Robert's small but quaint office, making herself at home in his leatherback desk chair. She propped her slippered feet on the corner of the desk and tapped them in an irregular, staccato rhythm with the tip of her closed parasol.

A few moments later, the door opened and in walked Robert, wearing a hunter green morning coat and tan trousers.

"Willow," he welcomed her warmly. "What brings you here on such a sunny day?"

'Round and 'round and 'round they go, she thought. Robert definitely had something on his mind or he wouldn't be making small talk. She slid her feet from his desk and stood.

"I thought I would pay you a little visit," she answered in all honesty, giving him a peck on the cheek. "Any new developments in Charlie's case?"

"As a matter of fact, yes."

His answer surprised her. Biting back the myriad of questions swirling through her brain, she watched him walk around the desk and take a seat.

Robert focused on her, his lips drawing together in what could only be a smile held in check. "You'll get your petticoats all in a bunch if you keep your curiosity bottled up. Would you like me to explain?"

She released a pent-up breath. "Yes."

He laughed. "Take a seat and I'll tell you everything, from the beginning."

Willow moved to the nearest chair, forgetting all about her protruding bustle as she leaned closer to Robert.

"The police have turned the case over to us."

Willow inhaled sharply. The police were often willing to work with Pinkerton, but she had never heard of them actually turning a case over to the Agency.

"They're leaving it open on their end, mind you, but because Barker was one of ours, they're letting us take the reins. Yesterday we got a telegram from Union Pacific headquarters in Boston. Because the crime occurred on a train belonging to the Union Pacific Railroad, they've asked that we cooperate with the security agent being sent to conduct his own independent investigation."

"You aren't going to, though, are you?"

"I'm not going to what?" he asked.

"Let them investigate simultaneously. You don't know what kind of incompetent lummox they'll send. He'll impair our investigation, maybe even unknowingly destroy evidence."

"Come now, Willow, I'm sure Union Pacific hires very skilled men. Not as skilled as our people, of course," he added, "but competent enough to conduct a case without mistakenly overlooking a murder weapon, I hope. Besides, Francis and I have already discussed the matter and decided to cooperate fully with the Union Pacific officer."

Willow swallowed. If Francis Warner had been brought into this, her powers of persuasion mattered little. The superintendent had no time for her point of view or ideas. Robert, who trusted and believed in her, weighed the pros and cons, thought over her requests and propositions, and made a decision based on the merit of her argument. Warner, however, often made his decisions based on her gender rather than her reputation as a detective.

"Then at least let me get a head start. Let me see what I can come up with before the UP man gets here. That way he won't be stepping on any toes."

Robert shook his head. "The fact is, Willow, he's already here."

She sat in stunned silence, wondering when her life had begun to spin so out of control. Two weeks ago she'd been lurking around Jefferson City, keeping a close eye on Sammy the Snake. Now here she was, back in New York, officially taken off active duty, about to be stuffed into a windowless basement office, she was sure. Her next assignment would probably be dusting off old case files and putting them in alphabetical order. Maybe sweeping the front stoop on particularly leafy days.

Well, she had been a Pinkerton agent too long for such mundane chores. If she couldn't be a detective— investigating real crimes and not just "who took my sliced turkey on pumpernickel?"—then she would not investigate at all.

She straightened her spine as she stood, glaring at Robert with a no-nonsense look on her face. "Robert Allan Pinkerton, I have only two words for you. *I quit.*"

"What?" He jumped to his feet, racing past her to the door before her hand could grasp the knob. "You can't quit."

She took in his startled expression, eyes wide, mouth lax. A small smile touched her lips. She kissed first one cheek, then the other. "You are a precious, precious man, Robert Pinkerton. I love you dearly. But I most certainly *can* quit, and I have every intention of doing so."

Still, he blocked her exit. "Willow Elizabeth Hastings," he said in the same tone of voice. "You are a beautiful, outrageous, obstinate woman who sometimes makes my teeth perspire. You are also a wonderful friend."

"Robert," she interrupted, "I hope you know that whether I work for the Agency or not, you will always be my dearest confidant. I wouldn't lose touch with you for all the heather in Scotland."

"I know. But you didn't let me finish. Aside from being a beautiful woman and a wonderful friend, you are an even better detective. The gravest crime of all would be to let you slip through our fingers."

"Do you mean it?" she asked, holding back a smile.

"I'll do whatever it takes to keep you with the Agency."

The room fell into silence. A knowing grin spread

across her face. "I guess that leaves you only one choice then, doesn't it?"

His eyes narrowed warily. "And that is . . . ?"

"Put me on the Barker case."

Robert stared at her blankly. "Excuse me?"

"Your hearing isn't failing, Robert. I said that if you want me to stay with Pinkerton National Detective Agency, you'll assign me to Charlie's murder investigation."

He shook his head and made his way back to the desk. "You drive a hard bargain, Hastings."

"I'm a good detective, Pinkerton," she stated boldly.

Robert tapped a finger against his chin, in deep thought. After several long minutes, he raised his head and met her eyes. "I'll let you go after Charlie's murderer on one condition."

Uh-oh. Her staunch certainty slipped a notch. A condition. This could mean trouble. Nonetheless, she opened her mouth and heard herself ask to hear his bargain.

"A simple one, really," Robert said, a bit too smoothly for her peace of mind. He went to the door once again, calling for Mrs. Girard to send in the railroad security officer. "All I ask is that you work with the Union Pacific investigator."

Willow mulled it over for a moment, weighing her options carefully. But in the end she really had only two choices. Quit her job and, if she was lucky, find a position at a laundry house or as a governess. Or stay on with the Agency and—as painful as it might be—work with another (less competent, she was sure) investigator.

"You, sir, drive a hard bargain. But I agree."

Just then, someone tapped softly on the frosted plate glass of the office door.

"Come in," Robert called.

Willow kept her eyes on Robert, not bothering to turn around even when she heard a man move in behind her. An attitude of firm competence would set the tone with this so-called investigator.

"Willow Hastings," Robert said, "allow me to introduce you to Union Pacific Officer Brandt Donovan."

Chapter Seven

Willow whirled around. And promptly dropped her parasol. *"You!"* she hissed.

Brandt Donovan's mouth fell open. He thought he would have lost his tongue if it hadn't been fastened in back of his throat. *"You!"* he breathed.

"You know each other?" Robert asked innocently.

"Yes," Brandt responded affirmatively.

"No," Willow answered at the same time just as strongly.

Brandt saw icy daggers aimed at him from sparkling violet eyes.

"We met briefly," Willow amended.

"Where?" Robert asked.

"Jefferson City," Brandt said honestly.

"St. Louis," Willow said loudly, obviously trying to overshadow his answer.

When Brandt gave her a questioning glare, she smiled

prettily. "You must be mistaken, sir. I'm quite sure we met in St. Louis."

Cocking her head toward Robert, she continued. "The train stopped in St. Louis for a few hours and I took the opportunity to visit one of my favorite millinery shops. That's where I purchased this bonnet." Her hand fluttered toward the feathery concoction atop her head. "On the way out of the store, I nearly tripped on the hem of my gown. Mr. Donovan was kind enough to catch me before I embarrassed myself by falling flat on my face. I never did thank you properly, did I, sir?"

"No thanks necessary, ma'am," he said, catching on to her little game, though he had no idea why she felt the need to make up a story in the first place. He would be sure to ask once he managed to get her alone.

And he *would* get her alone.

"Still, I do appreciate your assistance," she continued. "If not for you, I might have seriously injured myself."

"Well, I'd like to think that if I hadn't been there to catch you, some other gentleman would have."

"True gentlemen are few and far between, it's sad to say. In fact—"

"All right, all right," Robert interrupted shortly. "Enough of this good-natured bantering. I appreciate that you saved her life, Mr. Donovan, and that she's thankful, but need I remind the two of you that there are more important issues at hand?"

"You're right, Robert," Willow said. "I'm sorry for losing sight of our true reason for being here."

Brandt almost lost consciousness when he heard her apology. She sounded almost like a lady. What happened to the Willow Hastings he'd met in Jefferson City? The one who tempted and teased a man into aching arousal by shamelessly removing her stockings in

65

front of him. The one who sang like an angel—then devilishly turned down his sexual proposition for fear of bruising him further.

His hand almost rose to his cheekbone. The injury had pained him for a good week. But thoughts of Willow had lingered longer, and involved another kind of physical ailment entirely.

"Willow. Mr. Donovan. If you'll have a seat."

The three of them sat in silence for a moment while Robert shuffled papers on his desk. Then he clasped his hands in front of him and looked at them. "As you both know, one of our operatives was killed two days ago. Stabbed to death on a Union Pacific railway car just after it pulled into Grand Central Station."

He passed them each a large brown envelope at least half an inch thick. "These are some of the photographs we have of the crime scene, along with notes taken by the investigators I sent. Some police information is included, and whatever else I thought imperative to the case."

Brandt pulled out the contents of his envelope to study but noticed that Willow didn't bother opening hers. Which caused another question to pop into his head. Why was she here?

"Excuse me, Mr. Pinkerton, but why are you apprising me of the situation in Miss Hastings's presence? I'm not sure the subject is appropriate for a lady," he said, aware that he used the word "lady" quite loosely. "Perhaps we should wait to speak of the case in private. No offense," he added, sliding a glance in Willow's direction.

Her lips pursed, but she said nothing.

Robert cleared his throat and looked sideways, coloring three different shades of red. "Well, Mr. Donovan," he began, "that's another reason I asked you in here. You see, Miss Hastings is . . . um, that is to say—I want you and—" He stopped to clear his throat.

"Oh, Robert," Willow said sweetly, batting her long brown lashes, "do let me tell him."

Brandt's eyes narrowed. He smelled a rat. "Tell me what?"

Willow came to her feet, that blasted grin painted on her face. She held out her hand. "Congratulations, Mr. Donovan. I'm your new partner."

Brandt stood so fast, he nearly forgot to unbend his knees. He started to raise his voice, then forced his emotions in check. "I do hope you're joking."

The cat-who-ate-the-canary-and-licked-clean-the-bowl-of-cream expression on her face told him she wasn't.

"Not in the least, sir," she replied.

His eyes swung to the man behind the desk. "Tell me she's joking, Pinkerton."

"I'm afraid not, Mr. Donovan."

"I work alone," he stated, though it had never been a particularly rigid requirement before.

"So do I," she said.

"You're both more than welcome to work alone," Robert said, "as long as you do it together."

"My office telegraphed you that I would be looking into the incident, did they not?" Brandt asked of Pinkerton.

"They did."

"Then you are well aware of the fact that I have investigated such cases before. I am completely capable of doing so now—without dragging some simpering female along."

Robert winced visibly. He opened his mouth to say something, but Willow cut him off.

"You do *not* want to turn that corner, Mr. Donovan," she told him, back ramrod straight.

He crossed his arms over his chest and fixed her with a stern gaze. "And just why not?"

"Because this 'simpering female,' as you so rudely put it, can investigate circles around you."

"Please," he scoffed. "Women belong at home, raising children and keeping their husbands happy, not tripping around in the detective business. I have five sisters," he added, "so I know about these things. Each one of them was courted and wed and never let a silly notion enter her head about solving crimes, or working to make her own money, for that matter."

Willow blanched. Her chest rose in indignation and a scarlet blush crept up her neckline. "You ignorant, foul-minded, obnoxious son of a—"

"Willow!" Robert shouted.

"—jackal," she finished. "If you had any idea just who you were dealing with, you'd amend your low opinion of women."

"I know exactly who I'm dealing with," Brandt said in a deep, intimate tone. "If you recall, I got quite an eyeful when we first met."

"Well, I wouldn't bet too much on your memory, Mr. Donovan, seeing as how your left eye was nearly swollen shut. Such an injury makes me wonder how good an investigator you really are. Perhaps *I* should be worried about working with *you.*"

Brandt bristled at that remark, most certainly aimed at his masculinity. He raised himself to his full height, towering over her as best he could since the top of the woman's head came even with his shoulders—higher if he included that damn hat.

"I'll have you know that I am a top-notch professional, Miss Hastings. I am head of Security for the Union Pacific Railroad."

"And I'm Catherine the Great," she retorted, "but that

is of no consequence here. It's how you operate, not who you are, that matters in this line of work."

"Is that right?" he challenged.

She held his gaze, not the least intimidated by his height or breadth. "That's right."

Behind them, Robert cleared his throat. "Are you quite finished?"

Willow broke eye contact first, lowering herself with the utmost grace into her chair. "Quite," she answered.

"I take it you're not thrilled with the idea of working with a woman," Robert said. It was a statement, not a question.

Brandt answered anyway. "I'd rather work alone."

"I agree," Willow said. "He'll only slow me down, Robert."

"*I* would slow *you* down?" Brandt regarded her with wide, disbelieving eyes. "I assure you, you would be running to catch up to my investigation."

"I would be running to get away from the disgrace of your investigation," she corrected, then turned her head to study the opposite wall with blatant disinterest.

Brandt decided against putting up further argument. "Mr. Pinkerton, I cannot work with this . . . *woman.*"

Willow's head whipped around. A scoffing sound rent the air as she stared at him, mouth open, nostrils flaring. "Robert, I cannot work with this . . . *man,*" she shot back.

Robert gave a long-suffering sigh. "I'm sorry you both feel that way. Because you either work on this case together, or neither of you works on it at all."

Willow caught her breath. So that was the crux of it. She either worked with this mule-headed, arrogant ignoramus or she found herself another occupation.

She glanced at Brandt through her peripheral vision.

Where would stubborn refusal get her, other than kicked into the street like a cur?

Robert implored her with a desperate expression. She inhaled deeply, counting to seven before a smile stretched across her tight lips.

"Fine," she said in a calm, decisive voice. "If Mr. Donovan will lower his standards and agree to work with me, then I guess I can do the same." She waited only a heartbeat before adding, "My standards were never all that high to begin with."

Brandt ignored her. "The Union Pacific will not be happy to hear that you refused to allow me to investigate," he threatened.

Her first inclination had been right, Willow thought: brainless Neanderthal. *Never threaten Robert* was very high on her list of things not to do.

Robert's jaw clamped shut, all but chipping teeth. "I'm sorry to hear that, Mr. Donovan," he said in a tight, clipped tone. "But then, your presence is not really necessary. A Pinkerton operative was murdered. That it happened on a Union Pacific passenger car is fairly insignificant at this point."

He stood, resting his closed fists on the desk. "Now, I am giving you the opportunity to investigate, as your company has requested. However, this offer hinges on your agreement to work with Agent Hastings. If you find this arrangement unacceptable, then I bid you *adieu*." He held his hand out to Brandt.

Au revoir. Bon voyage, Willow added silently. *Don't let the door hit you in the back on the way out.* Things were looking up. Robert would be so impressed by her ladylike behavior through all of this that he would assign her the case even after Brandt Donovan stormed out, refusing to work with a woman. Whoever said, "You can't have your cake and eat it, too," didn't know a fig about the art of manipulation.

"If that's your position," Brandt said to Robert, "then I have only one thing to say."

Willow stood, holding out her hand to Brandt. He was taking entirely too much time to turn down Robert's offer. "It was nice to see you again, sir." That lie was the hardest she'd had to swallow in a while.

"What is it?" Robert asked, continuing the conversation around Willow's rush to see Brandt Donovan on a train bound for Boston.

Ivory teeth gleamed as Brandt grinned. He took her proffered hand and brought it to his lips for a light kiss.

Uh-oh.

"Where do we begin?"

Chapter Eight

Candles burned all around. The smell of flame and wax permeated the shimmering darkness. The uneven gray stones that made up the walls of this dark dungeon sent a sharp chill through the room.

A whimper of fright reached his ears. He stared hard at the woman tied and gagged on the altar before him. Her arms were spread out on either side of her body, her legs bound tightly together at the ankles. A feminine replication of the crucifix that hung on the wall above her head, she represented a sacrifice like that of Jesus on the cross.

She struggled against her bonds, trying to scream past the thick cloth stuffed in her mouth.

"She is ready," the man said to his companion, who stood alone in a dark corner. "Bring me my cloak."

A cloud of black material fell about his shoulders. He reached up with gnarled fingers to fasten the clasp at his neck.

"For your sins you must pay. To God you must repent." He circled the altar, swinging the aspergillum back and forth over her naked form, sprinkling her flesh with Holy water. *"Asperges me, Domine, hyssopo, et mundabor: lavabis me, et super nivem dealbabor,"* he chanted in the language of the Old Church. *"Thou shalt sprinkle me with hyssop, Lord, and I shall be cleansed,"* he repeated for her benefit. *"Thou shalt wash me, and I shall be whiter than snow."*

The petite woman shivered in terror.

He stopped beside her head, removing the cloth from her mouth. *"For your sins you must pay,"* he intoned. *"To God you must repent. Do you regret your wicked ways?"*

Tears rolled from the girl's eyes, into the dark hair at her temples. She nodded weakly.

"Do you regret your wicked ways?" he asked again, his voice gaining strength.

"Y-yes," she managed, teeth chattering with fear.

"For your sins you must pay. To God you must repent. Repent. Ask God to forgive you your trespasses."

"For . . . give me."

"The Lord cannot hear you. Speak louder, my child."

"Forgive me."

"Beg His forgiveness for your sins." His words echoed through the dungeon room.

"Forgive me."

"Forgive us, Lord, for we know not what we do!" From inside the cloak, he produced a long sword, its golden hilt engraved with a crescent moon. He grasped the weapon in his white-knuckled hand.

"Again, my child."

Her chest heaved with the effort to speak. "Forgive me."

"Misereatur vestri omnipotens, Deus, et, dimissis peccatis vestris, perducat vos ad vitam aeternam. *May almighty God have mercy upon you, forgive you your sins, and bring you to everlasting life."*

Raising the sword, he looked down into her terrified eyes. "Amen," he said, and drove the sharp point home. Life's blood poured from her body as her heart beat its last.

He removed the blade from her chest, wiping it clean with a soft linen cloth.

"This child of God has been forgiven, Outram. Take her home."

Chapter Nine

Willow stormed into her room at the Astor House hotel, slamming the door closed with a clatter that reverberated off the walls. She hurtled her parasol across the room, just missing the flowered porcelain vase on the floor beside the fireplace.

Moving from the sitting room into the bedroom, she continued to vent her frustration. Hat, gloves, shoes, all were thrown in one direction or another, their flight punctuated by curses aimed at Brandt Donovan.

The only thing that didn't receive the full force of her fury was the portfolio of photos that Robert had given her, which she tossed with uncommon gentleness onto the bed.

With an angry yank, she pulled open the jacket of her gown, hanging it and the matching skirt in the mahogany claw-footed wardrobe. Petticoats and corset soon followed, along with her silk stockings.

By the time she stood in only her knee-length chemise, her anger had dissipated somewhat. But she still hated Brandt Donovan with a passion. Her foot tapped impatiently on the thick mulberry carpeting, arms across her chest.

Why did he have to be the only person in the state of New York reasonable enough to agree to Robert's ultimatum? Any other man would have fought it tooth and nail, too proud to work with a female operative.

But not Brandt. He made it perfectly clear that he didn't like the idea of being on a case with a woman, but he wasn't going to let that small inconvenience keep him from doing his job.

When he had turned to her and asked, "Where do we begin?" she'd wanted to smack the smug smile off his face. It had taken all of her willpower to bite her tongue and remain silent while Robert filled Brandt in on the Charlie Barker case. As soon as Robert had dismissed them, she'd stalked out of the office to the hotel without a backward glance.

Brandt claimed to be a detective; let him discover where she was staying.

Not that she cared to ever see him again. Her investigation would go much more smoothly without that boorish oaf getting in the way.

She wrapped the red satin robe about her shoulders and moved to the bed for the file. Propping fluffy pillows behind her back, she crossed her legs and began sorting through the contents of the envelope.

She spread the photos in an arc at the foot of the bed, paying little attention since she'd seen the crime scene firsthand. Then she started reading the enclosed profile of Charlie Barker. It included a wide range of facts: age, date of birth, family, details of his murder. But nothing that hinted as to *why* he'd been killed.

Willow worried a thumbnail, clicking it against her

front teeth, staring at all the information before her. She couldn't shake the feeling that Charlie's death had something to do with his last assignment. When she'd commented on his jumpiness, hadn't he told her that it was just a case he was working on? Why wouldn't Robert tell her what Charlie had been investigating? Surely he realized that the murder likely happened because Charlie stirred up a hornet's nest, got close enough to make someone nervous.

Robert had never been one to hold back, especially where an agent was concerned. So what made this time different? Who would have such a secret that they were willing to kill to keep it?

And who was Gideon?

She hopped off the bed to look for the peach slippers she'd earlier discarded in such a fit of temper. She found the left one and tossed it over her shoulder, continuing her search. She spotted the right slipper resting on its heel in the corner of the room. Pulling up the piece of fabric that lined the bottom, she freed the square of paper hidden at the toe.

She set it with the photos on the bed. Even with everything spread out in front of her, she still couldn't see any clues as to who murdered Charlie, or why.

A noise in the front room caught her attention. She cocked her head to listen more closely. The ping of glass touching glass sounded again.

Sweeping the papers and pictures beneath a pillow, Willow quietly slid open the top drawer of the bedside table and reached for her revolver. Fingers curled tightly around the butt of the gun, she crept forward, senses honed to pick up on the first sign of danger.

She paused at the sitting room entrance, listening. Silence. She turned the knob and eased the door open a fraction of an inch. Then another. Her eyes scanned the room.

Brandt Donovan stood in front of the sideboard, sipping a glass of brandy as if he belonged there.

She lowered the revolver, releasing a huff of ire. "What are you doing here?" she snapped.

"Having a drink." He held up his glass as proof while his eyes perused the length of her body, covered only in the thin red robe, and moved back to her face. "Can I fix you something?"

She tossed her pistol behind her onto the bed. "You can pour me a sherry," she said, "and then you can drag your mangy carcass out of my room."

He poured sparkling golden liquid into a crystal tumbler and handed it to her. "You left the office before I had the chance to ask where you were staying."

She took a long swallow of the sherry. "I see you found me anyway."

One side of his mouth turned up. "Robert told me."

"Remind me to thank him later," she muttered. Maybe an office full of rotten cabbage would be an appropriate gesture of gratitude.

"He seemed to think it might be a good idea to wait a day or two before dropping in, to give you time to cool off." He shrugged. "I told him that was nonsense. We're partners now."

Brandt stepped forward until there was only a hairsbreadth of space between them. Until Willow had to lean her head back to keep from breaking eye contact.

"Partners don't cool off," he continued.

His voice ran like warm molasses down her spine. She quickly shook off the comforting feeling.

"They stay close." He slipped an arm around her waist. His body pressed against her intimately. "And they stay hot. *Very* hot."

For a moment, she remained in his arms. Then, as his face lowered toward hers, she broke free.

"You stay hot," she said, moving to the bar to refill her glass. "I'll stay cool, and just maybe we'll be able to manage a lukewarm relationship." She fixed him with an icy stare. "A business relationship, that is."

"Of course." Carelessly, he moved across the room, taking a seat on the sofa, his feet propped upon the table before him. "I hope you don't think I was insinuating any other kind," he said before emptying his glass.

"I think you were trying to insinuate yourself into my bed," she told him with a brazen tilt of her chin. She delighted in the sudden pink that tinged his high cheekbones. "I also think that if we hope to form a successful alliance, you'd better stop seeing me as a woman and start seeing me as a detective."

"That's kind of hard when said detective is prancing around half naked in front of her partner." He looked pointedly at the lacy trim of her shift, visible through the gaping edges of her robe. "You may think of yourself as more detective than woman, Miss Hastings, but I assure you, I am all man."

A dare lay somewhere within those words, she was sure, but she refused to take the bait. Instead, she decided to throw out a thinly veiled challenge of her own.

She moved to stand over him, one hand grasping the wood trim at the back of the settee, the other resting on the curved sofa arm. The front of her red satin robe gaped open, showing even more of the thin ivory chemise and a good deal of bare flesh. "And I assure you, Mr. Donovan, that there is very little of me that is not entirely female. Should I ever decide to go about proving that point, it would be a most pleasurable experience for you."

His only reaction was the lifting of one russet brow.

A warm, firm hand moved around her back to caress the curve of her buttock. "Care to prove that now?"

She smiled seductively, leaned closer, and blew in his ear. Then whispered, "No."

With that, she pulled away, pointing to the door. "Now that you know where I'm staying, there's no need for us to remain in each others' company. Tomorrow morning will be soon enough to begin our investigation."

Brandt set his glass on the low table in front of the settee before rising. He smiled regretfully. "You could have experienced something truly amazing tonight," he told her.

"I doubt it," she said, "but you would have seen God."

Chapter Ten

Several hours after her confrontation with Brandt, Willow stood at the window of her room, overlooking City Hall Park. Earlier she had seen couples out for an evening stroll. Men and women walking hand in hand, riding in open carriages.

But with the shadows of darkness came a slight chill to the air, driving people inside to the toasty comfort of their homes. The street was littered with vehicles moving so fast that no one paid much attention to anyone else.

And certainly no one would notice a hunched and drunken man stumbling along the sidewalk.

Willow dressed slowly, watching the last orange-purple rays of daylight being swallowed by the black of night.

Knit cap pulled low to hide her face, she checked her pistol one last time before tucking it into the waistband of her pants. The matching knife pressed reassuringly against her calf inside the worn black boots.

She slipped a packet of tiny picks and pins into the pocket of her overlarge jacket and started from the room. As she approached the sitting room door, a knock sounded from the hall, followed by Brandt Donovan's cultured drawl.

A colorful oath passed her lips. The man was becoming an albatross. She could practically feel a length of thick hemp tightening about her neck.

Mumbling something unintelligible, she raced for the bedroom, tearing off the man's clothing in exchange for her trusty red robe. She pulled the edges close around her neck and returned to answer the door.

"What do you want?" she charged immediately, fixing him with a scathing glare. His polite gentleman's smile made her queasy.

He bowed slightly at the waist. "I came to escort you to dinner."

"You came all the way here to take me to dinner?" she asked.

" 'All the way here' isn't very far at all." He cocked his head in the direction of the door opposite hers. "I have the room across the hall."

Her face screwed up as though she'd been sucking on a lemon. It took all of her short temper to keep from kicking him in the shin. "I'm having my supper brought up," she lied easily.

"Nonsense. There's no reason for both of us to eat alone when we can have a pleasant meal in the dining room."

Pleasant was not the first word that came to mind when she thought of sitting through dinner with him. She cleared her throat. "I'm not feeling very well."

"It's no wonder, staying cooped up in this room all day. You need a hearty meal and a bit of fresh air. Per-

haps after dinner we could take a walk through the park.
I hear it's lovely this time of year."

She closed her eyes and took a deep breath. "You're
not going to leave me alone, are you?" When she looked
up, green eyes sparkled down at her.

"No," he answered.

"You're going to stand here until I agree to go to
dinner with you."

A smile was his only answer.

"I'm not even dressed," she tried one last, desperate
time.

"I'll wait."

"Of course you will," she muttered to herself. "Stay
here," she grumbled, and shut the door in his face.

She returned several minutes later, far from happy but
resigned. The sooner she tamped down any curiosity
Brandt might be harboring, the sooner she could get on
with her investigation.

She ran a hand over the front of her bodice, assuring
herself that she hadn't missed a button in her rush to
dress. "Let's go," she said and walked past him, the lack
of enthusiasm in her voice matched only by the sour
expression on her face.

Brandt stared after her for a moment, watching the
gentle sway of her hips as she moved down the hall,
lavender blue skirts trailing behind. He didn't know why
he should be attracted to a woman with such a surly
disposition, but he couldn't help the arousal that leapt in
his veins when he looked at her. Of course, with the
way Willow walked . . . and talked . . . and breathed, any
man would be hard-pressed not to feel a little something
stir to life below the belt.

In a few long strides, he caught up, taking her arm
despite an initial struggle. Neither of them spoke until
they reached the hotel dining room and were seated.

He studied Willow across the table, taking in her up-swept auburn hair, adorned with a small bouquet of violet fabric blossoms. The deep purple of the flowers blended attractively with the lighter periwinkle of her gown.

"You look lovely," he said.

Suspicious eyes peered over the top of the tall menu. She didn't respond.

"That color brings out the violet of your eyes."

Willow closed her menu with a flourish. She opened her mouth, then snapped it shut as the waiter approached.

Good timing, Brandt thought, positive Willow had intended a scornful reproach for his attempt at politeness.

Her brittle composure and angry demeanor never seemed to falter. From the moment they'd met in Robert Pinkerton's office, she had remained boldly confident and outwardly hostile, visibly seething over his interference in an investigation she deemed hers, and hers alone.

They would butt heads at every turn, he was sure. Willow would do everything in her power to keep him from discovering Charles Barker's murderer. He would do everything in his power to show her that he was in this to the end—even if it meant becoming her shadow.

Wouldn't that just rattle the hell out of her? Brandt smiled to himself as Willow ordered the coquilles St. Jacques Mornay. He requested the same, and a bottle of wine.

Willow downed her first glass of chilled chardonnay in one long swallow. He refilled her glass before commenting.

"You don't like me very much, do you?" he asked.

"Not very, no," she answered bluntly.

He chuckled, amused by her assertiveness. "Why not?"

84

She took a sip of wine, then licked the rosy liquid from her lips. The action burned a path straight from his eyeballs to the center of his groin. He shifted a bit to the left and awaited her answer.

"There are so many reasons not to like you, it would take me all night to list them."

"Try. If you're going to hate me, I at least deserve to know why." Perhaps what was sure to be her ice-cold honesty would douse the ardor that made it hard to find a comfortable position.

Willow set her glass aside, brows knit in concentration. "Let's see," she said. "You are obnoxious."

He threw a hand over his heart and fell back against the chair, giving her his best wounded look. "You cut me to the quick, madam." Volley number one had no affect whatsoever on his arousal.

A feminine brow winged upward at his theatrics. "I guess I can add *melodramatic* to the list," she quipped. "You are obnoxious."

"You said that already."

"It bears repeating," she replied dryly. "You are arrogant, self-centered, and self-serving."

Volley number two had the blood in his loins thinning a fraction and moving out in other directions. "I'm not sure how you can come to such a conclusion after our few short meetings, but I think those can be thrown together into one category," Brandt offered.

"I'm a very good judge of character," she answered primly. "And, no, they cannot be thrown together, because you are each one of those things individually. You are also a bigot."

That was the one. Volley number three did it. His desire cooled completely, possibly lost forever, given the sudden fall of his . . . er . . . pride.

The waiter came then with their meal. As soon as he

85

left, Brandt leaned forward and fixed her with what he hoped was a cross look. "How do you figure that?"

"You don't believe women can be good investigators," Willow told him as she popped a tender scallop smothered in lemon butter into her mouth.

"They can't," he replied honestly. Just because a woman had the ability to incite a man's lust didn't mean she could hold her own against the criminal mind.

"There!" she cried, her fork clanging against the side of her dish. "You are a bigot."

"It is not bigoted to believe that women can't do the job of a man. It's the truth."

Her mouth fell open in indignation; her eyes bulged. "That is the most outrageous thing I have ever heard. I will have you know that I have solved in weeks cases that would take a man months to figure out."

He scoffed. "Impossible. The only way that you or any other woman could solve a crime before a man is if you used your feminine wiles to wheedle information out of some unsuspecting fool."

If possible, her mouth fell open even farther than before. Her eyes all but sprang from their sockets. "That is the crudest thing I have ever heard. I definitely have to add *crude* to my list. And boorish. You are crude, rude, and boorish. I'm surprised you manage to walk upright. Most apes drag around on their knuckles, scratching at themselves. Although in the privacy of your room I'm sure that's something in which you take great pleasure."

Brandt allowed himself a small smile. The blood was flowing back to his nether regions, heated by the surprising invigoration of battling with Willow Hastings and watching her skin flush, her breasts rise and fall in angry breaths while she argued with him. Who could have known squabbling with a woman could be so sexually stimulating?

"Touché," he said. "Are there any other reasons for your dislike of me, or is that it?" He took a bite of Duchess potato, unperturbed because he was beginning to enjoy this. Immensely.

"Oh, Mr. Donovan," Willow crooned, "I have not even begun to convey my dislike."

By the time they finished their meal, Brandt's ears were nearly on fire. He imagined that Willow had a dictionary under the table and was reading off every negative trait from *A* to *Z*. He didn't offer to refill her wine, but emptied the last of the bottle into his own glass and tossed it down in one giant gulp.

When she fell silent, he stared at her with wide, somewhat cloudy, disbelieving eyes. "You're through?" he asked, astonished. "Are you sure you wouldn't like to add one more *obnoxious* just for good measure?"

She tossed him a sugary-sweet smile. "I don't suppose it would hurt," she said. "You are also obnoxious."

"Thank you. I was almost beginning to feel above a garden slug."

Willow sighed. "It's a shame you had to say that."

"Why? Wasn't it obnoxious enough for you?"

"Oh, it was plenty obnoxious," she said. "It's just that—to spare your feelings, of course—I overlooked *sarcastic*. But after both of those rather snide remarks, I think it's only fair that I add it."

"Very well. Are you finished?" he asked.

"That's all I can think of for now."

Brandt rolled his eyes. "I meant, are you finished eating?"

"Oh." She dabbed the corners of her mouth with the white fabric napkin. "Yes, I believe so. It was delicious."

He grunted. His meal had been far from enjoyable.

Oh, the food tasted fine and at first he'd been more amused than offended by Willow's remarks. But even the most tender of broiled scallops tended to upset his stomach when he was forced to listen to a long, detailed list of his faults.

Taking her arm, he led her from the table and back upstairs to her room. At the door he bowed over her hand and pressed his lips to the warm skin.

"Though the conversation rankled," he said softly, "the company remained utterly magnificent." Then he turned for his room across the hall.

"You know," Willow said, stopping him, "if I had a list of reasons to like you—which I don't, of course, because there simply isn't cause—but if I did have such a list . . ." Her voice grew quiet. "I would have to put *polite* at the very top."

What had caused this sudden about-face? Brandt wondered. Was she feeling guilty for having run him through the wringer?

He took in her stately figure as she stood unmoving in front of her hotel room door. The lavender blue material of her gown hugged every nuance of her body, every straight line and gentle curve. Her bright eyes shimmered in the dusky lamplight of the hall, deep, dark violet orbs dancing with vivacity.

With erotic images of a night spent in Willow's bed firmly ensconced in his brain, Brandt stalked forward, closing in until her back hit the solid width of the door with a cushioned thump.

"Polite, hm?" He grinned wickedly. Not one to pass up an opportunity when it presented itself, his hands settled on her waist. "What else would you add to that list?"

Willow held his gaze, her expression giving no hint of the thoughts inside her head. "I would have to say that you can be very charming when you want to be. Of course I can see through the act."

"What act?" He pressed closer, until he could feel the smooth expanse of her skin through the material of her gown, no stiff corset bones crimping and binding her perfect flesh.

"Your charm is all an act," she stated. "You bow gracefully, smile beguilingly, playing the role of gentleman to the hilt. You use your charm to manipulate people—to get your way. And once you have people completely won over, once you've seduced a woman into a swoon, you go in for the kill."

"Is that so?"

"I believe so."

"And have I got you nearly won over?" His hand moved higher on her waist. His fingers brushed beneath the swell of her breast. "Shall I swoop in for the kill?"

"You can try," she said, neither putting a halt to his caress nor encouraging it. "But you won't succeed."

"Why is that?"

"Because I've got you figured out. Your ploy of honor and chivalry can't work if the prey is wise to the trap."

"We'll see," was his only response. He ran the back of his hand across her temple, leaning close enough to smell the rose-scented shampoo she must surely use to wash her hair. His lips grazed her cheekbone, the lobe of her ear.

"Care to invite me in?" he whispered.

She turned away so quickly that he stumbled.

"If we're going to begin our investigation first thing in the morning, I'll need my rest." Her key turned in the lock. "Good night, Mr. Donovan. Sleep well."

With that, she disappeared into the room, leaving a disappointed Brandt in the deserted hallway.

Chapter Eleven

Willow pulled the black knit cap farther down around her ears. With the back of her jacket stuffed with old rags to produce an artificial hump, she stumbled across Broadway, incorporating a rattling, hacking cough to her guise as an excuse to cover her face with gloved hands.

By the time she reached the Pinkerton offices, the streets were empty. Her fear of being discovered lessened considerably, but still she continued with her hunched, irregular gait and an occasional rumble from her chest. She fell against the side of the building, staggering drunkenly up the few steps to the front stoop.

Fumbling around in her pocket, she removed one of the lock-picking devices from her collection. To conceal it from the view of anyone who might glance in her direction, she lifted a half-empty bottle of rum to her lips, at the same time working a tiny gadget into the keyhole. Just as she felt the lock begin to give, the pick slipped. She let loose with a sailor's curse.

Bringing the bottle to her lips once again, she dug into her pocket for an older, more reliable tool. A hairpin.

With the skill of an experienced craftsman, she slipped the pin inside and wiggled it around. Seconds later, she felt the lock loosen. Leaving the rum on the doorstep, she turned the knob and sneaked inside the dark building. From memory, she moved through the outer office, using her hands to avoid running into Mrs. Girard's desk.

Once she reached Robert's office, her trepidation eased. This room had only one small window with a view of the alley and the brick building next door. With the curtains drawn, no one would ever notice the low glow of lamplight inside an establishment supposedly abandoned for the night.

She struck a match and held it to the wick of the crystal-domed lamp on the corner of Robert's desk. Soft yellow illuminated the center of the room, casting only the slightest glimmer of light into the corners.

Willow moved to the file cabinets, searching for the employee file on Charles Barker. Seated behind the desk, she began scanning the information found there. At first she saw nothing of significance. Employment history, personal facts—all information she had already been given. Nothing that would have gotten him killed.

She wondered if Robert had already gutted Charlie's file. It was a well-known fact within the Agency that case information remained in the file of the assigned agent until the situation was resolved. Then, it was all moved to a separate file under the case name and identification number.

Had Robert already transferred the paperwork? If so, she would never find out what Charlie was working on. She could spend a week's worth of evenings going through case files and she still might never stumble across the one that got Charlie killed. It would be like searching for a rat in a rattler's nest.

She was about to give up when a thought hit her: What if Superintendent Warner was keeping the paperwork on his desk? Willow balked at the idea of rifling through his possessions. At least if she got caught in Robert's office, she was pretty sure she could talk her way out of it. But Francis Warner was not known for his tolerant nature. He would not only pepper her with a harsh reprimand, but she would probably find herself without a job by morning.

Which, if the Ambassador clock hanging on the wall next to the door could be relied upon, was fewer than seven hours away. It had seemed like forever before she was sure Brandt would stay in his room and she could sneak out of the hotel. And she would have to be back in her room, in her nightdress, before sunup. Brandt would arrive at her door not long after, expecting her to be rested and ready to get to work.

She sifted through the rest of Charlie's file and found nothing. Disappointed but determined, she tried to think of where else Robert might be keeping the information.

Probably under lock and key, she thought.

Of course. Under lock and key. Hadn't Robert once confided in her that there was a secret wall safe in his office? Behind a painting of some kind?

She whirled around. There were pictures on every wall.

Starting with the one closest to her, she began tilting them sideways to look beneath. Finally she found the safe, tucked away behind a large painting of men and women playing croquet. She lifted the frame from its hook and set it aside, climbing onto the sofa to get a better look at the numbered dial.

She had never broken into a safe before. She had no idea how to figure out the combination. *But*, she reminded herself, *it's easier to break into the safe of someone you know than of someone you don't.* She had to think like Robert.

Robert was protective. He always kept an eye out for his friends and family. He was predictable. She could always tell what he was thinking, how he would react.

So what would Robert do with the combination to his office safe? He would take it home with him. But he would also leave a copy at work, just in case.

She went to his desk, rooting around in the drawers. Then she began pulling them out and feeling underneath for hidden slips of paper. She looked under the desk blotter, inside his cup of pencils. She even upended the chair to search around the heel base.

Nothing.

The Ambassador clock chimed one. If she didn't find the combination soon, she would have to give up and try another night. Muttering to herself, she set the place to rights and turned down the wick of the lamp. Robert would notice immediately if even one thing was out of order. Cursing him for being so damn secretive, she started out of the office, giving the floor plant by the door a swift kick of frustration.

She adjusted the hump of rags in her jacket, replaced the knit cap, and slowly opened the front door, checking for observers before stepping out of the building. She had one foot on the front step when it dawned on her.

Robert hated plants.

Mrs. Girard filled the outer office with flowerpots of every shape and size, pruned and watered them like they were her children. But she wasn't allowed to give the shrub in Robert's office so much as a sip of water. He

93

took care of it himself, complaining every time a leaf turned brown and died.

Willow ducked back through the door and ran to his office. On her knees beside the less-than-healthy plant, she began turning over each huge, oval-shaped leaf. When that failed to turn up anything new, she tore off her gloves and sank her hands wrist-deep into the soil. She ignored the moist stickiness, turning the dirt over and over in her hands, letting it sift through her fingers. Finally her nails ran into something solid and cool.

She brushed it off, feeling its shape. A key.

That sneaky bastard.

It made sense now. Robert memorized the safe's combination, but left the master key in the office in case something ever happened.

She took down the painting again and felt the cool metal until she found a small keyhole just below the combination dial. It turned smoothly. The safe popped open. She piled the safe's contents in the middle of the desk and lit the lamp.

The top file was marked XAVIER, YVONNE in bold black letters. Below, in a lighter, penciled scrawl was the name of the investigator assigned to the case: Charles W. Barker.

She browsed through the file, taking in pages upon pages of a murder report, as well as several photographs of the crime scene and a woman's body.

Knowing that Robert would notice if anything was missing from the file, she pulled a stack of Pinkerton stationery from the desk drawer and began copying the information, word for word.

When she finished, she sat staring at the pictures for several long minutes. They weren't gruesome photographs. She'd seen bodies far more mutilated. This victim was clean except for the blood on her chest.

Whoever killed her had taken the time to arrange the body just so, to place a flower—what looked to be a pale-colored rose—in her hands.

If only she could take the photos with her. She needed to study them. There could be a clue somewhere in the pictures that she wouldn't catch in only a second-long glance.

Duplicates. This file was probably Charlie's, recovered after his murder.

Willow went to the file cabinets, opening the bottom drawer marked *X*. Her eyes were drawn to the large letters at the top of the second, matching file. She couldn't take the entire portfolio, but she had already copied the information, so she didn't need the whole thing. She only needed the photographs. If anyone noticed the pictures were missing from this file, they would probably just think them misplaced.

She returned the contents of the safe, replaced the picture on the wall, reburied the key into the soil of the plant, and extinguished the lamp. Confident that Robert would never know someone had been in his office, she hurried from the building, heading back to the Astor House with the information she'd gathered tucked securely beneath her shirt and into the waistband of her trousers.

When she arrived, she slipped in through the back of the hotel: the same rear entrance she'd used to get out, and that Robert had used the night he came to her room. It wouldn't do to have people witness a man visiting a lone woman.

Willow breathed a sigh of relief as she ducked into her well-lit room and turned to close and lock the door. Now all she had to do was get a couple hours of sleep to convince Brandt that she'd been in her room all night. She would hide her newly found facts somewhere safe until she got the chance to look them over more thoroughly.

"How nice of you to drop by."

Willow whirled around. And came face-to-face with her nemesis. Anger and frustration warred within her. She felt like a delinquent toddler, followed every step by a hawkish nanny.

"What are you doing in my room?" Her voice was deceptively even, white-hot fury bubbling just below the surface.

Brandt sat reclining on the settee, feet propped in front of him, the epitome of nonchalance. Shimmers of light danced against a crystal tumbler as he raised it to his lips and drank before answering. "I'm just sitting here waiting for you," he replied easily. "Mind telling me where you've been? I assume you weren't at the theater, given your less-than-ladylike attire."

She resisted the urge to tug at her man clothes. "Where I go and what I do is none of your concern. Now get out of my room." She opened the door, leaving him more than enough space to make his exit.

But he didn't move. He stayed seated, took another sip of brandy, and pinned her with a steady gaze. His eyes shone with emerald clarity, cool and determined. He wasn't any more likely to leave of his own volition than she was to sprout wings and fly across City Hall Park.

She slammed the door shut. The sound reverberated through the room and, she was sure, down the hall. Giving him a withering glare, she crossed her arms over her chest, hitching one hip to the side in annoyance. She felt the file, warm and stiff against the bare skin of her torso.

"You seem to have forgotten that we're partners," Brandt observed.

"I forgot nothing."

"Then where were you?"

"That is none of your business," she told him, enunciating carefully so there was no chance that he would mistake her meaning.

"But we're partners," he said again. There was a sharp edge to his tone now, a steely glint in his eyes. "Therefore, your whereabouts most certainly *are* my business."

"I told you that we would start on the case in the morning. Tomorrow we become partners. At eight o'clock, and not a minute before." She moved toward the bedroom entrance with as much nonchalance as she could muster, considering she was dressed in ratty male clothing, clutching the stolen information to her breast like a hulk of driftwood on a raging sea.

"Don't you want to know what brought me to your room so late at night?"

The question stopped her in her tracks. Before, she had been too preoccupied with getting him out of the room to think about his reason for being there in the first place. But now that he brought it up . . .

He didn't wait for her to respond. Her pause a yard from the bedroom was answer enough.

"I was lying in bed, struggling to fall asleep, when an image formed in my mind. Can you guess what that image was?"

She shot him a frosty glare to convey that if he didn't hurry with this little anecdote, she wouldn't stick around to hear the ending.

His mouth lifted in a slight smile as he continued. "It was you," he informed her.

She managed to hide her surprise.

"Standing in front of the door, just as I last saw you. Your hair swept up in that flower-sprigged coronet, your dark violet eyes shining up at me." He rose from the sofa, moving to the bar to refill his glass. "A thought

I'd had earlier floated through my brain. That I had seen eyes that shade only once before in my life."

Tipping back his drink, he emptied it in one swallow and set the glass aside. He walked forward but stopped short of touching her.

"A very unique color, amethyst. It occurred to me that there are probably very few people in the world with eyes just that shade of purple. That I would happen to cross paths with two of them seems beyond belief.

"And then I thought, what if I didn't meet two different women with eyes that sparkled with amethyst fire? What if those magnificent orbs belonged to only one woman?"

His hand came up to cup her chin, tilting her head back so that he could look more deeply into her eyes. "Is it possible that, without realizing it, I've met the same woman twice? First in Missouri, now here in New York?"

Willow pulled away from his grasp, taking a step back to put more space between them. "I don't know what you're rambling on about, Donovan, but I'm tired. If you don't mind, I'm going to bed."

He shrugged a shoulder carelessly. "I was just wondering if maybe we had met somewhere before. Maybe in Missouri."

"Have you completely lost your senses? Of course we met in Missouri. You came there to check on me for Lucas and Megan, remember?" She rolled her eyes at him, then turned and took another step toward the bedroom door.

"Oh, I remember," Brandt answered. "I also remember getting into a slight scrape in an alleyway just inside Jefferson City."

Willow halted with her hand on the doorknob. She swallowed convulsively.

"You see," Brandt continued, "I thought I could help when I spotted two men in the alley, one being held at gunpoint. Imagine my surprise when the man with the gun got the drop on me. I was standing with my back to the wall, a knife at my groin. That's when I noticed the eyes. Bright, vibrant violet eyes. Now, when was the last time you saw a man with violet eyes?" he mocked.

His arms came up on either side of Willow's still form, imprisoning her against the door. She felt his chest brush her back but refused to turn around. Felt his hot breath on her neck but refused to respond.

"I didn't get a very good look at the woman in the alley. She was wearing a knit cap." His finger traced the thick band around her ears. "Kind of like the one you have on right now."

She shook her head, trying to dislodge his finger.

"She was dressed all in black. Much like you are. What a coincidence." He straightened, dropping his arms from her sides.

"It's a shame that I didn't get a better look," he sighed. "But all I really saw were her eyes." With two fingers against her cheek, he slanted her face toward his. Pointing directly at them, he said, "Eyes just that shade of purple."

Turning up his palms, he shrugged dramatically, then moved back to the settee. "Quite a coincidence, wouldn't you agree?" he asked, dropping onto the brocade cushion.

She didn't answer. Her mouth felt like she'd been chewing on sawdust. Her heart pounded in her breast. Her blood drummed through her veins in silent panic.

He knew. She had been lucky until now, but he'd finally put two and two together.

He knew. And he was sitting there, supremely pleased with himself. Playing with her like a cat after a mouse.

He knew. He was simply waiting her out. Letting it sink in. Giving her time to walk into the trap of her own volition.

Well, she wasn't going to give him the satisfaction. If he wanted her to panic and admit to being in that alley, then she would remain calm and keep her mouth shut.

Besides, maybe he really didn't know anything. Maybe he was grabbing at straws, trying to draw her into confessing something he only suspected.

"Good night," she said shortly and pushed open the bedroom door.

"Good night," he called after her. Then, before she closed the door behind her, "Oh, Willow, you wouldn't happen to own an ivory-handled revolver, would you? With a matching stiletto blade?"

Chapter Twelve

Willow leaned weakly against the bedroom door, covering her ears to block out the demonic sound of his mocking laughter.

So he knew. So what?

Brandt already knew she was a Pinkerton agent, so what did it matter if he also knew she'd been the one to accost him in that Jefferson City alleyway? If he hadn't been so blasted nosy in the first place, he wouldn't have gotten a knife put to his groin.

Willow was beginning to wish she'd done as threatened and cut it off.

But what if he told Robert?

Robert would have no problem with her trying to apprehend a criminal in such a manner, but if Brandt also related the circumstances of her residence in Jefferson City, Robert would have her guarding the mayor's poodle before the day was out.

And the only way to keep Brandt from letting the cat

out of the bag was to come clean, level with him, be . . . honest.

The thought made her shiver.

How long had it been since she'd practiced honesty? She couldn't quite remember. Lying had become second nature to her, a reflex. She lied to get out of sticky situations; she lied to get into them. She lied to keep her profession a secret, and she lied to cover up her family background.

She wasn't sure she could tell the truth if she tried.

But now was as good a time as any to find out.

She shrugged out of her heavy black coat and tossed it on the bed, covering the file she'd stolen from Robert's office. Spine stiff, shoulders braced, she held her head high and marched back into the sitting room.

Brandt lounged in the corner of the settee, eyes sparkling in merriment. "I didn't expect to see you again until morning," he said.

She had half a notion to ask why he was still here, in her room, then. Instead of gracing his arrogant presence with a reply, she remained silent. From her waistband, she pulled the pearl-handled Smith & Wesson American revolver, setting it on the low table in front of him. Next came the stiletto knife from inside her boot and the tiny derringer stuffed at the small of her back. The line of weaponry glowed in the lamplight, each positioned pointedly at Brandt's belly.

"I assume that answers your question," Willow said matter-of-factly.

He stared at the miniature munitions collection set before him. Each piece had ivory handles with the carving of a man and woman in seventeenth-century dress beneath a weeping willow tree.

He reached for the pistol, palming it, testing its weight. His eyes never left the ornate carving.

"I take it this is symbolic," he remarked.

"My name is Willow," she answered blandly.

"Was it your idea to have all of your weapons customized this way?"

"They were a gift."

That brought his head up. His green eyes drilled into her own. "From whom?"

"Is that a professional question, or a personal one?"

"I'd like to know who knows you well enough to present you with a veritable armory—all bearing the same scene, indicative of your name. Let me guess: Your parents were so proud of their little girl's decision to work for Pinkerton that they had them special made for you."

Her teeth clamped shut. "My parents were already dead when I joined the Agency."

A hint of remorse touched his eyes. "I'm sorry," he said. "I didn't mean to dredge up painful memories."

She shrugged indifferently, then took a deep breath and tried to relax, reminding herself that Brandt's opinion didn't matter. She was not here seeking his approval. Her stance, however, remained defensive.

"If not your parents, then who?" he asked, going back to his original question.

"Robert," she answered, preparing herself for the onslaught of his contempt.

Instead of lashing out, he simply queried, "Robert Pinkerton?"

She nodded.

Brandt replaced the revolver and picked up the knife. The silver blade attracted a ray of light and bounced it off the far wall. "I didn't realize the Agency gave such expensive gifts to their new operatives." His eyes rose to meet hers. "Or was this a gift of a more personal nature?"

"Robert and I are friends," she answered defensively. "Friends?" he asked. "Or lovers?"

Willow grabbed the knife out of his hand, tucking it back into her boot. In quick, agitated movements, she replaced the rest of the weapons on her person. "Your curiosity goes beyond business, Mr. Donovan. Robert and I are friends, and I resent your implication that there's more to it than that. Now, if you'll excuse me," she said, walking away, "I would like to get a few hours of sleep before I have to see your despicable face again."

"Willow," Brandt called after her. "Willow . . ." He caught up to her just as she crossed the threshold into her bedroom. His fingers curled around her arm, anchoring her in place. She remained facing in the other direction, holding herself rigid, still as a statue.

"I'm sorry," he whispered into the hair above her ear. "I didn't mean to suggest that anything inappropriate is going on between you and your supervisor."

She pulled away from him.

Brandt moved to the foot of the bed, pushed her earlier discarded coat out of the way—without uncovering the photos from Robert's office, thankfully—and sat down. "Now, how about enlightening me as to your presence in that alley the night we first met."

Willow turned, taking in his curious expression and relaxed pose. He sat on the edge of her bed, his back propped against a post, one boot heel digging mercilessly into the soft white of the bedspread.

How was it that this man seemed at home in any environment? She remembered his stance as he stood inside her room at the Silver Spur. The first time she'd found him helping himself to a glass of brandy in her hotel room. And now this. The man looked positively ridiculous perched there at the foot of the huge canopy bed, surrounded by ruffles of angelic white.

A devil on an angel's cloud popped into her head, quickly followed by the thought that she was definitely not an angel.

"Do you make a habit of barging into ladies' rooms?" she asked, her tone scornful.

In true devil's form, a wicked grin spread across his face. "Only when I'm invited."

"I didn't invite you," she pointed out.

"No," Brandt replied smoothly, "but, then, I wouldn't necessarily categorize you as a lady."

Her brows lifted for a moment, until she realized that he was probably right. At least she had never been much of a lady in his presence. She had held a knife to his groin, been found living in a brothel, purposely undressed in front of him, and any number of other very unladylike things.

Still, he wasn't much of a gentleman to say so.

"Besides," he continued, "I intend to discover just why you felt it necessary to nearly emasculate me."

"I didn't nearly emasculate you," Willow defended.

"You did!" he barked. "You broke the skin with that blasted knife of yours!"

Her eyes widened. She didn't recall pressing that hard against his manhood.

"Right here," he said, spreading his legs. He pointed to the very spot she'd supposedly injured, high up—very high up—on the inside of his left thigh.

His trousers covered the abrasion, but his outraged demeanor told her that she must have truly drawn blood. Pride swelled in her chest and she had to pull a straight face to hide her amusement. It wasn't often that she held a blade to a man's groin, but she now knew that when she did, she could do considerable damage.

She felt that she should make some sort of reparation.

The best she could manage was a nearly solemn, "I'm sorry."

Brandt snorted.

"I was on a case," Willow explained. "I'd been following that man for quite a while. So when you interfered, I was not only afraid you'd figure out that I was a woman but furious that you let him get away."

His soulful emerald eyes burned into her. "You weren't the least bit worried that I'd turn you over to the law, were you?"

She smiled, feeling more at ease with this man. She kicked off her boots and perched at the head of the bed. "No."

"Why not?"

"Because all I had to do was show them my Pinkerton badge."

"That wouldn't have blown your cover?"

She shrugged a shoulder. "Probably, but the man from the alley was already long gone. My case was blown."

"All because of me?"

"All because of you," she answered bluntly.

His brow creased as he concentrated. "Robert was awfully nice to me, being the guy who'd botched your case."

Willow averted her gaze, rubbing an imaginary itch beneath the rough fabric of her trousers.

"You didn't tell him, did you?"

She turned back to find Brandt staring at her intently. "No, all right? No, I didn't tell Robert that you interfered and made me lose Sammy the Snake."

"Why not?"

"Because the only thing Robert hates more than hearing about a fouled-up case is hearing a load of excuses for fouling up in the first place."

"But it wouldn't have been an excuse," he pressed. "It's the truth."

She waved a hand in the air. "It doesn't matter. I shouldn't have let you get the drop on me. It was my own fault that Sammy got away."

"Willow," Brandt said with a chuckle, "I'm twice your size. How, exactly, were you supposed to keep me from getting the drop on you?"

"For being only half your size, I'd say I did a pretty good job of defending myself. Or weren't you afraid of becoming a eunuch?"

He winced. "All right, so you had me a little concerned," he admitted. "Who taught you that, anyway?"

"Robert."

"Robert," he repeated. "Of course. You two really must be good friends," he acquiesced, but she thought she detected a note of rancor in his voice. "A man wouldn't show just any woman that move. He'd be too afraid of having her turn it on him."

"I would never hurt Robert," Willow vowed. "I *like* him."

"And you don't like me very much, do you, Willow?" he asked quietly.

She flushed. It was one thing to possess uncharitable feelings, another matter entirely to be called on them. "It's not that I don't like you," she explained. "It's just that I don't particularly like you being around."

Brandt frowned. "What's the difference?"

"Well, I imagine that if we had met under different circumstances, we might have gotten along very well."

"You might have fallen into my arms rather than kicking me in the shin, you mean?"

She sniffed, raising her chin a notch. "I wouldn't go that far."

"So why don't you like me being around?" he asked.

"Because you're compromising my investigation," she answered honestly.

"Charles Barker might have been one of your operatives, but he was killed on one of our trains," he reminded her.

Willow shifted on the bed, sitting up a bit straighter against the headboard. "Charlie was my friend. That makes this case personal."

"Then maybe you shouldn't be working on it at all," Brandt ventured.

She shot him a furious glare.

"If you're planning to make this into some sort of personal quest for revenge, then you're more likely to mess up. You may end up just like Charlie Barker, bleeding to death on the floor of a passenger car with a hundred strangers standing around, staring."

Willow leapt off the bed to pace, shaking an angry hand in Brandt's direction. "Just because I knew Charlie does not mean I'm going to make mistakes. If anything, I'll be more careful and more aware. *You're* the one who's going to foul things up for me."

"Why do you say that?" he asked, not the least offended by her accusation.

"Because this is just another case to you, a problem you need to deal with before you can go back to Boston. You're likely to overlook significant facts, important points that could pull this case together."

He stiffened at the insult, but all he said was, "Then it's a good thing we're partners."

His quiet statement stalled her pacing. She looked at him for some explanation. Hands on hips, she asked, "What does that have to do with anything?"

"You're worried that I'm going to overlook something because I'm not close enough to this case. I'm concerned that you're too close. Since we're partners, we'll be able to keep each other in check."

She didn't want to keep him in check, she wanted to throw him out the nearest window.

"I guess this means you're not reconsidering," she said.

"Reconsidering what?"

"Going back to Boston."

The corners of his mouth lifted. "Not until we wrap this up. And we're never going to do that if you don't tell me where you were this evening."

She sighed wearily. This was one discussion she really didn't want to get into—not this late at night. "Do you think we could talk about it in the morning? I'm awfully tired, Brandt." She felt as though she had been awake for seventy-two hours. All she wanted to do was peel out of her pants and sink into the soft cushion of the bed.

"How do I know you'll still be here in the morning?"

"Because I don't intend to go any farther than that mattress."

"Why don't you give me whatever you found tonight and let me go through it? You can get some sleep and we'll discuss things in the morning."

Willow bristled at that suggestion. She had broken into the Pinkerton building, defiled her best friend's office, and stolen files kept under lock and key. She'd be damned if she would let someone else get the first real look at that information.

"No."

His eyes narrowed. His arms went across his broad chest in an irritated fashion. "Don't tell me you intend to keep it from me. I thought we fought this battle already."

"We did. And I am resigned to the fact that I have to

put up with your miserable hide until we solve Charlie's murder. But I'll be damned if I'm going to let you study that stolen file without me."

His muscular frame lurched up from the bed. "*Stolen?* You didn't tell me you *stole* it. From where?"

She swallowed, cursing herself for a slip of the tongue. "Really, Brandt," she said, licking her lips nervously. "One would think you'd never investigated a murder before."

"I've never *stolen* information before. Where did you get it?"

Sighing, she averted her eyes before answering in a low voice. "The office."

"What office?" he pressed.

"The Executive Office!" she snapped sarcastically. Then, honestly, "The Pinkerton office, where do you think?"

A frown appeared, making the skin around his eyes pucker. "Wait a minute. You broke into your own office? Why, for God's sake? You work there."

"Yes, but I felt there was something about Charlie's murder that Robert wasn't telling me."

"So you broke into his office."

"Yes."

"And stole the information he wouldn't give you freely."

"Yes."

"Do you know that's a crime?"

She clamped her jaw shut. "Yes."

"You could go to jail."

Her teeth ground together. "Yes."

Brandt paused, taking in her tall form, the straggling knot of hair pinned atop her head, the loose black shirt and trousers encasing her body. The thought of her getting caught, being sent to jail, soured his stomach.

110

And yet she had broken the law. For a case. For a friend.

He just hoped the authorities didn't come looking for her. Because, God knew—the way his body tightened at the very thought of touching her—that if the police came knocking at the door, he'd confess to the whole blasted thing and let them drag him away instead.

Chapter Thirteen

Willow covered her mouth as a huge yawn escaped.

Brandt insisted he be allowed to go through the file she'd filched, and since she didn't want him looking at it by himself, she had no choice but to stay awake. She'd exchanged the pants and shirt for her shift and robe and now sat on the floor in front of the settee, photographs and papers cluttering the table.

Brandt sat beside her, sifting through the pages of files she'd copied. For some reason she didn't understand, he found it easier to concentrate while keeping up a normal, totally unrelated conversation. More than once while studying the photographs of the dead girl, he'd hit her with obscure questions like, "What's your favorite color?" and "What do you think you'll want for breakfast?"

Without looking up from her scribbled notes, he said, "Why did you tell Robert we met in St. Louis?"

Vaguely, through the foggy web of drowsiness, she heard him.

He nudged her in the ribs with his elbow. Her head fell off the pillow of her hand and her eyes popped open. "What?" she asked, startled. And then she remembered where she was, and who was with her.

She ran a hand over her face, stifling another yawn. "What did you say?"

"I asked why you told Robert we met in St. Louis."

Willow's mouth turned down. "When?"

"At his office. When he asked where we'd met before, you made a big production of covering up my answer. I was wondering why."

"Oh. Well, I'd already told him about losing Sammy, and your name hadn't come up. I didn't see any reason to alter my story."

His eyes darted to her for a fraction of a second before returning to their perusal of the papers in his hand. "Just because we happened to meet in Jefferson City doesn't necessarily mean I had anything to do with your failed assignment."

She groaned and buried her head in her hands. Logic. At five o'clock in the morning. It was almost too much to bear. Her mind had shut down hours ago. She couldn't even come up with a decent reason not to answer him.

"Do you remember where you found me in Jefferson City?" she asked.

"Yeah. In a dark alley, holding some guy at gunpoint."

"No," she said wearily. "I mean, after that. Before you knew who I was and you were simply looking for Willow Hastings. Where did you find me?"

A wide, wicked smile spread across his face. Straight

white teeth gleamed in the brightness of several burning oil lamps set throughout the room. "I seem to recall a rather seedy place by the name of the Silver Spur. A small, shadowy room, and a gorgeous brunette with legs that went all the way to Paradise."

"Yes, yes," she said, waving off his colorful description. "I'm sure Stella showed you the time of your life, but do you remember finding me?"

Brandt leaned close, until his breath caressed the side of her face and ear. "I was talking about you," he whispered. "And *your* legs."

She looked at him, wide awake now. Then a modest grin curved her lips. "I didn't think you'd noticed," she said.

He snorted, leaning back against the sofa. "A man would have to be dead not to notice," he scoffed. "And even then, I think he'd put a hold on Heaven just to get one last look."

The compliment, no matter how coated in pure male egotism, warmed her heart. It felt good to be appreciated—even for only her looks. Even by drunks in a barroom, or arrogant investigative partners.

"I didn't want Robert to know where we really met because I didn't want him to find out what I'd been doing or where I'd been staying. I was afraid you'd let it slip."

The papers in his hand forgotten, he focused his undivided attention on Willow. "You mean your supervisor didn't know you were singing in a brothel? Didn't know you kept a room there, as well?"

"Not exactly," she answered. "And it wasn't *only* a brothel. There was a saloon there, too."

"It was a whorehouse!" he bellowed.

She cringed at his harsh tone of voice.

"It's one thing for you to be singing for your supper

as part of your disguise, if your supervisor knows. But rooming with a bunch of prostitutes like it's a boarding house is another matter entirely. Especially if your supervisor doesn't have the faintest notion!"

"What are you getting so upset about?" Willow asked. "It's not like you're responsible for my welfare."

"You could have gotten hurt," he ranted. "Or worse, one of the customers could have decided that you were as good as any other whore in the place."

That rankled. "Beverly made sure everyone knew I wasn't for hire. And there were some rather large bouncers who kept an eye out for me."

"How convenient," Brandt snapped. "So why didn't these overly attentive bouncers happen to notice you sneaking in and out of the place dressed like a man?"

"Because I was dressed like a man!" she yelled back. "And because I was careful."

"Not careful enough, obviously, or you wouldn't have let me get the drop on you."

Her pride stung. Her hackles rose. "You may have gotten the drop on me, but you did not best me. Or did you forget that it was my knife that nearly unmanned you?"

By this time they were on their feet, hands on hips, faces red with anger. Mere inches of empty space separated them.

"You may have held a knife to my groin, but you didn't have the nerve to do anything about it."

Willow blanched at his tone of voice. "I'll show you nerve," she threatened. "Give me a knife and I'll gut and geld you before you have time to blink."

Brandt seemed at a loss for words after that declaration. His cheeks turned pink. His lips thinned into a chalky white slash across his face.

"You're a tease," he said with no real conviction.

"You're a cad," she tossed back, not in the least offended by his remark.

"You're a lying, conniving little harlot."

Her eyes widened for a moment at that one. "You're an obnoxious, conceited bastard."

"You're a manipulative little twit."

"You're an arrogant scoundrel."

"You're a dim-witted old maid."

"You're a brainless Neanderthal."

His jaw locked. His voice became rough. "I want you."

She swallowed hard, feeling an undeniable heat climb its way up through her stomach. "What are you waiting for?"

Brandt reached her in one stride. His arms came around her in a vicelike grip, cradling her close to his chest. His lips were like fire, licking, burning her tender skin. Their mouths met in a powerful, passionate kiss, scorching in its intensity.

Willow moaned as her legs gave out. Without breaking the kiss, Brandt swept her up in his arms and made his way to the bedroom. He whipped back the covers and deposited her in the middle of the bed, following her down. His lips trailed away from her mouth, marking a path of wet, sucking kisses down her throat.

Her head fell back, granting him greater access. The weight of his torso resting between her legs sent shivers of excitement through her limbs. Her fingers went to the front of his shirt, deftly releasing the buttons and pulling the tails from the waistband of his trousers.

His hands smoothed down her sides, stopping at the belt of her robe. With a quick tug, the narrow tie came loose. The red satin fell open to reveal the nearly transparent material of her shift. He slipped an arm around

Willow's waist and lifted her so that the robe fluttered from her arms to the sheets.

He eased her back onto the mattress, then moved away. Willow cried out at his sudden absence and then took a sharp breath when she saw that he was only discarding his own constricting clothing. He came back to her, splendorously naked.

A hand raked beneath the shift, forcing the material up as his hand stroked her hip, belly, the underside of her breast. She lifted her arms and allowed him to slip the annoying article over her head.

"Brandt," she whispered. And the sound was swallowed up by his mouth. His tongue delved deep, tangling with her own, drawing her into a maelstrom of hot, fevered emotions and tiny, mewling cries.

His hands kneaded her breasts, his thumbs making devastatingly arousing circles over each nipple, drawing them into hard, pebbled peaks.

"Brandt," she breathed again as his lips closed over one aching tip. His mouth was so warm on her breast, his hands so strong and sure as they grasped her hips. He positioned himself between her legs, his shaft pulsing at the opening of her desire. His fingers brushed through the downy auburn curls, seeking the hidden nub of pleasure within.

He found her slick and ready, her need so strong that she arched into his hand. He had never been with a woman who became so hot so fast. The urge to drive into her, to let himself be swept away in a tide of pleasure was so great, he had to bite down on his lower lip to maintain a thin strand of composure.

As far as he knew, she was a virgin, he reminded himself. He had to go slow. He had to make it good for her, too.

She whimpered and twisted beneath him, nearly severing his last tenuous thread of control. "Shh," he whispered, tucking a strand of hair behind her ear. "It's all right," he told her. "I'll be gentle, I promise."

She answered by tangling her fingers in his own hair and tugging his mouth down to hers. Her breasts pressed flat between them. Her legs wrapped around his hips.

Brandt slid into her easily, groaning with the exquisite pleasure that simple motion brought. He buried his face in her neck until he thought he could breathe without coming apart. Then he began to move. Slowly at first, giving her body time to adjust to his invasion. Her nails dug into his back, urging him to continue.

He kissed her ear, nipping the lobe, let his tongue trail across her jaw until he reached her mouth. Her lips opened beneath his and he kissed her, wrapping his tongue around hers, licking the edge of her teeth while one hand toyed with a pert nipple and the other delved between their bodies.

His fingertips skirted the mat of hair between her legs, drawing a line straight to the source of her enjoyment. While he moved inside her, increasing his rhythm and movements, he touched the bud of sensation and felt Willow tense with pleasure. Her breath caught in her throat and it took a full minute for her to begin breathing again. All the while, his finger flicked and whirled, drawing agonizing cries from her near-frozen lungs.

He wanted to give her fulfillment. Wanted her to come before he did, but as her cries and undulations increased, his control began to slip. He grit his teeth, hanging on with a silk-thin strand of control. If she didn't reach her climax soon, he would be forced to go before her—and then backtrack to give her her pleasure.

Willow's nails dug into his shoulders, her head arched into the pillows, and her hips rose to meet his thrusts. "Now," she whispered raggedly. "Please, now."

And that was all it took for Brandt to grant her wish. He clutched an arm around her waist, pulling her closer, at the same time locking his mouth to hers. And as her legs wrapped more tightly about his waist and her cries of delight reached a crescendo, he held a thumb to her clitoris and took one last, hard thrust.

Tremors of satisfaction wracked them both and he rolled to his side to keep from falling off the edge of the bed. Willow went with him easily, her arms around his neck, her face pillowed in the curve of his neck. He was still inside her, but she didn't seem to mind. She simply pulled her knees up to accommodate their position.

Which made him wonder . . .

Had she seemed a touch too passionate for an untried virgin? Had she fallen into bed with him just a little too easily? Had his passage been a bit too smooth?

He gave his head a mental shake. Of course she'd been a virgin. Willow might possess the smartest mouth he'd ever encountered on a woman, she may even toss around innuendoes like they were confetti, but she had only been in that brothel on a job for the Pinkerton Agency, not as a working girl. She had to be . . .

Then again, did it matter? It shouldn't. But in the recesses of his mind, he couldn't help thinking that it did.

He wasn't used to deflowering virgins—avoided them like the plague most times. But then, he wasn't used to smart-mouthed, hot-blooded female Pinkerton agents, either. And he damn well didn't like the idea of Willow being with other men. One or a dozen, it didn't matter. He damn well didn't like it.

With hot coals of anger suddenly burning a hole in his gut, he shifted to roll Willow away from him and then moved to the other side of the mattress to get out of bed. He didn't bother looking back as he rounded the bed and picked up his discarded clothes, then began to dress with quick, efficient movements.

He heard a soft rustle and assumed Willow was shrugging into her robe. He was glad. He wasn't sure he could maintain this level of moral outrage if he turned to see her still naked and lovely on that soft, warm mattress.

He waited until he was fully dressed, until he had his disappointment sufficiently tamped down, until his breathing was slow and even. Then he turned to face her.

She sat with her back to the ornately carved headboard, that bloody red robe wrapped around her lithe form once again. And in her eyes . . . in her eyes was a flicker of passion that had nothing to do with what they'd just shared in that bed. No, he suspected the passion burning in those amethyst orbs had more to do with anger than lust. Anger and betrayal. He had used her, seduced her, dragged her into bed. Only to roll away and abandon her moments after he'd gained satisfaction.

He was a heel. Lower than gutter swine, rooting through day-old trash and refuse.

And even though he was miserably unhappy about her past experience with men and her . . . well, her past in general, he was no better for treating her so abominably.

He opened his mouth to apologize. And couldn't think of a single thing to say. Was he sorry he'd slept with her, or sorry she hadn't been a virgin? Sorry he'd moved away like that, or sorry they'd tainted their working relationship with passion?

Truth be told, he wasn't sure he was sorry for any of those things. He certainly couldn't be sorry they'd made love; he'd wanted to do that since he opened the door to her room at the Silver Spur and caught a glimpse of her long, luxurious legs while she removed her stockings.

And he should be *glad* she hadn't been a virgin. For God's sake, he'd made a practice of avoiding innocents since soon after he'd been one himself. An experienced woman could give a man untold pleasures in bed. They also knew enough about secret liaisons to not catch a child in their bellies.

Granted, neither of them had had much time for, nor given much thought to, that sort of thing, but in the future, an experienced woman like Willow would know how to be more cautious so that they could enjoy the company of each others' bodies without the risk of serious and unwanted consequences.

He *was* sorry he'd moved away from her so quickly. His rioting emotions had gotten the better of him and caused him to bolt instead of thinking things through while remaining in the warm comfort of her embrace. And the fact that she apparently thought he'd moved away from *her* and not simply what—in his mind—she represented, caused a sharp pang of regret.

It did concern him a bit that their relationship had crossed a line from professional to personal. They hadn't been getting along very well as investigative partners; what had they—*he*—been thinking to let things get so far out of control? He'd wanted her, true. But he'd wanted other women before and been able to avoid them. How were he and Willow going to work together now that they'd slept together? As though Willow hadn't harbored enough animosity toward him before . . . one look at her hard, stern face told him that her demeanor toward him earlier was nothing compared to what it would be from this moment forward.

"Willow, I—"

She cut him off before he got two words out, holding up a hand and swinging her legs over the mattress. "Don't bother," she clipped out. She tugged the robe

121

more tightly around her body as her feet touched the floor. Her chemise was left behind, crumpled on the mattress where they'd made love.

"But I want—"

"I know what you want," she snapped, her eyes shooting fire. "You wanted me—or so you say. You wanted to fulfill your base, animal desires and I was handy. Fine."

She plucked her wrinkled chemise from the bed and tossed it away. He felt sure she treated the garment as she wanted to treat what had happened between them; throw it into a corner and forget about it.

"Now that you've had your satisfaction, I suggest we forget this ghastly mistake ever occurred and go back to investigating Charlie's murder."

He'd been right, he thought, as his eyes darted to the crinkled-up ball of linen in the corner. But he'd be darned if he was going to let her toss him away as easily as she had her soiled chemise.

"Willow, listen."

Willow watched his lips move, watched his hands fist and unfist in the pockets of the trousers he'd donned so quickly after their little liaison. When would she learn? When would it ever sink into her thick skull that she and men were as volatile a combination as a stick of dynamite and a lit match?

She refused to meet his eyes as she marched past him toward the sitting room door. "No, thank you," she said in response to his request. "I've had about as much of you as I can stomach tonight. I'm tired and not in a particularly good mood, so I would really prefer you simply leave."

Although she refused to look directly at him, in her peripheral vision she saw his lips compress into a thin line, a muscle in his jaw jumping. He began to open his mouth, to again plead with her for . . . what? Sympathy? Understanding? Forgiveness? *Sorry,* she thought, *but I'm just not that good an actress.* And she wasn't in the habit of thanking men for making her feel like a paid companion.

"Go. Now," she said, before he could utter a word. "Please."

It was the please that got through to him. His shoulders slumped a fraction, his jaw relaxed, and he pulled his clenched hands from his pockets. She pulled the door wider as he walked past, and even though he turned toward her once he'd reached the other side, she didn't give him a chance to say anything more, but closed the door on his face.

If tears sprang to her eyes, she refused to acknowledge them. She'd never had time for tears and she'd be damned if an arrogant Union Pacific officer would be the one to bring them forth. No, if anything her sadness stemmed from a deep, gut-wrenching disappointment in herself. Hadn't she learned her lesson the last time she'd let a man into her heart—and her bed?

Robert was her best friend now, but back then, he'd been her . . . infatuation. Yes, that was the best word to describe how she'd felt about him. She'd been young. He'd been young, but still older and more sophisticated than she. He'd been her supervisor, the dapper son of Allan Pinkerton, whom she'd loved like a father. And she'd fallen in love with him. Or so she'd thought. In truth, it had been merely a girlish fascination. She'd given him her heart, and her virginity, but it had taken Allan Pinkerton's death and the realization that Robert was not the man for her for Willow to come to her senses.

It had been a hard, painful lesson, but she'd learned it well. And since then, she and Robert had been able to get through the embarrassment and insecurities of their past to not only continue working together but to care for each other like family. She loved him as a brother now and wouldn't change that for anything in the world.

She sighed and moved farther into the bedroom, avoiding the bed as she moved toward the luxurious lavatory. She looked at her reflection in the large oval, gilt-framed mirror hanging above the water basin. Her hair was a wild tangle and her normally pale skin turned an even deeper shade of pink as she thought about what she had done to turn her hair into such a wild mess.

At least with Brandt, she had the luxury of retaining her heart. He hadn't come remotely close to touching her there. And if she'd made a gargantuan mistake by getting swept up by his passion and letting him into her bed, at least there was no chance of losing her heart as well as her reputation and peace of mind.

He was a fine male specimen, she'd give him that. His tall, muscular form and broad shoulders had caught her attention the first time she'd seen him in that alley. And soon after, she'd taken notice of his hair, eyes, and strong hands. But she'd seen any number of handsome men in her life. Though they occasionally had the power to turn her head, they never turned more than that.

With her personal history, not to mention the responsibility of keeping her job in order to provide and care for Erik, she knew better than to let her head fill with any silly notions of love and happily-ever-after. Unless the man who turned her head was willing to accept her brother and support them both for the rest of their days, he had no place in her life.

Brandt had gotten past her defenses, that's all. A momentary lapse in diligence, brought on by their late night of looking over Charlie's files, too little sleep, losing

Sammy in Jefferson City, the fear of losing her job altogether, of living in the Silver Spur for too long . . . All of those things and a dozen more had compounded and worked against her better judgment. She'd suffered a setback, but it was nothing she couldn't work through.

After a few hours of sleep, she would wake, dress, and confront Brandt in a much more reasonable frame of mind. She would simply tell him that tonight . . . last night . . . had been a mistake. It would not happen again, so it would be best that they both put it behind them and move on. They would work together on Charlie's case if they must but would otherwise have nothing to do with each other.

Simple.

And if Brandt had a problem with that, she would just have to remind him exactly what she was capable of with her little pearl-handled stiletto. Only this time, a measly cut wouldn't be the extent of the damage.

Chapter Fourteen

At exactly midnight, beneath a crescent moon, the dark-haired prostitute was returned to the edge of the wharf, to the very spot where she had been standing not two hours earlier. A perfect white rose rested between her breasts, clasped tightly between hands folded in prayer.

Chapter Fifteen

Despite being tired enough to rest comfortably on a bed of nails, Brandt didn't sleep after leaving Willow's room. He'd lingered in her sitting room for several minutes, gathering and organizing the files and photos they'd been looking over. A part of him was relieved that Willow had kicked him out, saving him from having to say something when he wasn't quite sure what to say. But another part of him hoped she would come out and let him explain. Not that he had a clue how to go about that. If he had, he'd have done it much sooner.

He was used to sharing a few blindingly passionate moments with a woman—sometimes one he barely knew—and then walking away. But with Willow, he didn't want to walk away. He didn't want to leave with this animosity between them. And it had very little to do with the fact that they still had to work together.

So Brandt lingered in the sitting room. And when it became apparent that Willow wouldn't be coming out, he meandered across the hall to his own room. Then he lingered there, pouring himself a drink, staring into the flames of the fireplace, wondering how in God's name he could have bolted from one of the most pleasant sexual encounters of his life. Calling himself ten kinds of fool.

When the clock on the mantel chimed eight and he lifted his head to see daylight pouring in through the open drapes, he rubbed his tired eyes, threw back the last swallow of scotch in his glass, and steeled his resolve.

Willow had wanted them to begin their partnership at eight o'clock this morning, so they damn well would. He set his glass on the fireplace mantel with a clink and moved toward the hallway.

He opened the door, only to find Willow standing on the other side, a hand raised to knock. The moment he saw her, a spark of awareness flared in his belly and spread outward through his bloodstream. She wore a gown of deep, vibrant plum that perfectly matched her eyes. Her hair was braided and twisted into a complicated coronet that gathered at the back of her head, a few sprigs of flowers stuck in the strands for decoration. Except for the slight hint of shadows beneath her eyes, she looked entirely rested and ready to tackle another day.

Brandt, on the other hand, looked like hell, and he knew it. He hadn't gotten a wink of sleep, was still wearing the same clothes as last evening, and probably smelled like a distillery since he'd nursed a bottle of whiskey ever since returning to his room.

He immediately experienced another sharp jab of regret at the way they'd parted and tried to make amends. "Willow," he began, "about last night . . ."

A flare of hurt darkened her eyes a moment before

her shoulders pulled back and her spine snapped ramrod straight. "I'd rather not discuss last night, if it's all the same to you," she informed him in a lofty tone.

His jaw clenched, his fingers tightening around the doorknob under his hand. "No, it's not all the same to me," he told her, struggling to keep hold of his temper. "We need to talk about what happened, about where we go from here."

Willow toyed with the drawstrings of her matching purple reticule and shot him a glare filled with cool indifference. "Last night's incident isn't worthy of debate. It's over and done with and never should have happened in the first place."

A measure of her righteous indignation seemed to be replaced by modest chagrin as she turned her head away. Her eyes refused to meet his as her tone softened only a degree. "And since there's absolutely no chance of it happening again, I see no reason to waste time conferring over what occurred."

He could see she had no intention of uttering another word on the subject. And most times that would be just fine with him. This time, however, it wasn't. And damned if he knew why.

He only knew that his jaw throbbed from the grinding of his teeth. His hand squeezed the crystal-cut knob of the door hard enough to draw blood, and if he let himself touch her, he'd most likely rattle the teeth right out of her head.

So he would let the subject drop. For now.

After several seconds of tense silence, Willow crossed her arms beneath her breasts and assumed an agitated stance. "I take it you're once again planning to hold up my investigation," she stated primly, slanting a distasteful glance over his wrinkled shirt and breeches and summarily dismissing their prior topic of discussion.

Caught slightly off guard by the change of subject, he opened his mouth to correct her—it was *their* investigation, not hers alone—but realized he was too tired to pick up that argument once again.

"On the contrary," he said instead, deliberately relaxing his muscles and loosening his hold on the door. "I was just on my way over to wake you. I thought you might have slept in but knew how eager you were to get an early start this morning." He stepped out of the room, forcing her back a pace. "Shall we go?"

"Like that?" she asked. "You intend to walk around like that?"

He looked down at himself, wondering just how bad he must look for *her* to be offended. After all, this was the same woman who had stumbled in last night dressed in fisherman's garb and smelling like week-old carp.

A small amber stain marred the front of his shirt. Scotch, no doubt. Spilled when he was concentrating more on Willow than getting the liquid fully into his mouth. Lifting an arm, he took a quick sniff and admitted that he smelled none too pleasant this morning, himself.

Catching his subtle self-assessment, Willow raised a brow. Her haughty air set his teeth on edge. So he hadn't bathed or changed clothes since early yesterday morning and was beginning to turn ripe. She had lived in a brothel and sung to a roomful of cowpokes who smelled much worse than he, he was sure. Which didn't give her much room to judge, in his opinion.

"Come in," he ordered, pushing the door open once again. "I'll just be a minute." He turned and marched across the room, not bothering to make certain Willow followed. As he reached the bedroom, he heard the main door click shut and out of the corner of his eye saw the swish of her skirt across the room. He gave a silent huff of approval. At least she'd done one thing without argument.

"What do you have planned for today?" he asked as he discarded his wrinkled clothes and poured a bit of tepid water into the deep sink of the connected washroom.

"Does the name Yvonne Xavier ring any bells?" she asked from the other room, her voice raised to clearly reach his ears.

He rolled his eyes, wondering if Willow thought him daft. "The name on the file. Of course," he answered shortly.

"Yes, but I mean otherwise. Other than the fact that she was murdered, have you ever heard her family's name before?"

With a damp cloth and a sliver of soap, Brandt swabbed his chest and under his arms, trying to recall any recognition of the name. "I don't think so; why?"

"Being from Boston, you might not be familiar with some of the wealthier families here in New York. I didn't even catch the relation at first." Her voice drew closer and he quickly fastened the clean pair of trousers he'd just slipped on.

"The Xaviers live here in town. The father owns a local fabric mill. Yvonne was their only and very beloved daughter. This morning I remembered reading a newspaper article on the train back to New York about how she disappeared after a function at the family's home one evening last month. She was only nineteen years old."

Willow's form appeared in the doorway as she rested a shoulder against the jamb. She didn't bother glancing in his direction. Just as well, he decided as he tugged at the waistband of his clean pants.

"Since Charlie Barker was working Yvonne Xavier's

case, I can only assume her family hired Pinkerton to find her."

For a split second, as he looked up from tugging on his boots, he caught Willow staring at him, her eyes centered on his still-bare chest. As soon as she realized he'd raised his head, she quickly turned away. With her mouth turned down in a frown, she stared across the room, focusing on a rather unspectacular piece of artwork, in Brandt's opinion. Once again, she began to fidget with the strap of her satchel.

Like hell it was over, he thought, fighting a grin. She may think their bout of lovemaking was only a fluke. She might even believe it. But if he had anything to say about it, last night's events most certainly would occur again.

He turned toward the bureau for a clean shirt, nearly breaking out in a whistle. Willow could be determined and mule-stubborn, but she'd never yet run up against him when his mind was set. And right now, his mind was set on her.

"You were saying . . ." he prompted casually over his shoulder. He took his own sweet time deciding on a shirt. Studying first one, then another. Feeling the fabric and making sure to flex the muscles of his back as he moved.

After a moment he felt Willow's heated gaze on him and smiled. He'd known that water lily painting couldn't occupy her for long.

"I was saying . . . what?" she mumbled.

"You thought the Xavier family had hired the Pinkerton Agency to find Yvonne, since Charlie was working the case," he reminded her. He chose a shirt and turned, using slow motions to slip his arms into the sleeves, pull the sides closed, slide each button through its proper hole.

"Yes." She cleared her throat and forced her eyes to his. "Yes, that's what I thought," she said more strongly. "And when Yvonne was found dead, Charlie apparently stayed on to find the killer."

"Until someone murdered him," Brandt added, knowing Willow was thinking the same thing. He tucked the tails of his shirt into his pants, done toying with her. For the moment. "Do you think he figured out who killed the Xavier girl?"

"Possibly." The lines on her forehead deepened in distress.

"And whoever that person is, he killed Charlie to cover up his crime?"

"Most likely," she reluctantly agreed. "Otherwise . . ."

"Otherwise, there was no reason for Charlie to die." New York might be crowded and have a higher risk of crime than other cities, but even so, people did not go around stabbing innocent people on crowded passenger trains.

There was no reason for Charlie to die, regardless, Willow thought with a spurt of anger. Charlie had only been doing his job. And anyone who would murder a young girl deserved to be brought to justice.

"There was no mention in the file of who Charlie suspected of Yvonne's murder." She worried her bottom lip with her teeth.

Brandt finished dressing and moved to stand before her. She lifted her head absently, meeting his hazel eyes. Being so close to him brought back a wash of memories from the night before and she quickly looked away. She didn't care to think about last night. Nor did she care for a repeat performance.

And she didn't even want to consider why witnessing his bare torso had sent her pulse rate soaring. It was just a chest, for heaven's sake. She'd seen the male variety before and would no doubt see it again upon occasion.

If Brandt Donovan's bare chest seemed to be exceptionally well chiseled, if the muscles seemed to flex and flow a bit too gracefully, the smooth skin to glisten a golden bronze . . . why, that was just a trick of the early morning sunlight streaming through the open drapes.

She hadn't slept, was forced to deal with Brandt again this morning, still needed to find out who had killed Charlie, and had so far been unable to dispel the unfortunate memory of her misspent lust not two hours before. All of these things combined to lower her defenses. Otherwise, she was sure she would find Brandt Donovan loathsome rather than sinfully handsome.

Give her half a minute to gather her wits and she would. Turning the other way, she strode across the sitting room.

"Do you think she knew her attacker?" he asked from several feet behind her.

Willow's brows knit and she stopped, his pointed question bringing her back to the matter at hand. It was possible *she* knew Yvonne's attacker. *Gideon.* That was, if Charlie's note was accurate and connected to the girl's death, as she suspected. Unfortunately, she couldn't be sure. She couldn't even be certain Gideon was a person. It could just as easily be a social club, a street address, or the name of some man's horse.

"Why do you ask that?" she questioned Brandt, turning slightly to face him.

"You said she disappeared from a function at her family's home. Chances are, she remained at the house all night. She would have had no reason to be out where a stranger could abduct her."

"True. She could have known the person and gone willingly."

"Or known the person and not realized the danger she was in until it was too late. Which means that we may not be looking for just anyone. We may be looking for someone in Society. A wealthy aristocrat, an acquaintance of the Xavier family. What do you think?"

He had a good point, which might narrow the scope of their investigation. "There's something else I discovered in Yvonne's file this morning. A handwritten note on the back of one of the photographs, which is probably why we missed it the first time." She didn't bother to add that the only reason she'd spotted it at all was because she hadn't slept a wink last night and had ended up poring over all of the notes and evidence in the hours before she decided to get dressed and pretend nothing had happened between Brandt and herself.

Her eyes narrowed as she concentrated on the proper wording. "It said, 'Exactly like the others, but Yvonne wasn't a prostitute.' Do you have any idea what that might mean?"

Brandt stiffened, his spread-legged stance growing even more rigid. With his hands on his hips and his eyes narrowed, he said, "I believe it means we're in more trouble than we thought."

Chapter Sixteen

"And might I ask just how you came by this information?" Robert stood behind his desk, hands on hips, fixing a pointed gaze at Willow.

"You might," Willow replied, "but I would rather you didn't."

Robert's nostrils flared as his eyes shot daggers. "Allow me to rephrase that," he clipped out through lips stiffened in outrage. "How—*exactly*—did you come by the information?"

His tone brooked no arguments, but Willow wasn't about to admit to having broken into his office. "I dropped by to visit Charlie's widow yesterday," Willow told him, the lie falling easily from her lips. "Once I told her I was working to find Charlie's killer, she gave me his most recent case file in hopes that it would aid the investigation."

She glanced absently at Brandt, only to find him staring back at her, eyes wide, mouth agape. She widened her own eyes for a fraction of a second, silently urging him not to naysay her. If he did, if Robert caught so much as a whiff of deceit, they would both be thrown out on their ears.

Robert's brows winged downward at her account. "It's Agency policy to keep only two copies of everything involved in a case—one for the agent's supervisor, the other for the archived records room after the agent has closed the case. We have both copies of Charlie's most recent files here in the office. Are you saying he had a third at home?"

"Yes, there was a third," she responded readily with the answer that Robert himself had provided. She refused to look in Brandt's direction again, for fear he would give something away.

Lips pursed, Robert began to pace the short space behind his desk.

"Excuse me," Brandt finally spoke, shifting in his chair. "It's beginning to look as though Charlie was killed because of his work on the Xavier case. Are we all in agreement on that fact?" He glanced at Robert, then Willow, not waiting for affirmation. "So regardless of how many copies of the file exist, I'm wondering why we weren't simply given the information in the beginning," he said with a pointed glance at Robert. "We might have tracked down the killer by now, if we'd known what Charlie was working on."

"It didn't seem pertinent at the time," was Robert's reply.

It was Brandt's turn to raise a brow, Willow noted.

Robert had the grace to look contrite. "This was my lack of foresight, and I apologize," he said, nobly taking the blame. "I didn't realize that Charlie's connection to the Xavier case had anything to do with his death. I should have, but I didn't."

He took a deep breath and let it out on a sigh. "Charlie didn't report any of this to me. Which is not to say he wouldn't have; he may not have had the chance before he was killed."

When Brandt and Willow had told Robert of Charlie's scrawled note and the other details they were beginning to piece together, Robert had immediately informed them of the recent string of killings down by the docks. Apparently, someone was murdering working girls and leaving their bodies on the wharf to be found. The authorities suspected the same man of committing all the crimes because of the similarities in the way the girls were killed, as well as how the bodies were arranged. A recent newspaper article that Robert showed them mentioned the victims' arms being crossed over their chests, a single white rose found clutched in their hands.

The very thought made Willow's stomach revolt.

"The Xaviers are a very influential family. They wanted their daughter found, and after her death, they wanted her killer found. They did not, however, want the details of Yvonne's death or the subsequent investigation revealed." He shook his head sadly. "I didn't even have much knowledge of the case myself. It never occurred to me that her murder was connected to the others."

Willow understood Robert's regret and sense of failure. "Apparently, it only recently occurred to Charlie. Yvonne wasn't like the other girls; she hadn't been walking the docks. It's understandable that no one put the two incidents together."

The paper in Brandt's hand crinkled as he clutched it, his knuckles going white in anger. "Another body was found just two nights ago. What the hell is going on in this town? Five women are dead and no one seems to be out looking for the bastard who's murdering them."

"We've got a problem," Robert said, clearing his throat at the understatement. "That much is obvious. Unfortunately, because all of the victims were prostitutes, no one seems eager to find the killer. The wealthier citizens who could raise enough of a fuss to form a full-scale manhunt aren't overly concerned. They consider themselves far enough removed from that element to be perfectly safe going about their everyday lives." He cast his eyes downward before continuing in a low tone, "And frankly, some people think these women deserve it. Being morally corrupt and all."

"Nobody deserves this," Brandt spat and slapped the newspaper on the desktop.

"And Yvonne Xavier wasn't a prostitute," Willow reminded them softly. "She was the daughter of a wealthy merchant. Her status in Society didn't save her."

"You're right," Robert agreed. "But I don't think people realize that. The details of Yvonne's death were covered up. Partially by us, at the family's request, but mostly by the family themselves. They didn't want it known that she was found down by the docks. It was bad enough that she'd gone missing and was then found dead; they didn't want her memory and reputation tarnished any further."

"The point is," Brandt put in, "whoever is committing these murders *isn't* limiting himself to only dock whores."

"Unless Yvonne's death was simply made to look like the others." Willow lifted her head and exchanged glances with both men. "She could have been killed by someone else, for another reason entirely, and then dumped by the docks to throw off the authorities' suspicions."

"In which case, it was probably by someone she knew. Someone who traveled in the same circles."

Brandt picked up the stack of newspapers Robert had shown them, each containing a different article about the dockside killings, and began rifling through the pages. "Wasn't a carriage seen near the scene of one of the murders? An expensive carriage, with some sort of crest that the witness couldn't quite make out?"

He continued hunting until he found the information he was looking for. "Yes. An expensive, black, personal carriage was seen shortly before a body was found."

"That doesn't prove anything." Robert cleared his throat, casting a quick glance at Willow before looking away and adding, "Wealthy gentlemen are often seen in that area of the city, picking up and dropping off..." He cleared his throat again. "Um, women."

Willow ignored Robert's discomfort with the subject of women bartering their bodies for money. He'd been fine discussing the case when the victims had been anonymous prostitutes. But now that he had to discuss the actual events that took place when a man paid for a woman's favors, he seemed decidedly uncomfortable.

"Maybe that's exactly what he was doing," she said. "Dropping someone off. Only this time, she was dead."

"So you really believe the killer is someone in high society," Robert remarked. It was more of a statement than a question. "Not a drunken sailor or a prisoner escaped from the asylum, but someone with enough money to have my job if you're wrong."

"It's a distinct possibility," Brandt said simply, bringing one booted leg up to rest on the opposite knee.

Robert sighed. "I was afraid of that. So what do you propose we do?"

"I think our first plan of action should be to talk to Yvonne Xavier's family," Willow said. "They might remember someone who attended the ball at their home the night Yvonne disappeared. Or recall a gentleman who paid their daughter a bit too much attention."

Robert nodded. "It's a delicate situation, but hopefully the Xaviers will cooperate if they think it will help bring their daughter's killer to justice."

Willow turned her focus to Brandt. He seemed to be deep in thought, tapping his steepled hands against his lips. Full, pale lips that had touched her flesh just last evening. Touched her everywhere.

But she didn't want to think about that. She didn't want to think about any part of what had passed between them. Especially since she was determined that it would never happen again.

She tamped down on the warm rush of sensation that threatened to flood her belly . . . and lower . . . and forced herself to look elsewhere. Which caused her to notice a slight frown marring his brow.

She gave a silent sigh and watched him for a moment, awaiting the inevitable. Waiting for him to disagree with her suggestion, as she knew he would.

"I have a better idea," he said finally, his hands falling to the arms of his chair. "Or rather, one that might work with your suggestion."

"And just what might that be?" She wanted to sound annoyed. She *was* annoyed, but only slightly. More than that, she was resigned. She and Brandt hadn't agreed on anything thus far, why should their subsequent actions concerning the case be any different?

"I think we should infiltrate the circle of friends Yvonne Xavier would have been in contact with. We might learn more if people thought they were confiding in their equals rather than answering questions for outsiders."

Willow blinked. "How do you propose we do that?" she asked. She had never been a part of high society. Pretending to be a songbird was simple. Even disguising herself as a man barely posed a problem. But convincing mannered, sometimes snobbish citizens that she was one of them would be nearly impossible.

Brandt cast a meaningful glance over her body, starting at her eyes and traveling well below her breasts. "You fill out that dress rather nicely," he commented with obvious double meaning. "Provided you can keep your temper under control, I have no doubt you can convince everyone that you're a new member of the upper crust, just arrived in town."

His flagrant perusal of her form raised just enough annoyance for her to snap, *"Temper?* I do not have a temper."

It wasn't until Brandt raised a brow and Robert tried— unsuccessfully—to stifle a laugh that she realized her voice had risen. She immediately grew silent, pursing her lips and smoothing a hand serenely over the bodice of her gown. "What does my lack of temper have to do with being accepted within Society?"

Brandt chuckled. "If you can get a handle on that temper you claim not to possess, I don't think we'll have a problem. All you have to do is pretend that you adore me."

As hard as Willow tried, she couldn't muffle a dissenting snort. She could barely tolerate being in the same room with him. It would take all of the Argonauts in Jason's army and the Hounds of Hell besides to drag anything even resembling adoration from her.

She fixed him with a glare that she hoped displayed the likelihood of her compliance with his request. She imagined birds would talk and man would fly long before she ever learned to adore anything about this man. "And why, pray tell, would I want to do that?"

He flashed her a grin that warned her only a moment in advance that she was in trouble. Deep, dark trouble.

"Don't all blushing new brides adore their husbands?"

Chapter Seventeen

Willow didn't blush. She did curse, beg, rant, and feign tears on Robert's arm. Anything to get out of the asinine plan Brandt had concocted—and of which Robert seemed highly enamored. To no avail. It seemed that she would soon become Mrs. Brandt Donovan—at least as far as New York's upper crust was concerned. Most of whom she would meet in only a few more minutes.

The gown she wore tonight was emerald green, a shade Mary Xavier—who had insisted on a whole new wardrobe, made up of mostly French designs, of course—claimed suited Willow's coloring perfectly, especially her long, auburn hair. The dress was beautiful, Willow admitted, but the cut was somewhat risqué.

Thin, braided strips of material held to the very curve of her shoulder, with strands of sparkling beads dangling another few inches down her arms. Her bosom, with the rather unnecessary aid of a bust-improver, was pushed high into the top of the bodice, which sloped down far enough to reveal a deep shadowing between her breasts. The back of the dress was cut even lower and flared out over her bottom with the help of a small bustle.

Her only covering at the moment was a thin, black lace shawl that she alternately kept about her shoulders or let fall to the small of her back to drape over her arms. But once she arrived at their destination, the hosts would take her wrap and she would once again be virtually exposed to anyone who cared to look.

Except when she'd worked at the Silver Spur, Willow didn't think she'd ever walked around baring quite so much flesh. Such were the ways of the French, Mrs. Xavier had assured her. And while she didn't know if that was true, she did assume she looked rather stunning—if Brandt's reaction when he'd first seen her could be taken as complimentary. He'd basically stopped his conversation with James Xavier in midsentence and stared at her like a hungry wolf during the rest of her descent of the stairs to the foyer, where the men awaited the ladies for their outing.

His mouth had turned down in a momentary frown when she'd moved close enough for him to see the full effects of her combined décolletage, corset, and bust-improver, but had straightened a bit when she'd covered herself with the shawl.

Judging by his expression, she'd been surprised he hadn't demanded she change. Not that it would have done him any good. She would have refused, simply on principle. And after the time and exertion it took to get into her current ensemble, she'd have walked Fifth Avenue naked before changing into another.

So here she sat, laced into a corset so tight she could barely breathe, trying to remember the French she'd hastily studied, and praying they would be able to pull off their ruse.

Brandt had come up with the idea of infiltrating Yvonne Xavier's circle of friends by pretending to be Society darlings themselves, but Robert had been the one to actually establish their false backgrounds. He'd discussed the plan with the Xaviers and procured their agreement to go along with the investigation, wherever it might lead. Brandt and Willow were to stay at their home, and the Xaviers would introduce them as a newly married couple just returned from an extended honeymoon in Paris. Brandt was to be of the St. Louis Donovans—at Mary Xavier's suggestion—while Willow would be touted as an American heiress who had been vacationing abroad . . . until she'd met and been swept away by the handsome and irresistible son of a wealthy riverboat family.

The idea of Brandt sweeping her away on anything other than a wave of fury and annoyance made Willow nearly choke on her tongue. The fact that he had indeed swept her away that fateful night in her room at the Astor House was of no consequence. But she'd had very little say in the matter once Brandt and Robert put their heads together. And when Mrs. Xavier joined the fray, Willow had known arguing about her role in the charade was a lost cause.

Robert and Brandt had even decided that it was necessary for Brandt and Willow to share a bedroom—to avoid even a hint of something amiss about the visiting couple. They were worried unwitting servants would carry damning gossip from one household to another, tipping the killer off to Brandt's and Willow's true identities and purpose.

Taking a short, shallow breath—the only kind that could be taken when she was tied up like a Christmas goose—she gave her low décolletage another yank upward and cursed her sudden run of bad luck.

"Something wrong, darling?" Brandt sat on the opposite side of the carriage, his legs loosely splayed, his entire body a study of relaxation. They had moved into the Xavier home earlier that afternoon and were now accompanying the family to a neighboring fête. To avoid offending the moral sensibilities of the Xaviers, Robert had bent the truth a bit about Brandt's and Willow's true relationship. He'd told the Xaviers that though they were *posing* as newlyweds, they were, in actuality, already married, and had been for years. James and Mary Xavier were enamored with the idea of a married couple participating in the same, somewhat dangerous career as investigators. They had not only supplied Brandt and Willow with a suite of rooms to share, but with a private coach so that they could come and go as they pleased. The latter convenience left Brandt and Willow alone during the short drive to this evening's event—a luxury Willow could well have done without. She wanted to spend as little time alone with Brandt Donovan as possible.

The very idea that he seemed so comfortable in his tailored breeches and suit while she was so *un*comfortable in her new gown, made her want to drive a fist into his belly. The sound of him calling her by such an intimate endearment made her want to aim much lower.

"I am fine," she said shortly.

"Nervous?"

She was, but she'd be damned if she would admit it. "Not at all. You?"

A smile of pure male confidence crossed his face. "Not at all. Are you clear on your fictitious background?"

She rolled her eyes. "As the dim-witted daughter of a wealthy shipping magnate, I'm an innocent lady who had the misfortune of crossing paths with the likes of you."

He chuckled, shifting his gaze from the open window of the carriage to her. "On the contrary. As the quite intelligent, ravishing daughter of a shipping magnate, you are the lucky lady who had the *exceptional* fortune of falling madly in love with me."

"There are two sides to every story," she put in, raising her nose slightly in the air.

Brandt shifted on the cushioned seat. "Just be sure that you come around to my side by the time the Xaviers begin introducing us at the Burton ball." Not giving her a chance to retort, he continued, "It will be interesting during this little adventure to see how well we share a bedroom . . . and a bed, don't you think?"

What little oxygen the tight corset allowed froze in her lungs. She had done an admirable job thus far of pushing aside the incident that had taken place in her room at the Astor House. And of ignoring Brandt's occasional suggestive looks and innuendos.

But to have him bring up the topic in so casual a way . . . and to know that they would indeed be sharing a room in the Xavier household . . . made her go hot and slightly light-headed.

She thought about how well he filled his clothes. And how good he looked out of them. How he'd touched her and brought long-buried passions to the surface in such a short amount of time, when she'd spent years tamping them down and denying they even existed.

Swallowing hard, she forced herself to look him in the eye. His lips were crooked in a sexy, suggestive grin, but she steeled herself against his charm. "We'll share accommodations by necessity, not by choice. And I'm trusting you to keep your hands—as well as your lascivious thoughts—to yourself," she added with what she hoped was a firm, hands-off glare. "I don't let personal issues muddle the clear lines of an investigation."

The cocky grin remained while his eyes drifted over her face, her shoulders, down to the swell of her breasts. "Usually," he said softly.

She raised a brow. "Excuse me?"

"Usually," he repeated. "You don't *usually* let personal issues conflict with professional ones."

"I *never* do," she reiterated, teeth tight, shoulders stiff.

"But you did the night we were together," he reminded her softly.

She gasped. Just as softly, but she gasped all the same. The audacity of the man, to bring up their little indiscretion. As though it weren't difficult enough to be near him every hour of the day without wanting to either banish him to the farthest reaches of Hell or repeat the performance. She certainly didn't need him reminding her of one of the biggest mistakes of her life.

"I know you'd like to put it behind you," he continued. "Forget it ever happened." He shifted again, his hands clenching and unclenching where they rested high on his upper thighs. "But we're going to be together indefinitely. Pretending to be husband and wife."

His gaze held hers, his hazel eyes burning like hot coals. "And the plain fact is, I wouldn't mind if it happened again." He paused for a moment, letting those words sink in. "You're a woman, I'm a man. It's obvious we're attracted to one another. It's going to be hard to ignore that attraction while sharing a chamber, a bed, a marriage—however fraudulent."

The carriage came to a halt while Willow tried to grasp the meaning of his declaration. She stared at him, unblinking, her fingers digging into the soft leather of the cushion beneath her.

What could she say? She shared his feelings and at

least a fraction of his sentiments. But she couldn't admit that, couldn't allow him to think that anything further could happen between them. If it did, her head would likely fill with fancy notions of love and marriage and forever. And while she was sure Brandt wasn't looking for any one of those things, she was even more certain that *she* didn't want them.

A quick tumble with an attractive man was preferable any day over the idea of sharing her life with someone. Of letting him close enough to know the real her, to learn her secrets.

She thought of her brother, tucked away where he was safe and cared for, and where only she knew of his existence. It was best that way, considering her occupation. A man—this man, especially—would only complicate her carefully constructed lifestyle.

Startling her out of her deep contemplation, the driver opened the carriage door and awaited their descent. She slid across the seat toward the door, then turned back to Brandt. "It may be difficult," she said, responding to his earlier comment, "but I do hope you'll try." Because God knew, she didn't have the strength to resist him alone.

He would try, all right, but it certainly wouldn't be to ignore his attraction to her. Rather, Brandt thought it might be interesting to try seducing her.

It wouldn't be difficult. He had already made love to her once; how hard could it be to topple her into bed again? This time, though, he planned to take things slow. To enjoy himself fully and be assured that she did, as well. And when it was over, he wouldn't roll away as he had so foolishly done before. No, if he got the chance to experience the delights of Willow's lovely body again, he would be sure to linger.

149

Of course, this time, she would shield herself against him. Any impetuousness on Willow's part that had worked in his favor before would now be working against him. She would suspect his every action and combat against it.

So he simply needed to be extra innovative. And diligent.

And he would begin now, tonight.

Ignoring the tenseness of her body, Brandt kept Willow's arm folded within his as they made their way into the Burtons' elegant town house. James and Mary Xavier walked a few steps ahead, nodding to acquaintances, stopping to chat and introduce their guests, newly arrived in the United States.

Brandt was learning that Willow was a competent detective and could easily infiltrate any situation, as the need arose. But he knew her disguise called for more than her usual talents. And he could tell she was nervous about their plan, especially her part in it. She was anxious and fidgety, and he'd heard her practicing basic French from the other room, over and over, until even he felt fluent in the language.

Brandt smiled broadly and saw that Willow did the same. She was a consummate actress when she needed to be and knew her role well. He wondered how he ever could have doubted her abilities. She seemed born to this type of work. But because she seemed more apprehensive tonight, he made a mental note to help her along. Make things easier for her whenever he could.

When Mary Xavier spotted the Burtons, who were mingling with their guests, she immediately led Willow and Brandt in their direction, while James moved off to a circle of his old cronies standing near the entrance of the ballroom.

Before leaving their home that evening, Mr. and Mrs. Xavier had given them an extensive list of everyone who had attended the soiree at their house the night Yvonne disappeared. They had also informed them that many of the same people would be at the Burton gala tonight.

Brandt and Willow were attending this event simply to begin their entrée into society, but the Xaviers had offered to host another gathering at their home if they felt it necessary to aid their investigation.

"William. Claudia. What a lovely party." The petite, fair-haired Mary swept up to the hosts and pressed light kisses to the air at each side of their faces. "I must introduce you to our houseguests. William and Claudia Burton, this is Brandt Donovan—of the St. Louis Donovans," she added proudly, "and his lovely new bride, Willow. Willow had been on holiday in Paris this past year, until she met Brandt and the two fell madly in love. Isn't that right, dear?" she asked, resting a hand on Willow's arm.

Willow opened her mouth, but Mary turned back to the Burtons before she had a chance to respond. "It's terribly romantic. And we've been lucky enough to entertain them while they're in town."

Mary's loud and embellished speech brought others to crowd around them, wanting to meet the world travelers and gawk at the newcomers.

"Did I hear that you've just returned from Paris?" a woman asked over Willow's right shoulder. "Oh, I've always dreamed of visiting France. You must have loved it."

"*Oui,*" Willow answered, drawing a round of chuckles and titters from the group. "Truly, it was lovely. But the most wonderful thing about Paris was that I met Brandt there. The city paled in comparison." She fluttered her lashes, cocking her head to gaze adoringly at her supposed husband.

"Au contraire, mon amour," Brandt returned in nearly flawless French. "It was you who put even the moonlit waters of the River Seine to shame."

Willow's cheeks heated at his compliment, but she saw that it had done its job; he had charmed his audience and endeared them both to this sometimes close-knit community.

For the next few hours, they mingled with the crowd, telling fictitious stories and charming as many guests as they could. While Willow enjoyed the refreshments and an occasional dance with Brandt or another male guest, she mostly felt fettered and frustrated.

Everyone here was a suspect. And no one was a suspect. She had no idea where they were supposed to begin their investigation within the Xaviers' circle of friends when they all seemed so friendly and harmless. And yet it was very likely that someone in this very room had abducted and murdered Yvonne.

And she had to find that person before he could kill again.

Brandt's arm tightened on her waist as they spun around to the last strains of a waltz. Through a smile, he asked softly, "Anything suspicious?"

"Nothing," she returned with an equally bright smile. "You?"

"Nothing."

She let her lips loosen a bit, moistening them with the tip of her tongue. "I could use a drink, though. All of this politeness is making me as parched as sand."

Brandt chuckled and pulled her away from the dance floor. "Well, then, allow me to find the punch bowl and bring you a beverage."

She reached into the small velvet handbag on her

wrist and removed a fan that matched her gown. "I'll make my way around the room," she told him, beginning to circulate air near her face and neck. "Shall we meet at one of the back windows?"

He nodded once, then turned toward the refreshment table.

Smiling and otherwise trying to avoid the same people she had spoken with earlier, Willow moved along the edge of the room, passing small clusters of women who were criticizing certain guests' gowns or stirring up more dirt on the latest public scandal.

She skirted several of these groups, using her waiting husband as an excuse not to linger. Leaving the crowded ballroom, she escaped into the nearly empty foyer. Stopping for a moment to catch her breath, she leaned against the opposite wall and closed her eyes.

She wasn't meant to frequent this type of event, she thought. She was much better off keeping to herself and only battling a few saloon girls from time to time over breathing space and personal items of clothing.

After this evening, she was never again wearing a corset, either. The blasted thing made her dizzy, and the bones were digging into her flesh like knife blades.

Raised male voices in the drawing room across the hall caught her attention. At first she thought the men might be laughing over some joke, but as she listened, she realized one of the voices, at least, seemed to be mounting in anger.

With a sigh, she pushed away from the wall and crossed the parquet floor. Making sure there was no one else in the foyer to see her eavesdropping, she placed an ear near the mahogany door panel and listened.

". . . dirty whores, I tell you. Every one of them deserved what they got."

153

"Do you really believe that, Chatham? Or are you just blustering again?"

"It's not blustering to possess moral principles and the conviction to stand by them." Willow envisioned this first man clutching his lapels and puffing up his chest while he delivered the obviously overused diatribe.

"I've used the doxies down on the wharf a time or two myself, I don't mind telling you," another fellow put in. "Worth every penny . . . which is precisely what I paid for them."

A round of masculine guffaws echoed into the hall.

"If they weren't out there, strutting about half-naked, we wouldn't be tempted," the first man put in again. "It's about time someone has begun to put a stop to the debauchery they're selling. Good riddance, I say."

"Good God, Virgil. You don't mean to imply that they *deserved* to die." The man who said this sounded truly aghast, and Willow wished she could see what was going on. She wanted to know who was saying what, the expressions on their faces, and who it was who seemed to relish the deaths of five innocent women, including a young lady from their own walk of life.

"That's exactly what I'm saying," the one they'd called Chatham chimed in. "Those who sin deserve to be punished."

"I guess that depends on your definition of sin," the jovial one piped up again, apparently trying to break the note of tension in the room.

But Chatham refused to be swayed. "What this city needs is a liberator, like in the Old Testament. A reformer. Someone who isn't afraid to dole out justice wherever and however necessary. Just like Gideon."

Chapter Eighteen

Gideon.

The name struck Willow's blood cold and made her gasp aloud.

Could that be what Charlie meant? Could it be that Gideon wasn't a person or place at all, but a reference to the Hebrew judge named in the Bible?

She had to get into the room and get a good look at this Virgil Chatham. The man seemed to have more than just a passing interest in the dockside killings. And more importantly, in the women who "deserved" to die for their sins.

Taking as deep a breath as she could manage to steel her courage, she squared her shoulders and barged into the room.

Every head in the room turned toward her.

"Oh, pardon me, gentlemen," she said, purposely making her voice sound slightly short-winded. She made a slow sweep of the room, taking in the features of each face. Some she recognized from earlier introductions, but not all. She needed names to put to the rest.

"I'm sorry for interrupting, but I thought my husband might be about." It was as good an excuse as any. When no one immediately offered directions to her wandering spouse, she stepped forward and held out a gloved hand to the closest gentleman. "I'm Willow Donovan. My husband is Brandt Donovan . . . of the St. Louis Donovans," she added, remembering the awe it seemed to inspire when Mrs. Xavier divulged that particular piece of information.

As she'd hoped, her one introduction led to nods and names from the rest. Stephen Bishop, Clarence Price, Harry Sheffield, Hadden Wellsboro. And finally, the last man, Virgil Chatham. He took her hand briefly, a loose hold that—luckily for Willow—didn't last long.

He gave her the shivers. She wondered if that was because she'd overheard his conversation and knew how he felt about the deaths of the girls on the wharf, or if she would have experienced the same reaction had she met him at the start of the evening, before she knew his views on the "ills" of society.

She took in his mutton-chop sideburns and long jowls. The wide girth pressing behind the buttons of his stylish waistcoat. The way he stared through her rather than at her. No, she suspected she would have disliked this man regardless of the words that tumbled from his mouth.

She cleared her throat and forced herself to ignore the chill that raced down her spine. With a smile, she said, "Since it's obvious my husband didn't join the rest of you here for a cigar, does anyone know where he's disappeared to?"

A simultaneous round of negative replies and head shakes met her query.

"He's probably off charming our hosts with more stories of Europe," she offered with a quick laugh. "I'll just go back to the main ballroom and wait for him. So sorry to have interrupted, gentlemen. Please, carry on." And with a quick toss of her head, she departed the room and pulled the door firmly closed behind her.

Consciously letting the tension wash from her body, she marched across the well-waxed floor, her heels clicking along the way. From the open doorway to the ballroom, she spotted Brandt immediately, standing at one of the far windows with two glasses in his hand, exchanging pleasantries with a middle-aged matron who seemed to have cornered him. Making her way around the room with quick, determined strides, she came up behind Brandt and put a hand on his arm.

"Ah, here she is now," he said with a smile, turning away from the other woman. He held out a glass to her. "Here's your punch, darling."

Absently, she took the glass, pressing her free hand to her forehead. "I'm so sorry about this, darling, but would you mind terribly if we went home early? I seem to have come down with a dreadful headache and think I need to lie down."

Concern and a bit of suspicion etched his brow. "Of course." He turned back to the older woman. "If you'll excuse us, Mrs. Flourant. I'll get your cloak and meet you at the front doors," he told Willow, taking both glasses and crossing the room.

Willow smiled a quick good-bye to the lady beside her and began to follow after Brandt.

"Are you leaving already?" Mrs. Burton asked with a frown as she reached the front of the house.

"I'm afraid so." Willow once again placed the back of her hand to her temple as Brandt moved behind her to cover her shoulders with the black shawl. "I seem to be suffering a touch of *réveiller lascif.*"

A choked sound escaped Mrs. Burton and her eyes widened.

Behind her, Brandt released a small snort. Turning, she saw the corners of his mouth lifted in amusement.

Willow frowned. "Thank you for a lovely evening, Mrs. Burton, but I'm afraid we must take care of this little malady before it gets any worse."

His mouth curved into a full-out grin and Willow's frown deepened. Whatever did he find so amusing?

"Yes," he put in. "It's best if we get home and get her directly into bed."

Leading her out of the house and down the concrete steps to the sidewalk, he began to laugh aloud. "You may want to study your French a bit more thoroughly," he told her as their carriage was brought around.

"And why is that?" she asked as he lifted her into the coach and took a seat across from her.

"Because you just told Mrs. Burton that you were . . . sexually excited." He quirked a brow and practically leered. "*Réveiller lascif* means 'randy.' *Horny. Aroused.* Essentially. Literally, it means something more along the lines of 'arousing lasciviousness.' "

Willow's mouth dropped open. "Oh, my God," she gasped in horror. "You mean . . . she thinks . . . that we're leaving to . . ."

"Uh-huh."

"And you told her we needed to get straight to bed. Oh, my God," she breathed again. "You *knew*. You knew what I'd said and you encouraged her to believe that we're going home to . . . to . . ." She turned a scowl on him and demanded, "How *could* you?"

"How was I to know that's not what you meant?" he asked, deciding to play innocent. "I thought perhaps this was my lucky night." After a brief pause, he ventured hopefully, "So are we leaving to, ah . . . ?" He was certainly more than a little sexually excited, now that she'd mentioned it and gotten his mind moving in all sorts of erotic directions.

"*No!* Absolutely not! I thought I was telling her I had a headache. Dear God, she must think I'm a lunatic."

"A very forward-thinking one, I'd guess."

Willow's lips flattened and she glared daggers at him through the semidarkness of the coach's interior. "If you're so prolific with other languages, will you please tell me why *I'm* the one who's supposed to drop a French phrase here or there?"

"Because you're the one who was supposed to have been vacationing in Paris for several months before my arrival. It wouldn't do for me to be more fluent in the language than my lovely part-Parisian bride."

"*Hmph.*" Willow crossed her arms over her chest and scowled, her gaze concentrating on the view out the window rather than on him.

"I take it your *headache* has gone away, then."

"My *lascif* never existed, if that's what you mean. The headache, however, is only growing stronger." She rubbed her temples and wondered how she managed to get herself into these situations. If she ever had to face Mrs. Burton again, she would surely burst into flames of mortification. And if Mrs. Burton told Mrs. Xavier of her faux pas . . . well, she would never be able to look either woman in the eye again.

The remainder of the ride back to the Xavier home passed in silence, for which Willow was infinitely grateful. Brandt was overbearing enough without thinking he'd been crowned the prince of passion, with everyone at the soiree believing him so virile that she couldn't wait to get him home and into bed.

If only they knew. Even though they were pretending to be man and wife, and sharing a room at the Xaviers',

Willow found the hard floor preferable to sleeping next to this man. Better yet, let *him* sleep on the floor.

The carriage slowed and pulled up at the sidewalk in front of the red brick town house. The driver hopped down to open the door and Brandt exited, turning back to offer his hand for Willow's descent.

She took it out of obligation, he suspected, quickly releasing his hold and moving up the short set of stairs at the front of the house. Without waiting for him to join her, she let herself in the unlocked door and headed for the second floor, the train of her dress rustling behind her.

Willow was upset and had every right to be. He shouldn't have teased her about her incorrect translation. Better yet, he should have smoothed things over by offering a plausible explanation for Willow's mistake. Instead, he'd made matters worse by not only finding her blunder amusing, but by further implying that he was taking his wife directly home to put an end to her arousal.

Though the foyer was still well-lit, the house was quiet, the servants having been instructed not to wait up for their employers' return.

At a slower pace, Brandt followed his perturbed bride to the guest room they'd been appointed and watched as she discarded her cloak. With a flick of her wrist, she tossed it over the back of the nearest brocade chair, then immediately began to light every lamp in the room.

So much for his expectations of a dark and amorous evening spent in her arms. On the other hand, making love in a well-lit room did have a certain appeal.

They'd already moved their possessions from the two rooms at the Astor House, which he assumed made Willow feel right at home. That, and the fact that she was apparently used to moving. He wasn't even sure if she had apartments of her own here in the city, but he did know she seemed quick to make herself at home wherever she ended up, be it a small room in a Jefferson City brothel, a hotel room on Broadway, or here in the Xavier household.

Brandt wished he adjusted to new surroundings as easily. His suite at the Astor House had been nice, as was this. But frankly, he missed his own room back in Boston. He missed his lumpy but familiar bed. He missed his landlady, Widow Jeffries, who met him every time he entered or exited the house, and the breakfasts she provided for each of her four boarders. He even missed the proximity to his sisters and their weekly, unannounced visits to check on him, rearrange his furnishings, and ask for the thousandth time when he was going to meet a pleasant young girl who could take over the duty of cooking and cleaning for him so that they wouldn't have to come over all the time and complain about the build-up of dust he didn't even seem to notice.

He watched Willow march into the adjoining bedroom and imagined she would be the one woman of whom his sisters *wouldn't* approve. Oh, they would find her lovely enough, in both appearance and personality. It was her occupation that would alarm them. And the fact that it would most likely take a herd of wild elephants, buffalo, *and* horses to get her anywhere near either a cookstove or a dust rag. She just didn't strike him as the domestic sort.

He followed her, pushing open the door that had drifted half closed after her entrance. And then froze two steps into the room.

Willow stood with her back to him, the unhooked sides of her gown gaping, the smooth flesh of her shoulders and back bare except for the small area covered by a stark-white corset.

161

This moment would remain locked in Brandt's memory until he cocked up his toes and went to meet his Maker. He'd gazed upon her bare shoulders and back before, of course. In this very gown that, since the moment he'd first seen her in it, had caused him to have the unreasonable urge to order her back upstairs to change into something more decent.

The difference now was that she was apparently disrobing. Right in front of him. The thought made his mouth dry, and his mind as barren as a desert wasteland.

With her arms bent at an odd angle, she struggled to untie the tight laces of the abominable undergarment. The small grunts and groans of her efforts met his ears and caused his eyes to dart directly to the bed.

It was made, the pale yellow coverlet flat and unwrinkled. And on one flower-sprigged corner rested Charlie Barker's file. She had apparently come in to retrieve it first, then decided to disrobe.

Brandt had no problems with the latter, but the former caused him to wonder if the investigation hadn't been her real reason for departing the Burton festivities early. Perhaps she'd had something on her mind that required immediate attention.

Sensing his presence—or perhaps hearing his shallow breathing, which felt laborious enough for his lungs to burst through his rib cage—Willow turned and let her arms fall to her sides. She speared him with a sharp, questioning glare but didn't chide him for entering the room while she was undressing.

"If you're going to stand there staring, the least you could do is stand over *here* and help me get out of this blasted thing. I can barely breathe."

That made two of them.

She shrugged the thin straps that passed as sleeves down her arms and let the stiffened material of the bod-

ice, separate from the matching skirt, fall to the floor.
She stood before him in nothing more than her skirt and
corset. Another shift of weight and her jeweled, satin
evening slippers slid across the carpet.

"Ahh," she sighed.

He envisioned her wiggling her toes underneath the
hem of her skirt, and a bolt of desire hit him square in
the groin.

"Are you going to unlace me?" she asked, tossing an
impatient glance over her shoulder.

Taking a step forward, he swallowed hard. With only
the tips of his fingers, he grasped the ties of her corset
and set about loosening them. He was careful to graze
only fabric and not flesh, not wanting to touch her any
more than necessary.

Oh, he *wanted* to touch her. Only St. Peter himself
wouldn't—if St. Peter were truly that strong a man. But
Brandt knew physical contact for the disastrous idea that
it was. Just brushing her back as he undid her stays
would bring on a desire to caress her shoulders, which
would urge him to run his hands down toward her
breasts. And who knew what he might want to touch
then.

Ha! He knew precisely what he would want to touch
next.

No, that way lay madness. That way lay the soft
moans and whispered pleas he knew she uttered during
lovemaking, and the pleasure he knew could be found
within her supple body.

Just untie her corset and back away, he told himself.
*Turn around and walk into the other room before you
do or say something you'll regret.*

Once she felt an inch of give in the too-tight undergarment, she gave a sigh of relief and stepped away from
him, toward the tall wardrobe in the corner. Opening one

of the double doors, she found her red satin wrap and pulled it on, keeping her back to him. He watched the long, oriental dragon design wriggle and sway as she did. Soon, the corset slid past her hips to her feet and she kicked it aside with derision.

"You don't need that thing, you know," he heard himself say.

Her head turned slightly at his assertion, but she didn't look at him or turn around. "I do if I expect to fit into these bloody French gowns. I think Mary ordered them a size too small on purpose."

With that, she pulled another undergarment out from beneath the red robe and tossed it away.

His eyes widened and then narrowed as he studied the object. Could it be what he thought it was? "And you certainly don't need *that*," he added, taking a chance that his knowledge of ladies' underthings was up to snuff.

She turned sideways and spared a glance for the discarded piece of clothing before grinning at him. "Now on that, I will agree with you. Another insistence on Mrs. Xavier's part, though how anyone could think I need to enhance these"—she brought her hands up to encompass the region of her more than adequate bosom—"is a mystery."

He laughed. He couldn't help himself. Both her expression and her sentiment as she stood there framing her own ample charms struck him funny. Though now his attention was focused on the exact spot he'd been so determined to avoid. Blast and damn.

Willow tightened the belt of her robe and turned away from him once again, fiddling beneath the material with what he assumed was her remaining skirt, which hadn't been removed earlier. With a soft *swoosh*, the emerald taffeta pooled at her feet, followed by her garters and stockings. She did a bit more fiddling and then stepped away from the entire mess.

And Brandt's mouth went dry for the second . . . no, the third time that evening. On top of the pile sat Willow's drawers, discarded like just one more annoying piece of frippery.

Which meant that beneath that robe the color of sin . . . The rest of that thought stuck in his brain. But the results of the image seemed to have no trouble reaching his already throbbing manhood.

Brandt had never met a woman so uninhibited, so unconcerned with modesty. One of the first times he'd seen her, before he knew who she really was, she'd been dressed much like this . . . in her fire-breathing dragon robe, with nothing underneath.

He'd wanted her then, and he wanted her now. He wondered if she would even be able to fathom how very *much* he wanted her. And he was beginning to think his desire for her stretched a bit farther than just the bedroom.

But before that train of thought could lead him down a track he'd rather not traverse at the moment, he cleared his throat, took a step backwards, and prayed she wouldn't turn and notice the prominent bulge in his trousers.

He tried to force his thoughts in another direction. If such a thing was possible while standing this close to Willow. All of his attention was captured by her warmth and vitality, the hint of her rose-scented perfume invading his nostrils, the wispy strands of coppery hair running in rivulets against the pale flesh of her neck.

Willow moved to the bed and scooped up the file he'd noticed earlier. Work. The perfect topic of conversation—something far from desire and sensations and sex.

"So it wasn't a headache that drove you from the

party, after all," he ventured, glad his vocal chords hadn't dried up completely from the parched feel of his mouth.

She avoided his gaze and answered with an evasive, "Not exactly." Resting her bottom on the edge of the bed, she opened the folder and began running one slim finger down the first page, obviously looking for something specific.

He loosened the cravat at his neck and shrugged out of his dress coat, tossing it over a nearby chair. It wasn't easy, but he did his best to ignore the slim strip of bare leg that had become visible when she'd sat and the sides of her robe fell open a fraction. "Mind telling me what you're looking for?"

"A name," she muttered, absorbed in scanning every line of writing before her.

He undid the cuffs at his wrists and rolled up his shirtsleeves. If she could be so undressed and comfortable, so could he. Then he came around to lean a hip on the mattress beside her. It was a dangerous place to be, he knew that. He also wanted to know just what she was looking for that had been so important that they'd needed to leave a gathering—a gathering where a killer might very well have been in their midst—unfashionably early. "What name?"

"Virgil Chatham. Do you recall any mention of the name Virgil Chatham in Charlie's notes?" she asked distractedly.

His brows knit as he thought back. The name struck a familiar chord. "Wasn't he at this evening's function?"

She nodded, flipped a page, and continued to study every word.

"Big, blustering bloke with long sideburns and a belly that enters the room five minutes before he does," Brandt recalled. He let his other hip rest on the bed as well, snug beside Willow. She shifted slightly, as though troubled by his proximity. But her robe was caught beneath him and if she continued to move away, she risked baring even more skin than she had already. She sat still, clearly choosing to abandon the fray.

"What is it about him that has you so agitated?" he asked, making no move to release her. His position also gave him a prime view of her inner knee. Just a spot of shadowed skin, but quite a lovely spot, he decided, and well worth his concentration.

And then Willow slapped the file in her hands closed, pulled her robe free with a no-nonsense yank, and stood to face him. "If you can focus on the matter at hand for just a moment," she stated with annoyance, "I think he's the killer."

Chapter Nineteen

Brandt blinked in surprise, all thought of bedding Willow fleeing at this turn of events. Well, not *all,* but her words certainly had a dousing effect on his ardor.

He rubbed a finger in his ear to be sure he was hearing correctly and blinked again. "Excuse me? Did you say you think he's the killer?"

She gave a fervent nod, then turned and left the room. He raced after her, wanting to get to the bottom of her sudden deduction.

"And just how did you come to this monumental conclusion?" he asked as she plopped down on the sofa, folded her legs beneath her, and once again opened Charlie's file. "Did he confess? Or better yet, perhaps you took one look at his long jowls and decided he looked evil enough to have committed such heinous crimes."

Willow looked up from her endeavor long enough to spear him with an irritated glare. "If you must know, I overheard him talking about the murders and thought he sounded a bit . . . zealous about the entire situation." She returned her attention to the papers in front of her, adding with a hint of arrogance, "But I would have suspected him anyway. The man makes my skin crawl."

An unexpected wave of protectiveness rolled over Brandt, followed quickly by a spurt of anger. He moved close enough to comfort her, his hand curling around her wrist and lifting it from where it rested on her lap. "Did he touch you?" he demanded.

She looked down at his fingers wrapped about her thin arm, dark against light, masculine against feminine, powerful against delicate.

Instead of loosening, his grip tightened. If he had been with her this evening, if he had refused to leave her side, he would *know* if the bastard had put his hands on her. Brandt's jaw clenched as he repeated the question. "Did he touch you?"

"No." She raised her head until their eyes met. "No more than a brush of his hand when we were introduced," she assured him.

It took a moment, but the rage finally ebbed out of him and he released his hold. He felt a modicum of relief that Virgil Chatham hadn't made a move toward her, hadn't hurt or threatened her in any way. And more than a modicum of peculiarity regarding his sudden sense of protectiveness over a woman who was his partner in this investigation only, and who made no secret of the fact that she wanted nothing more from their relationship than to find Charlie's killer.

Still, he wouldn't let her out of his sight again. If he had to perpetuate her earlier claim to everyone at the Burtons' party that she desired him beyond reason and tie a rope around her waist to keep her at arm's length, so be it. She'd bristle at the very idea, he was sure, but he'd do it anyway, if that was what it took to keep her safe.

Calmer now, he asked, "So what did he say that got your hackles up?"

"He said the women down by the docks deserved to die," she told him, derision tainting her voice. "While everyone else in the room was discussing the murders as just a passing event, he talked about sinners and the Bible and . . ." She stopped suddenly, pressed her lips together, rattled a few papers, then licked her lips and continued. "And he just seemed a little *too* fervent about it."

She was good, he'd give her that. Truly talented and quick on her feet. But he was beginning to know her too well to be drawn in as easily as before by her fast thinking and innocent looks.

He knew she was lying now, the same way he'd known she was lying a few days ago in Robert's office, when she'd told her employer that she'd been to visit Charlie's widow—and Brandt knew she'd done no such thing. She'd licked her lips, something he noticed she didn't do on a regular basis otherwise.

As tells went, it was a good one. Not terribly noticeable or out of place. And if the target of her lie was of the male persuasion, Brandt was sure the fellow would be drawn in by the sight of that lovely pink tongue darting across those lush pink lips and not pay a whit of attention to the falsehoods tumbling out of Willow's tempting mouth.

But Brandt liked to think he was heartier than the average man, and if not immune to Willow's charms, at least cognizant of them.

"What are you not telling me?" he inquired.

Her head jerked up and she regarded him through wide, falsely faultless eyes. "I don't know what you

170

mean," she said with a quick swipe of her tongue at the corner of her mouth. And then she snatched up a handful of papers and shoved them in his direction. "Here, help me look for Virgil Chatham's name in Charlie's notes," she ordered, hoping to distract him, Brandt was sure.

Brandt moved in front of her, taking a seat on the low mahogany table before the sofa to face her. "Have I ever told you how much I enjoy looking at you?" he asked innocently.

Her head whipped up again so fast, he imagined he heard the bones in her neck snap. This time, she didn't lick her lips, but her eyes did narrow as her mouth fell open in disbelief.

"You're quite beautiful," he continued. "A pleasure to gaze upon."

At that, suspicion began to creep into her expression. Her mouth closed in a flat line and her brows met in consternation. "If you're hoping to seduce me again, or catch more of a show than you were treated to in the bedroom, I'm afraid you're going to be sorely disappointed."

"I wasn't aware that *I* seduced *you* the first time," he clarified. "But regardless, that wasn't my intention." *Yet.* "I was merely pointing out how much time I've devoted to the simple act of studying your features. How familiar I've become with the nuances of your face."

Her shoulders lifted as she inhaled deeply, and then fell when she let out a disgusted sigh. "Are you going to help me look for Chatham's name or are you going to sit there all cow-eyed for the rest of the night?"

Cow-eyed? Never in his life had he been *cow-eyed.* He'd have taken offense at the very suggestion if he hadn't noticed the look on her face and the way her fingers clutched the papers in her lap. From her apparent discomfort, he imagined she hadn't had much flattery aimed in her direction lately. Or rather, that such flattery had been less than sincere.

He meant every word, and wished seduction was his intent at the moment. But first, he had to find out what she was hiding from him.

"I'm going to help you look for his name," he assured her. "But I'm also going to tell you that because I've spent so much time admiring your beauty, I've begun to notice a few things about you."

"And what might those be?" she asked, back to searching the documents before her.

"Besides the tiny mole at the very corner of your upper lip and the slight scar above your right temple," he began, earning another sharp glance and her full attention, "I'm beginning to know when you're lying."

She licked her lips, an action that tempted Brandt to capture her moist lips with his own. "I don't lie," she said with a strained laugh, the words firm. Her lashes swept down to veil her eyes, and any thoughts that might be visible in them. "But if I did lie," she ventured cautiously, meeting his gaze once again, "which I don't, mind you—how is it that you think you can tell?"

Holding her gaze, he leaned forward a fraction of an inch, until he could feel her rapid breath against his skin, until the satin of her robe brushed his chest and he could smell the rosewater she'd dabbed behind her ears hours earlier. Until her lips parted slightly and he felt her chest hitch as she struggled for air. And then he touched his tongue to her lips and showed her exactly what he was talking about.

Willow blinked, every muscle in her body unmoving, every cell on alert. The minute she saw Brandt moving toward her in that sleek, predatory way of his, she knew she was in trouble. She knew she should run but couldn't seem to move, even as she watched his face nearing.

Even as she saw his lips part and knew he was going to kiss her.

And then the tip of his warm, wet tongue touched her bottom lip, and every thought in her head dissipated into a fine mist of nothingness. Her blood, which had been simmering well enough at only his close proximity beside her in the bedroom and now in front of her here, shot to a full boil. And her skin, already heated and prickly, tightened in expectation.

Her eyes remained open, as did his, and she watched his already green irises darken to a deep shade of moss.

His tongue lingered at one corner of her mouth, then slowly stroked to the other, following the line of her lip. Letting just the tip rest there for a moment, he stared at her, and she wondered what he planned to do next. Wondered why he didn't simply kiss her, when that was what she—*he,* she corrected—obviously wanted. She held her breath and waited, her lips parted slightly in as much of an invitation as she could muster.

A part of her didn't want him to kiss her, didn't want him to touch or even be near her. While another part— the louder, more insistent part, it seemed—wanted nothing more. She fought the voice in her head that urged her to lean forward, closer, and take the initiative. To kiss him, by God, if he was only going to sit there and *not* kiss her.

But as she was about to do just that, he moved back, his wicked and cruel tongue disappearing into his equally sinful mouth. Her jaw snapped closed and she sat back, squaring her shoulders against the lingering signs of weakness she feared might be evident on her face.

"And just what was that, pray tell?" She was relieved when the words didn't waver.

"Your one and only flaw. The one and only that I've discovered thus far, at least."

She raised a brow and fixed him with what she hoped was an aggravated glare.

"When you lie, you lick your lips. It's damn sexy, by the way," he added in a husky growl, "but telling all the same." He raised his hand and tucked a loose tendril of hair behind her ear. "When we were in Robert's office, you told him you'd gotten a copy of those files from Charlie's widow. We both know full well that isn't true. Which is when I noticed that you licked your lips both before and after you misled your boss."

He smiled faintly, showing a thin line of straight white teeth. "You're very good. And in your line of business, I imagine the skill comes in handy."

She didn't respond. Couldn't decide whether to admit or deny it, and was more than a little annoyed that she *had* a telling sign, let alone that he'd figured it out.

If what he said was true and she actually did lick her lips—or make any other move that could be deciphered to her detriment—she would have to be more careful in the future. No one had ever accused her of lying before. In fact, she considered herself rather good at it. She could create new and plausible stories or excuses for just about anything, in the tightest of spots. She'd even caught herself, on more than one occasion, telling falsehoods simply because it was easier or—God help her—more fun than telling the truth.

"Since we've established that I can indeed tell when you're lying," Brandt continued, interrupting her thoughts, "I think it's safe to say that there's something about this Virgil Chatham fellow you're not telling me. Something he might have said that leads you to believe he's our killer. Words more incriminating than just him speaking less than kindly about the victims."

She narrowed her eyes to slits, her fingers tensing in annoyance. As she opened her mouth to reply, her tongue darted to the corner of her lip and his brows rose in obvious mockery.

Damn him, he'd been right. She *did* lick her lips before she began to lie.

She tried again, taking a deep breath and swallowing as she formed the words. And then she opened her mouth . . . and her blasted tongue darted right out to wet the opposite corner of her mouth. *Bloody hell!*

"Lick your lips and get it over with," he said with a smirk. "And then try telling me the truth for a change."

It was an order, not a request, and as much as she loathed telling him what she'd learned and why her gut was urging her to focus on Chatham as a suspect, she feared Brandt would know she lied, even if she cut out her traitorous tongue and scribbled her fabrication on paper.

With a huff, she all but threw the pile of papers from her lap to his and stalked across the carpeted floor. In the bedroom, she knelt down in front of the ornately carved armoire that housed her clothing and began to root around for her peach slippers. They were at the bottom somewhere, beneath the many new pairs of shoes Mary Xavier had ordered to match her newest gowns. Once she found them, she rose and turned to go back to the sitting room, only to find Brandt standing in the doorway, one shoulder resting against the frame, his feet crossed at the ankles. He'd removed his neckcloth and jacket and unbuttoned his shirt halfway down to bare a good portion of his sun-browned chest.

She sighed, as much at his tenacity as at the sight. Small wonder he was head of Security for the Union Pacific Railroad. He would make an equally successful Pinkerton agent. That same dogged determination was what made her a good investigator herself.

And even though it galled her to give away the last piece of this investigation that was entirely hers, to trust him with what might turn out to be the most vital key to this entire situation, she admitted that he did deserve to know. He was entitled to all the details so that he could see every angle of the case more clearly.

"Before he died, Charlie gave me something."

His mouth thinned as he studied her. "And you didn't see fit to share this with me until now?" he accused.

"No, I didn't," she answered firmly, hoping to put an end to his argument before it ever got started. "Charlie gave it to me, and I didn't know what it meant until tonight." She felt inside each shoe to determine which held the slip of paper and then pried up the lining at the toe to reveal the hidden clue. "In fact, I may be wrong about Virgil Chatham, in which case I still won't know what it means."

She unfolded the small bloodstained square and handed it to him.

"Gideon," he read aloud. "That's it, Gideon? What's that supposed to mean?"

"I don't know. Or at least I didn't until I overheard Virgil Chatham's tirade about the deaths of the girls by the wharf." She turned slightly and tossed the shoes back into the wardrobe, where they fell atop her many other pairs of slippers. "While he was ranting about them deserving to die for their sins, he mentioned the name *Gideon*. If I recall correctly, Gideon was one of the judges of Israel for forty years."

Brandt straightened, still studying the piece of paper in his hand. "Yes, but he didn't kill prostitutes. Did he?"

"Not that I'm aware. I wonder if Mrs. Xavier has a Bible we might borrow."

"I'm sure she does." Brandt turned and marched

through the sitting room, straight into the second-floor hallway.

Too curious to remain behind, Willow followed after him, clutching her robe more tightly about her naked form. "Where are you going?" she asked in a harsh whisper, even though she suspected there was no one around to hear them. She didn't think the Xaviers had returned home yet.

"To the library," he answered over his shoulder as he trotted down the stairs. She kept pace, her bare feet silent on the carpet and then on the hard foyer floor.

Sure enough, he found a small Bible—directly beside the much larger family Bible—after one quick perusal of the shelves. Drawing it down, he handed it to Willow and then placed a hand at the small of her back to usher her back upstairs.

She began flipping through the thick book on the way, wondering how she was ever to find a reference to Gideon among all the names and small black print.

"How do you use one of these things?" she asked in frustration as Brandt closed the chamber door behind them.

"Your guess would be better than mine." He shot her a chagrined half-smile. "It's been a while since I've had occasion to read the Good Book."

"Me, too." And at the moment, she regretted not keeping up with the lessons her mother had begun when she was a little girl.

Bending to gather the papers scattered on the settee, she handed the jumbled pile to Brandt and then took a seat on the sofa. "You look for Virgil Chatham's name in those while I try to find Gideon in here."

"How do you plan to do that?" he asked, leaning over the back of the sofa to peek past her shoulder.

"Well, I know it has to be in the Old Testament." She

flipped through the book until she found the section toward the middle marked New Testament and placed a hand flat against the leather cover, the other flat against what must be the final page of the Old Testament. "That cuts the difficult business in half."

Tilting her head back to look at him, she gave him a challenging grin. "Care to wager on who finds their quarry first?"

One russet brow rose with interest. "A betting gal, are you?" he teased. Coming around the long settee, he took a seat in the opposite corner, laying Charlie's file on the table in front of them. "And just what might you be willing to stake?"

She thought about it a moment but couldn't think of anything that might make a decent ante.

"Tell you what," Brandt suggested. "Why don't we leave the bet open-ended. Whoever wins gets to take a prize of his—or her—choosing, or ask a particular favor of the loser. The defeated player must comply, of course. No matter what."

Willow noted the wicked tilt of his lips, the predatory gleam that glittered in his eyes. If he won, he would ask something terrible of her, she just knew it. Something subservient . . . or worse yet, sexual.

A spark of pure lust burst in her belly. The fact that she didn't find that prospect as repulsive as she should frightened her more than the idea that he might take one of her possessions or ask her to polish his boots for a week.

But the bet had been her idea and she couldn't think of anything better to wager. She wasn't even entirely sure she didn't *want* him to take out his winnings in trade.

Besides, he wasn't guaranteed to succeed. She could

178

Thrill to the most sensual, adventure-filled Historical Romances on the market today…
FROM  LEISURE BOOKS

As a home subscriber to the Leisure Historical Romance Book Club, you'll enjoy the best in today's BRAND-NEW Historical Romance fiction. For over twenty-five years, Leisure Books has brought you the award-winning, high-quality authors you know and love to read. Each Leisure Historical Romance will sweep you away to a world of high adventure…and intimate romance. Discover for yourself all the passion and excitement millions of readers thrill to each and every month.

SAVE AT LEAST $5.00 EACH TIME YOU BUY!

Each month, the Leisure Historical Romance Book Club brings you four brand-new titles from Leisure Books, America's foremost publisher of Historical Romances. EACH PACKAGE WILL SAVE YOU AT LEAST $5.00 FROM THE BOOKSTORE PRICE! And you'll never miss a new title with our convenient home delivery service.

Here's how we do it. Each package will carry a 10-DAY EXAMINATION privilege. At the end of that time, if you decide to keep your books, simply pay the low invoice price of $16.96 ($17.75 US in Canada), no shipping or handling charges added*. HOME DELIVERY IS ALWAYS FREE*. With today's top Historical Romance novels selling for $5.99 and higher, our price SAVES YOU AT LEAST $5.00 with each shipment.

AND YOUR FIRST FOUR-BOOK SHIPMENT IS TOTALLY FREE

IT'S A BARGAIN YOU CAN'T BEAT! A Super $21.96 Value!

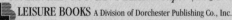 LEISURE BOOKS A Division of Dorchester Publishing Co., Inc.

GET YOUR 4 FREE* BOOKS NOW— A $21.96 VALUE!

Mail the Free* Book
Certificate
Today!

4 FREE* BOOKS 🌑 A $21.96 VALUE

Free *Books* *Certificate*

YES! I want to subscribe to the Leisure Historical Romance Book Club. Please send me my 4 FREE* BOOKS. Then each month I'll receive the four newest Leisure Historical Romance selections to Preview for 10 days. If I decide to keep them, I will pay the Special Member's Only discounted price of just $4.24 each, a total of $16.96 ($17.75 US in Canada). This is a SAVINGS OF AT LEAST $5.00 off the bookstore price. There are no shipping, handling, or other charges*. There is no minimum number of books I must buy and I may cancel the program at any time. In any case, the 4 FREE* BOOKS are mine to keep—A BIG $21.96 Value!

*In Canada, add $5.00 shipping and handling per order for first shipment. For all subsequent shipments to Canada, the cost of membership is $17.75 US, which includes $7.75 shipping and handling per month.[All payments must be made in US dollars]

Name _____

Address _____

City _____

State _____ *Country* _____ *Zip* _____

Telephone _____

Signature _____

If under 18, Parent or Guardian must sign. Terms, prices and conditions subject to change. Subscription subject to acceptance. Leisure Books reserves the right to reject any order or cancel any subscription.

Get Four Books Totally
F R E E* —
A $21.96 Value!

(Tear Here and Mail Your FREE* Book Card Today!)

PLEASE RUSH
MY FOUR FREE*
BOOKS TO ME
RIGHT AWAY!

Leisure Historical Romance Book Club

P.O. Box 6613
Edison, NJ 08818-6613

very well find the name she was looking for first. And then *he* would have to attend to her.

A small smile curved her lips. Now, that would be a triumph worthy of the battle, even though she had no idea what her request would be if she won. But she was willing to take the risk.

She held out her hand, waiting for Brandt to shake on their agreement. "You've got yourself a deal," she said, praying and hoping against hope that she wouldn't be sorry.

Chapter Twenty

"I found it. I think."

Instead of pleasing her, Brandt's words filled Willow with dread. He'd won the bet, and now she would have to do . . . something. Whatever he requested. Taking a deep breath, she leaned toward him, looking at the page where he pointed.

"It's not a full name, but *V.C.* could be Virgil Chatham's initials."

She looked at the initials, and at the name beside them: Outram. "Who's Outram?" she wondered aloud.

"I have no idea."

"Keep looking. Maybe Charlie made more notes than that, or wrote the full name for those initials somewhere."

"Yes, ma'am," Brandt said, grinning as he aimed a small salute in her direction.

She went back to searching chapters of the Bible for

any mention of Gideon, and after another fifteen minutes or so found what she was looking for.

"Here it is," she cried excitedly.

"Where?" Brandt slid closer, coming to rest with his hip against hers and one arm stretched behind her on the cushions. His warm breath tickled the side of her neck.

"*Ugh*," she groaned. "The Book of Judges; I should have known since Gideon was a judge. Why didn't I start there and save myself the past few hours?"

"Because neither of us are as familiar with the Holy Bible as we should be. What does it say?"

" 'And when Gideon perceived that he was an angel of the Lord . . .' " she began, reading each section that pertained to the name Charlie had found so important. " 'And Gideon said unto God, If thou wilt save Israel by mine hand, as thou hast said . . . The sword of the Lord, and of Gideon . . . And Gideon the son of Joash returned before the sun was up . . . Thus was Midian subdued before the children of Israel, so that they lifted up their heads no more. And the country was in quietness for forty years in the days of Gideon . . . ' "

"So Gideon led the Israelites to victory over the Midianites wielding the metaphorical 'sword of the Lord' and bringing about forty years of peace—quite simply put, he was a Hebrew judge who saved the Israelites during a time of strife. Something tells me that if this Virgil Chatham fellow is our killer, and if he fancies himself a modern-day Gideon, he's taking all this angel-of-God talk a little too literally."

"That's an understatement, if ever I heard one. He's twisting the real Gideon's motives to suit his own demented ambitions, I'd say." She cocked her head to look at Brandt. "Do you think he really believes he's wielding 'the sword of the Lord,' ridding the world of sin?"

181

Brandt chuckled. "He's got a lot of ground to cover if he's hoping to rid *the world* of sin. But if you're right, I'd say he's making a go of it here in New York. He'll be lucky if it lasts forty years, though."

Although she saw the humor in Brandt's words, she was too preoccupied to respond in kind. Her mind was racing ahead. If the killer sought to rid the world of sin, it seemed he planned to begin by eradicating a class of women many considered to embody all the ills of society: the fallen angels, the prostitutes. Willow felt sick to her stomach. They'd assumed the wounds in the women's chests had come from a knife. She suddenly knew the murderer was following the Bible verse to the letter and those slashes had been made by a sword.

"What are you thinking?" Brandt asked quietly, running the back of his hand over her cheek.

She closed her eyes briefly, fighting off images of the victims struggling for their lives, being stabbed through the heart by a man who thought himself an angel of God. A minion of Satan would be a more accurate description.

When she opened her eyes again, Brandt was still studying her, his face showing mild concern while his fingers continued to stroke calming patterns on her cheek and neck.

"I'm thinking we'd better stop Virgil Chatham before he kills another innocent girl. And that if we're wrong about him being the killer . . . God help us all."

"We will stop him," Brandt said, his tone more sure than hers would be at the moment. "But first we need some rest. You've been out and about all day, and sitting here searching for names most of the evening. You look as exhausted as I feel."

Standing, he took her arms and pulled her up beside him. "I say eight hours of sleep will do us both some good. We'll start fresh in the morning."

"But what if he goes out again tonight?" she asked, even though he was right. She felt ready to collapse.

"He won't."

There was no way Brandt could guarantee such a thing and they both knew it. "But what if he does?" she repeated as he pushed her toward the bedroom.

"Even if he does—which I'm praying he won't—there's nothing we could do about it. We don't even know where Chatham lives. We have to talk to Robert, see if he could get the man's address for us, and I doubt Robert'd appreciate being roused at this hour of the night."

Having reached the bed, he folded back the covers and applied a gentle pressure to her shoulder until she half sat on the soft mattress.

"First thing in the morning, we'll go down to the Pinkerton offices, tell Robert what we suspect, and enlist his help." He lowered his mouth to the curve of her ear and dropped his voice. "And then we'll stick to Virgil Chatham tighter than your corset."

She laughed and lifted her face to look at Brandt. He grinned down at her, only a hint of lasciviousness in his green eyes. Which, for him, was an improvement.

"First thing tomorrow?" she asked.

"First thing *tomorrow*," he promised. "As for tonight . . ."

Uh-oh. She'd forgotten about their bet. And the fact that, even though he'd only found Chatham's initials, he'd won.

She swallowed hard and forced herself to hold his gaze. "What is it that you want?"

He straightened and stood looking down at her. "Oh, sweetheart," he said with a chuckle, "you should never ask a man a question like that. You leave him too many options to factor into his answer."

She felt a flush of heat sweep up her cheeks and

darted a glance over his left shoulder to avoid the scrutiny of his gaze. "I meant as your prize to our wager. You did find those initials before I found any mention of Gideon."

"I know what you meant. But my warning holds true: Careful how you phrase things around a man willing to take advantage."

She brought her eyes back to his face and fixed him with a piercing stare. "Are you willing to take advantage?"

"Absolutely," he answered with an eager nod and a smile that would put Lucifer to shame. "Are you willing to comply?" he asked suggestively.

The air froze in her lungs as she realized she was. She'd been awaiting this moment all night. And she wasn't so sure that had she won the bet, she wouldn't have requested the same boon.

She'd been with him before, and even though she'd sworn not to make herself vulnerable to him again, she knew the sensations he could evoke, the pure pleasure to be found in his arms. And tonight she longed for his embrace. She told herself that as long as he understood that anything that occurred between them during the course of this investigation was simply a pleasurable little diversion, it would be all right. As long as they both understood their relationship was nothing serious, nothing leading to any kind of permanence, they could just enjoy it and both walk away unscathed at the end.

Thankfully, Brandt didn't appear to be a man seeking ties.

Digging deep for the bravery she'd used any number of times during her stint as a Pinkerton, she met his gaze and told him, "You won. I have no choice." Her words sounded more dire than she'd intended. In truth, the tickle in her belly increased with every moment that passed as she waited to hear what sensual torture Brandt would demand.

"Fine. I know how you feel about us sharing a chamber and I know you expect me to stay on that hard sofa"—he jerked a thumb over his shoulder—"or the equally uncomfortable chaise"—he nodded toward the lounge behind them—"but the prize I want is to share the bed with you tonight."

Her eyes closed tightly and then opened wide. *"What?"*

"It will be a far cry more comfortable than my other options, that's for sure. And I promise not to touch you. I'll hug tight to my side of the mattress. I'll even let you have all the covers if that makes you more comfortable."

He promised not to touch her. She made a nasty face in her head. How gallant of him, when all she'd been dreaming of tonight was the moment when he would. The louse!

"You want to share the bed?" she snapped, jumping to her feet and twining her arms huffily across her chest. "That's it? You're not going to demand I give in to your sexual appetites, or ask me to do your bidding for the rest of the week?"

One dark brow winged upward as he observed her irritated pose. "Not unless you want me to." He waited a moment and then asked, *"Do* you want me to?"

For some reason that question upset her more than his earlier failure to ask something sordid and altogether wrong of her.

"Of course not," she replied briskly, turning her attention away from him as she crossed to the wardrobe. "You're welcome to share the bed. I wouldn't dream of asking you to sleep on the sofa." The floor maybe, she added to herself, but nothing so well-cushioned as the settee.

Finding the nightgown she'd had in mind, she loosened the belt of her robe and let the silky material fall to the floor. Let Brandt catch a glimpse of her naked backside, she thought—just to remind him what he was missing. Then she quickly shrugged into the sturdy sackcloth frock. The dress fell to all but an inch from the floor and covered both her arms to the wrist and all the way up her neck. Not a spare inch of flesh was showing anywhere.

She'd planned to sleep nude, as she often did. Especially since she'd expected Brandt to ask something entirely different of her in exchange for his winning their wager. But if he merely wanted to sleep beside her in the big bed, then it would be next to the cocoon of her body wrapped in this voluminous gown. If he so much as threw an arm out in her direction, he would be greeted by nothing but stiff, scratchy material. Itching all through the night herself would be well worth it just to sense his discomfort.

Without sparing a glance in his direction, she marched back across the room and to the side of the bed opposite where he was standing.

"You know, I'm not sure I was the clear winner of our little bargain," he offered, still rooted to his spot only a few feet from the other side of the bed. "I was the first to find something, of course, but we can't be sure those initials actually stand for Virgil Chatham. Whereas the reference to Gideon that you found is certainly right. Perhaps we're both winners and equally due a boon from the other."

She arched a brow at what sounded like a load of rubbish to her.

"Is there anything you'd like?" he pressed on. "Perhaps something that, in my ignorance, I was too short-sighted to ask for?"

186

She couldn't decide whether to laugh or throw something at his head. So, instead, she fluffed her pillow, shifted to her side facing away from him, and gave her answer—utter, stony silence.

"Suit yourself," he said behind her, and she thought she heard the distinct rustle of clothing as he began to undress. The clunk of what must be a boot hitting the floor. A second later, another clunk. And then she imagined him peeling down his trousers until he stood in the middle of the room completely naked.

She waited, listening for the sound of a drawer sliding open, almost praying that his habit was to wear full-length nightshirts to bed.

"You'd better not be naked," she warned.

His only response was a chuckle, and when the mattress dipped behind her, she knew her hopes to be futile. Brandt Donovan was not a man to dress for bed, but would crawl under the covers as bare as a newborn babe. And that was one image she did not want floating around in her head only moments before she drifted off to sleep.

Thankfully, she was well cocooned in both her most matronly nightdress and the pile of blankets tucked up to her chin, despite the comfortable temperature of the room. Her body was wrapped in a veritable fortress, regardless of what Brandt might be wearing—or not wearing—on his side of the bed.

Willow squeezed her eyes tight, willing herself to sleep. The room around them was too quiet. Try as she might, she could barely hear either of them breathing. Minutes ticked by, and with each, her lungs seemed to struggle for air as she pictured Brandt beside her.

Was he asleep already? Or wide awake, listening to her the way she was struggling to listen to him? And was he truly naked on top of the same sheets and beneath the same blankets as she? She was pretty sure of the answer to that, which only caused her heart to beat faster and slumber to further elude her.

Suddenly, the mattress lurched, causing her to list backwards before she caught her balance and curled forward again.

"Willow," she heard Brandt whisper.

She ignored him.

"Willow, are you awake?"

She wished she weren't. Perhaps if she continued to ignore him, he would think she'd already nodded off and leave her alone.

"I know you are," he said next, bursting that particular bubble.

Taking a weary breath, she rolled to her other side to face him, careful to shift back to the very edge of the bed, as far from him as possible.

"What do you want?" she asked brusquely, hoping to deter him from further conversation.

"I can't sleep. I thought maybe we could talk."

Another expectation shot down in its prime. "About what?"

One shoulder rolled in answer. He'd turned down the lamp, but she could still see the outline of his body in the thin shafts of moonlight shining through the lace draperies.

"Go to sleep, Brandt," she said softly. "We have a lot to do tomorrow."

He reached out to touch the high collar of her nightdress, buttoned straight up to her chin. "This is just about the ugliest thing I've ever seen," he told her as his fingers drifted down to touch the fabric covering her arm. "Especially on a woman. Especially on you."

She met his gaze in the darkness but forced herself not to respond. She didn't want his words to appeal to her. And she certainly didn't want to think about his callused hand caressing the material of her gown as though he wished it were her flesh.

"This feels like horsehair," he continued, his fingers trailing farther down her arm. "Doesn't it itch?"

God, yes, it itched. Over every inch of her body. And his reminder didn't help matters. But it was a far cry better than lying naked in the same vicinity as this man, who could probably charm the wimple off a nun.

"Not at all," she lied, only afterwards remembering that he could tell when she did. Had she licked her lip? She couldn't remember. And she couldn't see his eyes well enough to know if there'd been a change in his expression.

"A shirt like this would drive me daft," Brandt said, moving his hand so that the material slid up and down on Willow's skin, increasing what he knew must be an already maddening discomfort. "So stiff and scratchy, like little needles rubbing every inch of my body. I don't know how you can stand it."

She wiggled under the covers, trying to dislodge his touch or the feel of the rough fabric, he wasn't clear which.

"Are you sure you wouldn't be more comfortable out of that thing?"

She shook her head, her auburn hair falling over one eye. With the same hand he'd used to stroke her arm, he lifted the strands away from her face and tucked them behind her ear. And then he let his fingers drift down her neck, to the small pearl buttons of her starched lace collar, hiding all that lovely ivory flesh and the pulse points he knew must be throbbing with desire by now. His certainly were.

He hadn't intended to seduce her tonight. Tease her a little, maybe, taunt her enough to remind her of what they'd shared before and what she was missing now by refusing him at every turn. But he truly hadn't planned to climb into this bed and make love to her.

Now, though, he didn't think he had a choice. He wanted her. And he knew damn well she wanted him.

Earlier, he'd purposely picked something nonthreatening to ask as payment for the wager he'd won. He knew she'd expected him to ask for more, for her complete and total acquiescence in whatever depraved act he suggested. Which is why he hadn't. And it had delighted him to see her annoyance when he'd requested only to be allowed to sleep on the far side of the bed instead of the inadequate chaise.

That was when he'd known all of her denials were for naught. She desired him as well. She had not only prepared for him to demand sexual favors as payment but had counted on just that.

"You must have something less . . . abrasive to wear," he added, keeping his voice low as he slipped the top button through its hole.

"What are you wearing?" she asked, and he chuckled at her boldness. Particularly since he knew she'd already assumed he was wearing nothing at all.

"Cotton drawers," he said, hoping the answer would surprise her. "They weren't shipped all the way from France and have probably seen better days, but they do the job well enough."

That brought a smile to her lips. A reluctant one, but still a smile, and he took the opportunity to loose another button.

"I don't usually wear anything to bed," he informed her. "Too confining. But I kept my drawers on tonight out of respect for you. And I'm willing to stay . . . confined for you, but there's no sense in both of us being uncomfortable." A third button popped free, and the pale flesh of her throat shone in the moonlight.

"I'm getting a rash just from being in the same room with this dress," he said. "I can't imagine what it's doing to your poor, tender skin."

He raised his head to find her eyes locked on his. She wore a strange expression that gave him pause. She stared at him for so long, he began to feel discomfited. "What are you doing?" he asked, running the tip of his index finger over her sculpted cheekbone.

Her violet eyes sparkled in the darkness and she said, "Waiting for you to lick your lip."

He brought his brows together in a confused frown. "Why?"

"Because I've never heard such a bucket of balderdash in all my life." One side of her mouth shot up as she gave him a smug grin. "You're not the only person who can spot a liar, you know."

Brandt laughed and pulled her forward for a deep, impetuous kiss. Her mouth opened beneath his and she kissed him back, as warm and uninhibited as he remembered.

His hands made quick work of the remaining buttons, all the way down to the hem of the hideous nightdress; then he separated the two halves of the gown, baring her beautiful body beneath the sheet and quilt that covered them both.

Impatient and not content to be fettered, he tossed the blankets aside and stared down at her near-naked form. "I knew you would be beautiful under that foul piece of burlap," he whispered fiercely. "Whyever would you cover such perfection with something so profane?"

With her hands on his bare shoulders, unabashed by her nudity, her lips curved up sedately. "It was supposed to keep your carnal urges at bay."

He threw back his head and snorted with laughter. When he lowered his head once again, she was chuckling with him. "Sweetheart, it would take all of the Seventh Cavalry to do that. And maybe even then they'd lose."

Willow sat up and shrugged the open gown down her arms, pulling it out from under her and tossing it over her shoulder to the floor.

Brandt watched her movements with unabashed fascination. She was the most stunning woman he'd ever seen, from her fall of burnished hair to her full, round breasts to the smooth flatness of her belly and her long, sleek legs. If he looked at her for a hundred years, it still wouldn't be long enough to absorb the full effect of her loveliness.

"Are you going to spend all night hovering, or are you going to make love to me?"

He sobered instantly. He shouldn't have been surprised by her acts of boldness after all this time, but this request hit him like a punch to the solar plexus. "Do you want me to make love to you?"

A moment of silence followed his question while she seemed to consider every possible outcome of her answer. And then she quietly said, "Yes."

He pulled his head back a fraction to study her heart-shaped countenance. "Is that the prize you wish for winning your part of our bargain?"

Her lips lifted in a seductive half-grin. It didn't take her so long this time to decide. "Yes, I believe it is."

Whatever he'd done to deserve such a blessing, he vowed to keep at it. "Then I have no choice but to comply," he murmured as he swooped in for another heated kiss.

Chapter Twenty-one

His hand on her breast felt like heaven. The cool air on her bare torso caused goosebumps to break out along her arms, even as the heat of his flesh burned her fingertips. She ran her palms over the smooth, even planes of his chest, the firm pectoral muscles with their dark bronze medallions in the center of each. She traced the sides of her thumbs over the tiny nipples until they hardened and he uttered a cry of pleasure.

As if to sweeten the pot, he lowered his head to her breast and suckled her supple, puckering flesh. Groaning in ecstasy, she arched her back and drove her fingers through his soft, feathery hair. It felt like silk, and she pulled his face closer until the ends brushed the sides of her breasts.

Her legs parted of their own volition and Brandt shifted his weight to settle between them. A natural act that felt so suitable, she wondered why she'd fought it for so long. This was right. This was where she wanted to be.

Brandt's mouth drifted lower, his lips leaving a trail of moisture as he kissed his way under her breasts, over her rib cage, and along the line of her stomach. His tongue lapped at her navel, drawing a circle around the indentation and then delving into the deep center.

And then his mouth moved lower, into the triangle of tight curls between her legs. His hands followed, kneading her hips and thighs. He parted her legs even more while his mouth wreaked havoc with her nerve endings. His tongue licked and stroked and nipped, causing lightning bolts of sensation to rip through her body. Her hips rose off the bed, seeking more of the pleasure he seemed so adept at providing.

He was making her crazy. Bringing to life feelings and responses she hadn't known existed within her, and she was taking the time to fully experience each and every one.

"Brandt." She breathed his name and he answered by lifting his head and gifting her with a brilliant, satisfied smile.

"I hope you know how desirable you are." His voice was husky as he moved back up her body. "And the last time . . . I hope you know that I didn't leave because I was through with you." He ran a finger over her budded nipple. "Who could ever be done with something like this?"

"Then why did you?" she asked, though her throat throbbed with the urge to moan rather than speak.

"Would you believe that I was confused?" he asked with an air of smugness.

"You? Indeed not." She tried to smile but wasn't sure the response reached her lips.

He continued to trace meaningless shapes on her skin,

driving her wild and causing her to wriggle beneath him. "I expected you to be a virgin." When her eyes shot wide, he hurried on. "It was a biased conclusion, I know. And none of my concern to begin with. But when you weren't . . . it disconcerted me, that's all. I needed time to think."

His touch had less affect on her now, as she concentrated on his words and prepared to roll away from him. "And did you?" she asked, a note of anger seeping into her voice.

He nodded. "It doesn't matter. It didn't then, and it doesn't now. I just wasn't prepared for it, that's all."

She studied him for a moment, wondering how to reply. She appreciated his honesty and felt she owed him a bit in return.

"It was only one time," she said. "One man. In case you were wondering." Surprise filled his sea-green eyes, but he wisely remained silent. She didn't bother to mention Robert's name because—as Brandt had said—it was none of his concern. But she did tell him a bit more, just to ease his mind. "At the time, I believed I was in love with him, though I've since learned that it was most likely a small infatuation coupled with deep affection."

She threaded her hands into the hair on each side of his head, much the way he'd done to her. "Does that make you feel any better?"

He inclined his head, though not a full nod of agreement, which led her to suspect that he truly didn't care about her past, had simply wanted to explain the misconceptions that had tainted their first time together.

"You should count yourself fortunate," she told him, hoping to once again lighten the mood. "You're the first man I've permitted in my bed for quite some time."

Her attempt to amuse him worked. "Only in bed?" he asked, quirking a brow. "What a shame, considering

there are so many other fascinating places to make love.
We do have our work cut out for us, don't we? Luckily,
I am in the prime of health and fully prepared to show
you each and every one."

His mouth lowered to stifle her chuckle and she met
his kiss with enthusiasm, more than willing to *let* him
show her all the enticing places he promised existed. But
she wasn't ready to let him have complete control. Not
when he'd already turned her insides to oatmeal por-
ridge. So she began her own assault on his senses by
kissing his stubbled jaw and running her hands down his
tightly drawn sides, beneath the waist of his cotton drawers.

She made quick work of the thin string holding the
material fast and ran her hands under the soft fabric,
pushing the garment past his hips. As his manhood
sprang free, he rolled from side to side, shimmying the
drawers down and off his legs, leaving them somewhere
at the foot of the bed beneath the covers.

Her hands drew circles on his taut buttocks before
coming around to grasp his throbbing flesh. Brandt
moaned as her fingers closed about him, alternately applying gentle pressure and barely touching the velvet
flesh.

Lifting a thumb to her lips, she licked it and then
teased the tip of his shaft with the wet digit. His entire
body stiffened and he swore. "Christ, what are you trying to do to me?"

Willow chuckled and took a slow lap at his unshaven
jawline. "Just giving you a taste of your own medicine.
Would you like some more?"

"No." He grabbed her hands and forced them both flat
to the mattress above her head. "I'd like something else."
And he plunged into her, drawing a gasp from them
both.

"Ah, God, you feel so good," he whispered in her ear, releasing his hold.

"So do you."

"Let's stay like this forever. Never move, never get out of bed."

Willow's fingers danced over his spine, drawing little circles on his sweat-slicked back. "It's all right with me, but are you sure you can last that long?" To emphasize her point, she thrust her pelvis upward, driving him even deeper inside her.

The air left Brandt's lungs in a whoosh as she watched his eyes all but cross. "I changed my mind." His voice came out low and harsh with desire. "Let's move. Let's definitely move," he said, giving his hips a deliberate roll. "But I still never want to get out of this bed."

Willow laughed. "I thought you'd see it my way."

His fingers dug into the soft flesh of her bottom and he reversed their positions with a growl, coming to rest beneath her on the mattress while she sat above him. They remained connected, her thighs straddling his hips. Her breasts swayed as she shifted her weight, found the proper position. And then she placed her palms flat on his chest and slid an inch upward along his rigid length.

His hold moved to her waist, aiding her movements. And then he began to stroke a path to the undersides of her breasts, running his thumbs along the curve there and back down. As their pace increased, his hips rose farther off the bed. His grip tightened and her fingers curled almost clawlike into his chest.

She threw her head back and fastened her teeth on her bottom lip as the sensations inside her built to a fever pitch. Her stomach constricted and the muscles surrounding Brandt's shaft began to clench and release.

"That's it, sweetheart. Let it come." He clasped his hand around the nape of her neck and pulled her down to his mouth, swallowing her cry of release as her body shuddered above him.

The climax washed through her and into him. He flipped her back to the mattress, drawing her legs higher about his waist and thrusting into her once, twice, three times more before his own release overcame him.

Brandt rested his forehead against Willow's collarbone, concentrating on the almost impossible act of simply breathing in and out. He didn't want to crush her with his weight but couldn't seem to muster the energy to move.

Her fingers fanned through the hair at his temples and he smiled. He couldn't remember ever being so content. Willow had changed his life. Not always for the better, he admitted as he recalled her right hook to his face and the stiletto she'd held to his groin. But now . . . now he wasn't sure he could imagine his future without her in it. And frankly, he didn't want to.

Rather than putting the fear of God into him, as it had in the past, the thought of being with this woman for the rest of his life comforted him. That alone convinced him that he'd made an apt decision.

Rolling to his side, he brought her with him so that her body cushioned against his. He left her arm draped across his abdomen and lifted one of her legs to cover his thigh. "We'll have to do that again soon."

She laughed softly, sounding tired and, he hoped, satisfied. "I'll be ready when you are," she returned cheekily.

"Good. And how soon do you think you'll be ready to marry me?"

Willow sat bolt upright, staring at Brandt as though he'd grown a second head. "Excuse me?"

Surely she'd heard him incorrectly. Surely he hadn't just asked her to marry him. Surely he hadn't taken what they'd done as a sign of her eagerness to launch herself into the state of matrimonial bliss.

He wasn't that type of man, dammit. She'd come to that conclusion even before she'd let him make love to her the second time. *Dammit, dammit, dammit!*

He took her hand and brought the knuckles to his lips for a kiss; then he pressed the palm to his chest and gave her an earnest look. "I want you to be my wife. Marry me, Willow."

She wrenched her arm back to her side and then grabbed a handful of coverlet to wrap around her nude body. "Are you insane?" She leapt out of bed and charged to the front of the armoire, where her robe lay in a wrinkled ball. "*Why?*" she cried. "Why would you ask me to marry you? Why would you ruin a perfectly lovely, *simple* interlude with a stupid question like that? Why would you think I'd make a good wife?" She speared him with an icy glare. "I wouldn't. I'd be terrible at it."

Brandt was out of bed by this time, too, shrugging back into his discarded drawers and knotting the string at his waist with a furious yank. "I disagree. I think you'd make a wonderful wife. For me, at any rate. And it helps that I already think I'm in love with you."

"*What?*" She whirled away from him, only to whirl right back. "Why are you doing this?" she asked, a note of panic tinging her voice.

He scowled at her, his arms crossed mutinously across his chest. "I told you, I'm in love with you. Why the hell are you reacting this way? Surely I'm not the first man to propose marriage to you."

"The first sober one. You are sober, aren't you?" Taking a step forward, she took a sniff to smell his breath. And then she mumbled, "I'd rather you were drunk."

"What is it about marriage that scares you so much?"

he asked pointedly, his scowl melting into a more curious look.

"I'm not *afraid* of marriage," she answered, even as she rubbed the chill from her arms. "What a silly notion. Just because I'm not a great admirer of the sanctity of vows doesn't mean I'm *afraid,* for heaven's sake."

She set to pacing back and forth across the oriental carpet. "What I want to know is what brought on this sudden sense of honor. We were having a fine time. Weren't we having a fine time? And you had to go muddle it all with talk of love and marriage. Bah!" She waved a negating hand in front of her.

"You've already said you're not a great admirer of marriage. Do you take issue with the idea of love as well?"

"Not for other people," she answered carefully. "But it's not for me." Her eyes narrowed as she faced him. "And certainly not for you."

He raised a brow, taken aback by her claim. "Are you taking it upon yourself to decide my feelings now? Tell me, do I prefer rice pudding or fig?"

She ignored the derisive question. "You aren't any more interested in marriage than I am. Or at least you weren't before tonight."

"You're right; marriage wasn't something I wanted to consider even in my worst nightmares. Until I met you."

With a sound of frustration, she let her head fall back. This was getting worse by the minute. And he sounded so bloody sincere.

Brandt moved toward her, wrapping his hands around her upper arms and forcing her to meet his eyes. "I like being with you, Willow. I love making love to you. And despite some minor obstacles early on, I think we work well together. We make good investigative partners; I

200

can't help but imagine we'd make good partners in a marriage as well."

She held up a hand and shrugged out of his grasp. "Stop, just stop. I appreciate the offer, I really do. And I won't say that I don't have feelings for you, because you'd know it was a lie. I wouldn't have gone to bed with you if I didn't. But I can't marry you. I don't *want* to marry you, or anyone. Please understand that."

It was his turn to look belligerent. His arms went back across his broad chest and he glared at her. "I don't understand. It's not every day that I ask a woman to marry me and it damn well irritates me when she says no. Especially when I see no clear reason for her refusal."

His tone irked her once again. Just when she'd begun to weaken toward him, too. "I've told you my reasons. And I don't owe you any more of an explanation than I simply *don't want to marry.*"

"Fine." He turned and grabbed a pillow and the top coverlet from the bed. "I suppose this means I'm dispatched to the sitting room."

"I didn't say that," she said softly.

He gazed at her, eyes narrowed, the rumpled bedding clutched beneath his arm. "You won't marry me, but you're not sending me away either. Just what game are you playing here?"

"I'm not playing any game. That's what I'm trying to tell you. One of the reasons I let myself become involved with you in the first place is that I thought we could be together without either of us getting caught up in any misguided sentiments about love and marriage, which is certainly not what I want."

One dark brow winged up with interest. "Are you telling me that after all of this"—he threw out an arm to encompass the room and, she assumed, their rather vehement argument—"I'm still welcome in your bed?"

She grinned at him. He looked so adorable when he was befuddled. "Yes, I suppose it does. As long as you cease any talk of marriage."

He frowned. "I'm not sure I like this any better than your refusal to marry me. Do you mean to say that you have no qualms about continuing to make love without a hint of commitment in our future?"

"That's exactly what I'm saying," she answered, hoping he was finally coming round to her way of thinking. "And what's wrong with that? I would think you'd appreciate the freedom of such an arrangement. Most men would love it."

"Well, *I don't*," he bit out. The blankets fell to the floor as he stood there stiff, hands on hips, as he glowered at her. "I damn well dislike the idea. It would make our relationship feel . . . common . . . base . . . *cheap*. It's one thing to carry on with a mistress, knowing the arrangement is nothing more than a series of encounters based solely on physical pleasures. It's quite another to continue a sexual association with a woman you wish to marry."

"Stop saying that," she ordered. "You're making this entirely too complicated. There's nothing wrong with simply enjoying one another's company while we're working together on Charlie's case."

"And what of children?" he demanded. "Have you thought about that? You can't expect to lie with a man for long without finding yourself in a family way."

"Really, Brandt," she replied lightly, almost amused. "I would expect you to be a bit more well read on such matters. I'm a grown woman; I know how to protect myself. Besides, you can't spend long at the Silver Spur without learning a thing or two about preventing pregnancy. That's something you needn't be concerned about."

He remained silent, and she feared she'd lost the battle. That he would storm out and she would lose not only the touch of his warm body against hers, but a person she was becoming quite fond of—as a friend, as a lover, as a man.

"I won't stop you if you choose to leave," she told him softly. "In fact, I'll understand completely. But I'd rather you decide to stay. The only thing I ask is that you not bring up the topic of marriage again. That subject is definitely closed."

She watched him thinking, his face a careful blank while he weighed his options.

"So you think this is a situation any man would be delighted to find himself in," he commented.

"By all accounts, and given what I know about the male of the species, I would have to say yes."

He took a step forward, and then another. A strange light entered his eyes as he cupped her face in the palms of his hands. "Then I suppose I do my gender proud. I won't plague you further with talk of marriage," he agreed, "but I won't promise not to try luring you over to my way of thinking." A small smile lifted his mouth. "You can't fault a man for attempting to charm a beautiful woman, can you?"

Anticipation shivered through her. "I could," she said softly, already succumbing to his smooth seduction, "but I won't."

"Good. Because I have a plan."

"A plan?" she repeated, distracted by the touch of his lips on her cheek and the corner of her mouth.

"Mmm-hmm. To woo you." His kisses moved to the other side of her face, tormenting the lobe of her ear and the long line of her mandible.

"How do you . . . intend . . . to do that?" she asked breathlessly.

"I thought that I would start here . . ." He placed a kiss in the hollow of her neck. "And move down." He dragged his lips to the opening of her silk robe and the swell of one breast.

"Oh, yes," she moaned, her fingers clutching at his hair. "That could work."

He gave a low chuckle and backed her up to the bed. And then he proceeded to show her the rest of his plan.

Chapter Twenty-two

The next few days were spent tracking down and following Virgil Chatham, the evenings at assorted events set up by James and Mary Xavier, and the wee hours of the night . . . those were spent at the most pleasant of activities while Willow and Brandt did their best to convince the world they were newlyweds—in and out of the bedchamber. And, as promised, Brandt didn't bring up the topic of marriage to her again.

They sat now in Robert's office, giving what had turned into a weekly report of their progress, which at the moment was practically nonexistent.

"I don't know what else to do. We've spent every moment we can watching him. He barely leaves his house unless it's to attend religious services." After spying on him for a full week, Willow had told both Brandt and Robert that her instincts pointed more strongly than ever toward Chatham. The man went to church nearly every day, and she didn't think it was a coincidence that his town house was located only a few blocks from the wharves where all of the bodies had been discovered. "We've even followed his valet," she added.

"A frightening fellow," Brandt put in. "Seven feet if he's an inch, shaves his head down to the skull, and has never spoken a word in public as far as I can tell."

"What do you suggest we do next?" Robert asked, and Willow could feel his impatience. They all wanted to catch the murderer, and none of them were very good at waiting.

She hadn't discussed this option with Brandt, but she cast him only a darting glance before announcing her newest plan. "We're obviously getting nowhere by following Chatham, and just in case we're wrong about him, I think the best next step would be to bait the killer."

"How?" Robert asked.

Brandt scowled.

She took a deep breath, preparing herself for the opposition she was about to face, and rushed on. "I'll dress as a prostitute and walk the docks."

"No! Absolutely not." Brandt was out of his chair in a shot, towering over her and firing a glare so hot, it nearly singed her eyelashes.

"I think it's our best option," she stated calmly. "If the murderer is going to continue killing young women, he's going to eventually come to the dock to choose a new victim."

"No."

"Brandt's right," Robert said from behind his desk. "It's too dangerous. We don't have the resources to keep men at the docks round the clock, but if you want the docks watched a little more closely, I can assign a few additional agents to the area."

"You're not going to get anywhere that way," Willow

persisted. "The most the agents will see is a man—or men—paying women for their services. If they move to another location, or the woman gets in a carriage as we suspect, the agents will have to follow them. And what if Chatham isn't our man? The agents will either follow him and risk missing the real killer, or they'll follow each man who appears and risk missing Chatham." She met Robert's eyes. "I doubt you have enough men to cover the docks *and* chase down individual customers."

Robert didn't respond, but his lips pinched in displeasure.

Brandt wasn't so cooperative. "And what do *you* suggest we do? Allow you to parade the wharf and get picked up by God knows who? Possibly dragged off somewhere to be raped and murdered? Or are you willing to cooperate with the men if it means eliminating suspects?"

"Of course not." She shot him a chilling gaze, even though she suspected his animosity stemmed more from worry than anything else. "Don't be vulgar. The most I'll have to do is get in a carriage with some of these fellows. And if you're willing to have agents there, as you said, they won't have to follow everyone, they'll only have to follow *me*. Besides, it may not go that far," she added when she still met with opposition. "We may happen upon something quite helpful with me doing no more than walking around for an hour or two."

"I don't like it," Brandt put in doggedly. "I won't have it."

She sat back in astonishment. She turned to Robert for support, but he seemed content to let her fight this battle on her own. "You won't have it?" she repeated. "You won't *have* it?" She rose to her feet and stood nose to nose with the man who had shared her bed these past several nights. Apparently, that had given him some erroneous views about how much say he had over her life. "I'm sorry to have to point this out to you, but you are not my father. Nor are you my brother or husband. You have no say over what I can or cannot do. I'll do what I feel is best for the investigation, with or without your consent."

When a muscle low in his cheek jumped from the pressure he was applying to his jawbone, she expected him to argue further. Instead, he spat out a gritted, "Fine. But I'm going with you."

"Fine," she agreed. That had been easier than anticipated. "I already told you that I think it's a good idea for agents to be around. And having attended so many parties the past few weeks, you would be the one most qualified to identify Virgil Chatham, or any other Society gentlemen who find their way down to the docks."

"Oh, no." A cruel grin spread across Brandt's lips. "I'm not going to hide in the shadows while you're putting yourself in danger. I'm going to be right there beside you."

"You can't," she said simply, falling back into her chair in frustration. "No one will come anywhere near me if they think I'm already entertaining a customer. And if Chatham or anyone else recognizes you, it would destroy our entire case."

"Where you go, I go," he asserted stubbornly.

"Might I remind the both of you," Robert spoke from behind his desk, "that I haven't approved this idea yet. It may be too perilous for either of you."

"I can handle this, Robert." Willow had to cock her head to see around Brandt's rigid, unyielding figure, hands jammed angrily on his hips. "I've been in tighter situations than this, and your men will be there in case I run into trouble. I'm not worried."

A frown turned down Robert's mouth. "I am, but I'm

going to give you permission anyway." Brandt turned
on him, apparently redirecting the aim of the daggers
he'd been shooting at her these past five minutes.
"You'll go with her," Robert addressed him calmly.
"You'll stay as close to her as possible, provided you
two can come up with some way for you to remain
nearby without either being recognized or jeopardizing
the operation."

He shifted his gaze from Brandt's hard countenance
to Willow's much softer, approving expression. "Anything else?" he asked, even though the tone warned them
not to get into another argument in front of him. Neither
of them said a word. "Good. Let me know what your
plans are and how many agents you'll need. We'll be
ready when you are."

"No. Absolutely not." They were becoming Brandt's
three favorite words.

"I think it's a splendid idea," Mary Xavier put in. "It
may be a bit awkward, but it's sure to work."

He glowered at the two women and resumed shaking
his head. They were insane, both of them. Willow with
her outlandish ideas, and Mrs. Xavier for going along
with them. And Mrs. Xavier had only been brought into
the plan because Willow needed her help coming up
with the right accoutrements for tonight's masquerade.

"Cook is sure to have some things we can borrow,"
Mary continued. "And anything else, I'm sure we can
alter."

"We have to hurry." Willow moved around the room,
collecting articles of clothing and assembling them on
the bed. "We have to get our ensembles ready so that
we can take them along with us this evening and change
right after the play. We won't have much time, so every-

thing has to be nearly perfect before we leave for the theater."

"I'm not doing this," Brandt argued again. "I know what I said back in Robert's office, but this is going too far. I'll stay back with the other men."

A sparkle of amusement entered Willow's violet eyes and a dimple creased her cheek. "Oh, no," she practically crooned. "You promised Robert that you would stay with me every moment, and I'm holding you to it."

Brandt sat back on the bed with a plop and crossed his arms mutinously. He wouldn't go through with this. He wouldn't.

"I'll go down and see what I can get from Cook," Mrs. Xavier said, obviously ignoring Brandt's wishes altogether. "You start getting ready and we'll have him suited up in no time."

She moved to the door and had already opened it a crack when she turned back. A flash of pain fluttered over her face for a moment. "I can't thank you enough for this," she told them quietly. "It means the world to us that you're working so hard to find out who hurt our Yvonne." Her voice broke on the last few words of her statement and she quickly left the room.

When Willow's gaze met his, he saw sadness there, and an iron determination. At that moment, he knew all of his arguments were for naught. His pride, his resolve, the fear that someone would see him . . . None of that mattered when he recalled Mary's declaration and looked into Willow's eyes.

He was going to do it, despite his earlier blustering. *Please, God, let it be quick and painless.*

"So what do we need to do?" he asked.

Willow's face brightened at his resolve. "Get undressed and we'll see what I have that will fit."

He unbuttoned his shirt, kicked off his boots, and began shrugging out of his pants while she gathered several items from the pile on the bed. With him standing in nothing but his drawers, she studied him.

He pulled the muscles of his abdomen in a fraction. He knew there wasn't an inch of excess to be found on his hard, lean frame. But with Willow perusing his nearly nude body like a shank of beef at the meat vendor's, he wanted to present his very best form.

Her detailed scrutiny sent a bolt of desire rippling from the marrow of his bones out in every direction. His hunger rose another notch as he watched a tinge of pink darken her cheekbones and knew she was feeling the same deep longing as he.

"We have a few minutes before Mrs. Xavier gets back," he hinted. Though he knew the suggestion was futile; Mary was just downstairs running a quick errand and liable to return at any moment. If she hadn't been, Brandt would have plucked Willow up by the waist, deposited her on the bed, and kept her occupied well through both acts of the play they were supposed to attend that evening, as well as the lengthy intermission.

Willow shook her head and answered in a thick, passion-laden timbre. "We can't."

She cleared her throat, apparently hoping to douse the firelike sparks of sexual awareness flying between them—that *always* flew between them—and quickly returned her focus to the matter at hand. But not, he was pleased to note, without a great deal of effort.

"I don't think we should worry about stockings and shoes. You can wear your socks and boots and we'll try to be sure the skirt is long enough to cover them."

Being brought back to the task before them—rather unpleasantly, at that—Brandt fought a snort.

"We have to do something about your chest, though."

She came at him with the most frightening object in

her collection and he took a step back. "What are you going to do with that?"

"Your shoulders are too broad and your hips are too narrow; we need to even things out a bit. Add curves in all the right places."

She fiddled with the strings until the material was as loose and wide as possible, then she held it near the floor and tapped the back of his bare calf. "Here, step in."

He muttered and cursed beneath his breath but did as she ordered. The sides caught on his drawers, but she tugged it the rest of the way up until the stiff material rested around his waist and rib cage.

"All right, now hold it here," she said, and moved behind him. "Take a deep breath." She waited. "Now blow it out and suck in your stomach."

He did, and she pressed a knee to the base of his spine and gave a yank that nearly toppled him over backwards. "Jesus," he gasped.

Willow laughed. "Don't be a baby. Women go through this every day."

He didn't know how. The one time he'd seen the marks the whale bones left on Willow's skin, he'd condemned the blasted feminine undergarment. Now he was wearing one. And she was right; no one could draw a full breath while wearing a corset. "In case you haven't noticed, I am not a woman," he pointed out very succinctly.

"Oh, I noticed," she cooed with a laugh and let her hand brush the curve of one taut buttock as she readjusted her hold on the corset strings.

"Take another breath," she told him. When he exhaled, she yanked again, and again he swore. "There," she said, circling around to inspect her work. Moving to a drawer, she pulled out several pairs of his thick, woolen socks and began stuffing them into the loose front fabric high on his chest.

"Careful, sweetheart," he said with a drawl, "or mine might end up bigger than yours."

Her laughter tinkled through the room like chimes as she tucked in another pair of socks. "Don't worry, as long as your bosom is in proper proportion to your size, I promise not to turn competitive." She threw him a saucy grin. "Besides, if I become too envious of your generous attributes, I can always make use of my newly patented bust-improver.

"Now turn around," she said, shifting him in front of the full cheval glass arranged against one wall. "Very nice. Very nice, indeed."

Brandt caught a good look at himself and nearly keeled over in mortification. He stood encased in cotton drawers and a woman's corset with his very masculine bare arms and legs sticking out on all sides. The fact that his sock-laden bosom now rivaled that of the most well-endowed matriarch did little to lift his spirits.

"I cannot believe I'm doing this. I look like my mother, God rest her soul. She and my father both would turn over in their graves if they saw me prancing around in women's underclothes."

"You're not prancing," Willow said, trying to allay his misgivings. "You're adopting a disguise to further our investigation. Your parents would be proud that you're willing to go so far to catch a killer."

"You didn't know my parents," he muttered.

"Lord!" Mrs. Xavier gasped as she came back into the room, clutching a small pile of clothes to her breast. "We'd better get these things on you. No one will take you for a woman, standing there like that. I've never seen such hairy legs," she said, and then made a point of looking anywhere but below Brandt's waist. "Even

James's legs don't have that much fur on them, and he's a hairy man, he is."

She bustled forth and handed Willow several large, nondescript garments as they both began dressing him. Mary pushed his arms through the long sleeves of a once-white blouse, while Willow wrapped a dark skirt around his waist. And then Willow delivered the coup de grace, a flowing blond wig that had come from her personal collection—bought and paid for by the Pinkerton National Detective Agency, of course—which she attached to his head with several sharp hairpins.

When they finished, he almost looked like a female. A large, not very attractive, not overly feminine female, but nonetheless, he could pass for a woman from a distance. He hoped.

"We don't have time to fix your face," Willow told him. "You'll have to shave before we go to the theater to avoid any signs of a beard, and then we can both change clothes in the carriage on the way to the docks."

A beard was the least of his problems. Right now, he was more concerned about getting enough air to avoid passing out.

"How am I supposed to breathe in this thing?" he questioned the women, giving the clawlike contraption an uncomfortable tug.

"Very carefully," they answered in unison, and then shared a chuckle at their mutual understanding.

"He's going to need a shawl to cover those big arms and chest," Mrs. Xavier commented, and bustled out of the room to find one.

"I hope you're enjoying yourself," he said darkly, staring at the top of Willow's head while she fussed with the pleats of his skirt. "Because when we're finished, I'm going to make you very, very sorry for doing this to me."

She looked up, meeting his eyes as she crouched in front of him, her face even with the general area of his groin. Corset or no corset, a man's body had no choice but to respond to a woman in such a position.

"I'll look forward to it," she returned saucily, then gifted him with a grin that would drive a saint to sin.

And there, before the full-length mirror, in women's clothes, a bulge appeared at the front of his skirt that in *no way* would help him pass as a female.

Chapter Twenty-three

No matter how many of these filthy harlots he dispensed with, a dozen more seemed to take her place. His task would never be done unless he increased his efforts.

And he was beginning to feel it was a mistake to concentrate on only the overt sinners. Granted, he had ended dear Yvonne's wickedness, but that hadn't been planned. He hadn't recognized her true corruption until he'd caught her en flagrante with that young upstart Parker Cunnington. Until that moment, he'd thought Yvonne pure of heart, unsullied. He'd intended to join with her and make their marriage one of pureness, dedicated to the eradication of evil.

He regretted having had to kill her. She had been a beauty. And down deep, he still believed there had been a touch of purity in her soul. But sinners must be punished, regardless of their comeliness or standing in society.

Which is why he'd begun to look more closely at those

around him. Prostitutes could be found at any time down by the docks, but there were whores all around him, dressed in fancy finery, holding their heads high, secure with their social status. Yet they corrupted community mores from the inside out, perhaps more insidiously even than those who sold their wares so blatantly to any man with a few coins and a place to carry out their dirty deeds.

A face took shape before his mind's eye. A delightful piece, if ever he'd seen one. He'd spotted her at several assemblages lately and had been told she was married to the strapping fellow who seemed to never be far from her side. Yet he still suspected her of great transgressions against God.

She was too exquisite not to have sinned. And she was more brazen than was wise for someone so young. Why, he'd been standing just around the corner when she'd boldly told Claudia Burton that she and her husband were leaving the party early so that they could go home and fornicate.

He would watch her carefully. It wouldn't be hard, considering the couple seemed to be at all of the same functions he attended.

And soon, after Outram disposed of the body that even now occupied the dark cellar room, the time would be right to rid the world of another transgressor, and he would make sure it was Willow Donovan.

Chapter Twenty-four

"I don't know how you stand these bloody things," Brandt complained for the fourth time in ten minutes, digging at the lower edge of his corset.

She experienced an almost sadistic glee over the fact that someone else—especially a man—was suffering the same nuisance she usually did. Of course, Brandt was much more vocal about his discomfort than the women who trussed themselves up in similar trappings every day of their lives.

For once, Willow wasn't wearing a corset herself. She was dressed in a rather shabby, dull brown skirt that fell to mid-calf and was pinned to the side at her knee to show even more of her stocking-clad leg. Her camisole, with pink ribbon woven into the border, left her arms and much of her chest bare, and the faded gray shawl draped about her shoulders acted as more of a shield against the chill air coming off the waterfront than a cover for her exposed skin. Her hair was knotted at the top of her head, with several long strands left to straggle around her face in what she hoped was an alluring yet beggared style.

"I don't want you wearing this monstrosity anymore," he put in, still on the fevered topic of corsets. "Or anything like it. I don't care if you grow as fat as a suckling hog. To think of you in this kind of pain for the sake of fashion . . ." he growled, tugging at another part of the garment. "No. I'm burning this damn thing and any others you have as soon as we get back."

Even though she'd come to much the same conclusion the night of the Burtons' ball, she wasn't about to let Brandt begin dictating to her. It would give him a false sense of authority and possibly lead to other demands she would feel less charitable about carrying out. So she thrust her hands on her hips and cocked her head in what she hoped was a challenging pose. "Just because you're laced up in my best girdle, don't think you can start dictating how I'm to dress, Brandt Donovan."

He huffed but didn't argue. Instead he concentrated his efforts on scratching at a particularly annoying stay, and grumbling all the while.

"Will you please hush. You're going to draw the wrong kind of attention to us. And can't you pitch your voice a bit higher? No one is going to believe you're a woman with that gruff tone."

"How's this?" he asked, two octaves higher and with a distinct Southern drawl that Willow couldn't help but find funny.

She turned away to keep from bursting into laughter, even though she couldn't stifle a chuckle at both his histrionics and the way he fluttered his lashes coquettishly.

As much as he'd balked at dressing in women's clothing for this assignment, he was now playing his part to the hilt. Throughout the night, he'd added a wide sashay to his walk, primped his long blond hair, and adjusted and readjusted his false bosom. Even his razor stubble seemed under control, since he'd shaved just before they left for the theater not four hours before.

She was about to comment on how often he reached a hand between his legs to feel his member—as though checking to see that is was still there, even though he was wearing a dress—when she heard a carriage approaching.

"Listen," Brandt whispered.

"I hear." She stepped away so they wouldn't appear huddled together and watched for the advancing vehicle. Letting the shawl fall to her elbows, she put her hands on her hips to tighten the front of her sleeveless camisole and accentuate her chest. A move Brandt would no doubt chastise her for later, having warned her more than once not to be *too* enticing.

But the coach stopped several yards away, in front of a woman who had been standing in the same warehouse doorway all evening. A well-dressed gentleman stepped out of the black landau, and Willow noticed immediately that it was not Virgil Chatham. Her heart plummeted; she had so hoped he would appear and do or say something to convince them that he was, indeed, the killer.

"La, but it must be Thursday if the likes of you are visiting me," the prostitute said with a seductive smile, moving forward to place a hand on the man's chest.

Brandt's voice reached her ear from just over one shoulder. "Isn't that Martin Proctor? The fellow we met at the Wellington soirée who announced every five minutes, rather vocally, how much he adored his new bride?"

"Hello, Ginni." The man pressed a kiss to the back of the woman's hand, as though he was greeting a lady at a party rather than picking up the prostitute he paid to pleasure him. "I've been anticipating this all week. Shall we?" He stepped back and ushered her into the carriage, and Ginni went willingly.

Willow took a closer look. "So much for wedded bliss," she replied dryly, realizing Brandt was right. "I wonder if Mrs. Proctor knows how her husband spends his Thursday evenings."

"Doubtful. Highly doubtful," Brandt answered.

She released a sigh of regret, realizing that this assignation was an old and routine one, not something she and Brandt needed to be concerned with. And not someone they needed to follow.

The coach drove off, and Brandt went back to alternating between checking his masculinity and "puffing" his breasts. Willow stared out across the water, well used to the fish- and rubbish-laden odor by now.

It frightened her to think of the poor, defenseless women who had been murdered here. Or possibly picked up here and murdered elsewhere. But it frightened her even more to think of the women who hadn't been killed, the ones who were still forced to sell their bodies for money.

Because it could so easily be her. *There but for the grace of God,* as the saying went. If it weren't for her job with the Pinkerton National Detective Agency, she might very well be in the same position, especially with Erik to care for.

And it wasn't so far-fetched a possibility that when Francis Warner finally got his way and edged her out of the Agency, she could still end up here.

Her teeth clenched, her hands balled into fists at her sides. She wouldn't do so willingly, she vowed. She would do anything else first—be a governess, a laundress, enter into a loveless marriage to a wealthy man—

221

but it was not unfathomable that she could one day find herself in the exact same situation as some of these women, just trying to make enough to buy food, keep a roof over their heads, provide for their children.

She only prayed that—before she did lose her job— she would be able to save enough to buy a nice little house somewhere and bring Erik to live with her. It had always been her most fervent dream and her primary goal. Lord, but she missed that boy.

Once again, her thoughts were interrupted by the sound of wheels and hooves on cobblestone, this time from the other end of the wharf. The carriage stopped too far away for them to make out details. But strangely it did not appear to come to a rest near any prostitutes that she noticed.

Brandt, too, appeared to find this odd. His hand clamped over her arm and dragged her back against the shadowed wall of a dark, empty warehouse. From there, he led her closer to the coach, putting a finger to his lips and gesturing for her to be silent.

They sneaked along the connected buildings, listening for any sound, watching for any movement. As they got close enough to see more clearly, the driver climbed down from his perch and opened the door. But rather than someone stepping out, he leaned inside and pulled out a large, bulky sack. He tossed the heavy parcel over his shoulder and turned so that Willow and Brandt could see his face.

Willow gasped, and then threw a hand over her mouth to smother the sound. Brandt's grip tightened about her wrist and Willow knew he was thinking the same thing: Outram Kyne. Virgil Chatham's tall, bald valet, at the docks, apparently . . . dumping something.

She remained perfectly still, waiting for the man's next move. While they watched, he carried his burden down one of the landing docks and laid it gently on the ground. He untied the ropes at each end and rolled the contents until the brown burlap came loose.

"Oh, my God!" This time Willow didn't bother stifling her cry of alarm, but the sound was still too low to carry.

A woman's body toppled onto the splintered wood of the pier. Outram began arranging the pale, lifeless form, folding her arms and adding a single white rose between her clasped hands.

As he started to bundle up the coarse cloth and ropes, Brandt stormed forward, raising his arms to signal the numerous Pinkerton agents stationed in various spots along the wharf. "Hold it!" he called out, making his way to where Outram stood.

Willow hurried behind Brandt, already reaching beneath her skirt for the derringer hidden in her garter. She wasn't sure whether Brandt carried a weapon or not, but she didn't intend to be caught defenseless in the company of this obviously unstable creature.

The valet straightened, stunned at being caught near the body of a dead woman. His eyes darted from side to side, looking for an escape. But Brandt was already there, tackling him and throwing his imposing frame to the ground.

Outram fought, kicking, hitting, and scratching. But Willow kept the barrel of her gun trained on him, and Brandt did his best to keep the man down. Then they were surrounded by running, shouting Pinkertons, all coming to aid in Brandt's fight.

Two men lifted Kyne; another helped Brandt to his feet. And they all stared at the young, dark-haired girl lying still on the dock.

Willow returned the pistol to her garter and moved toward Brandt. His wig was askew, the blond strands covering one eye. His chest heaved as he tried to catch his breath within the tight confines of the corset, and she noticed that one side of the lacy material was flat where his sock breast had fallen out during the struggle.

He stretched a hand out to her and she grasped it. In one motion, he pulled her against him, burying his lips in her hair. She wrapped her arms around his waist and squeezed tight while she rested her head on his shoulder.

Several of the agents led the servant away. Others remained with the body, covering her with the discarded sheet of burlap.

Willow couldn't pull her eyes from the body lying immobile not three feet away. Her heart squeezed in sadness, for who she was and who she could have been. She looked to be no older than Willow's age, petite, pretty, probably vibrant and lovely at one time, with her whole life ahead of her.

And now . . . she was dead.

Willow wondered when this girl had been killed, and her stomach gave a violent lurch at the thought that she and Brandt might have been able to prevent it. They might have saved her.

With his free hand, Brandt dragged the now straggling wig off his head. "Let's go change. We'll meet Robert at the police station and see what we can learn when they question the suspect."

"We're going to have a bit of trouble getting a confession out of him," Robert told them as he closed the door of a private interrogation room behind him.

"Why?" Brandt asked. He was back in his own clothes, a pair of buff-colored trousers and a plain white shirt, the cuffs rolled to just below his elbows. Willow was still wearing her outfit from the dock, simply because it had been easier than undressing and then dressing again. And unlike Brandt, she didn't mind if people saw her in rather ratty old feminine clothes. But she'd covered her bare arms with a long-sleeved shirtwaist and lowered the hem of her skirt so that her legs were no longer visible.

"It turns out the man has no tongue."

Willow's eyes widened as she looked at Robert. That *would* explain why they'd never seen or heard him speak to anyone, not even his master. Nor had he uttered a cry of outrage while being captured, which Willow had found odd.

"We did bring in Mr. Chatham to get his statement. He's visibly shaken and claims not to know anything about his employee's activities."

"Do you believe him?" Brandt wanted to know.

"We have no reason not to," Robert said, though he sounded less than enthusiastic about it. "Chatham also claims to have alibis for the nights of each woman's death, though it will take some time to verify them."

Robert turned to Willow. "What do you think?"

She didn't know what to think. She'd been so sure Virgil Chatham was the murderer, and now she was being told the man was innocent. Whether it was doubt or simply the fact that she hated being wrong, a chill swept over her skin at the idea.

"I'd like to know why Outram Kyne killed all those women. And what his connection is to Gideon." She shot Brandt a meaningful glance, knowing that Charlie's note and all their research had not been misleading. It meant something.

Robert, who was up-to-date on even the most minor detail of the case by now, said, "Perhaps the valet picked up on his employer's fascination with the Bible. Kyne has been with Chatham for several years now; perhaps he felt he was doing his master's bidding. We won't know until we talk to Chatham a bit more and somehow get a few answers from Kyne himself, but I'd guess that's the direction in which the police will be leaning."

"And what about Charlie?" Willow persisted. "If Outram killed him, *why?* And if he didn't, who did?"

Robert shifted his weight to another foot but held her gaze. "You said it yourself, Willow. Charlie figured out what was going on, got too close to discovering that Yvonne Xavier's killer had also murdered all of those women on the wharves. Kyne probably got scared and killed Charlie to protect himself. I don't think it's any more complicated than that."

Willow chewed the inside of her lip. She still had her doubts, still felt a niggling suspicion that all was not quite as simple as Robert and the police liked to think. But there was nothing she could do about it now, not with Kyne in custody and Chatham being questioned— and most likely released.

"I guess we should just be grateful there won't be any more killings," she said softly. Even if she wasn't completely satisfied with the guilt of their prisoner—or the innocence of his employer.

"As far as the police are concerned," Robert put in, "they have their killer. Virgil Chatham will be sent home as soon as they're confident he's told them all he can about Outram Kyne."

That should have made her happy. It didn't. But she sighed, gave a cursory lift of her shoulders, and turned to walk away. "At least it's over," she said to no one in particular.

"Is this yours, or was it here when we arrived?"

Willow looked up to see Brandt holding a leather-bound book. She didn't recognize the volume. "It must have been here when we arrived."

They were in the process of packing to leave the Xavier house, now that their investigation was officially over. It made her a little sad and she wasn't sure why. Possibly because she still had a nagging feeling that all was not right with the Outram Kyne situation. But more likely—and she was loathe to admit this, even to herself—it was because this was where she and Brandt had begun . . . whatever it was they shared. A relationship? A love affair? A friendship?

Perhaps a little of each. And she couldn't help but worry that once they left this house, this room—this room that had become *their* room—whatever it was they shared would all be over.

Not that she cared, she reminded herself with an intentional straightening of her spine. As she'd told Brandt, she wasn't interested in marriage or anything remotely similar. But she couldn't help hoping that their relationship would continue.

Only upon occasion, since Brandt would be returning to Boston now that their assignment was finished. But perhaps he would return to New York on business once or twice, and if she was also in town, they could get together. Maybe she would even be sent to Boston for the Agency and could drop in to see him.

She glanced at Brandt out of the corner of her eye as she folded a lacy lisle chemise. He hadn't said anything about what would happen between them after they moved out of the Xavier household. She wondered if he'd given it any thought, or even cared.

Right now, he only seemed to care about making all of his belongings fit into his single valise. Willow, on the other hand, needed a trunk and several bags for all the things she'd brought, as well as those Mrs. Xavier had thrust upon her during their stay. She would have to store some of them at the Pinkerton offices, since she couldn't possibly travel with this many parcels.

Mary Xavier chose that moment to breeze through the open doorway. "Mrs. Hullpepper has some of your laundry downstairs, fresh and clean," she told Brandt. "You can go down for it, if you like, or I can have it sent up."

Willow saw him scowl, probably contemplating how he would get anything more stuffed into his small, well-worn carpetbag. Without a word, he moved past Mrs. Xavier and out of the room to retrieve his things.

"Oh, I can't believe you're leaving so soon," Mary said sadly. "I've so enjoyed having you."

"Thank you," Willow returned with a smile. "We've appreciated your hospitality."

"It's been our pleasure. And thank you again for all you did to catch that horrible man." Her voice softened and her eyes misted at the mention of her daughter's killer. Or perhaps simply at the thought of her daughter.

"Oh, I nearly forgot." She pulled a slip of paper from the pocket of her dress and held it out to Willow. "This came for you not an hour ago."

Willow took the note and unfolded it, quickly reading the wired telegram. "Oh, no." She felt all the blood rush out of her head, felt herself sway, felt her heart lurch in panic.

Grabbing an already packed valise from the floor at her feet, she gathered only a few more articles before heading past Mrs. Xavier for the door.

"My dear, where are you going?"

Willow barely registered Mary's concern. Her mind spun in a thousand directions at once as she raced into the hall and down the wide, carpeted stairs. Mrs. Xavier followed close behind, repeating her question, frantically trying to get an answer.

"I have to go. I have to leave," Willow mumbled as she threw open the front door and raced down the steps. "My brother needs me."

228

Chapter Twenty-five

"What do you mean *she's gone?*" Brandt bellowed. They stood in the foyer, where Brandt, carrying a pile of newly laundered clothes, had come upon Mrs. Xavier staring out the open door after Willow's sudden disappearance.

The woman wrung her hands, anxiety causing the lines of her face to run deeper than usual. "I don't know what happened. I handed her the telegram she'd received and she read it and ran out of the house."

Brandt's fingers tightened on the fabric of his starched, folded shirts. "Did she say anything? Did she say why she was leaving, or where she was going?"

Mary shook her head, eyes frantic. "She only said that she had to leave." Her brow furrowed in thought. "And I believe she mentioned her brother. I didn't know she had a brother."

Brandt did, but he thought the young man was missing. How was it that Willow had suddenly found him?

Or was it that the telegram had contained some urgent piece of new information about her lost relation?

He shoved the pile of laundry into Mrs. Xavier's arms and headed out the door. He didn't know what was going on, but he thought he knew who would.

"You don't think she's in trouble, do you?" Mrs. Xavier called after him.

He shook his head, but in truth, he wasn't sure. Outram Kyne might have been captured, but the less-than-pristine Virgil Chatham was still out there, and Brandt wasn't taking any chances.

In record time, he made it through the busy city streets and up the front steps of the Pinkerton National Detective Agency. Without waiting for the secretary to announce him, he burst into Robert's office and speared him with a withering glance.

A startled Robert sat up straighter in his chair and slowly laid down the pen with which he'd been writing.

"Where is she?" Brandt charged.

"Where is who? And who gave you the right to break into my office like this?"

With his color rising and annoyance clear on his face, Robert rose to his feet to meet Brandt eye-to-eye. They would be nose-to-nose in a minute if Robert didn't start giving him the answers he sought.

"Willow is missing. She received a wire at the Xaviers' and has disappeared, and I suspect you know exactly where she is."

"I don't know what you're talking about," Robert replied calmly. But Brandt didn't miss the slight shift in his posture.

Brandt lowered his voice to an intimidating pitch and spoke each word slowly, so as not to be misunderstood. "I'm not a patient man, Robert, especially when it comes to Willow. And I'm afraid that if you don't tell me

where she is—within the next ten seconds, mind you—
I'll have to put you through that wall." He nodded his
head in the direction of the hardwood panel behind Robert's upright frame.

He expected Robert to balk, to take exception at being
spoken to in such a manner, as he'd taken exception to
having his office door kicked in, and Brandt was prepared to deal with that, too. He was prepared to deal
with anything if it would only help him find Willow.
But instead, Robert's gaze darted to the side, as though
trying to decide whether or not to reveal what he knew.

"She mentioned her brother," Brandt prompted. "I
know he's missing and that she's been looking for him
for several years. If anyone knows where he is—and
where she's gone—it's you." A sudden thought entered
his head and he blurted it out. "Knowing how much
Willow travels for the Agency, I suspect that any information or correspondence would come through this office. Through you," he added pointedly.

Robert's cheeks reddened and Brandt knew he'd hit a
nerve. "The wire she received . . . You sent it to her at
the Xavier home, didn't you?"

With obvious reluctance, Robert nodded. "It's not exactly as you think," he began. "Willow does have a
brother, but he's not missing. And he's not as old as she
lets on. Erik—"

"Erik? She told me her brother's name was Jeremy."

"Yes, well, the missing brother story is one she uses
often in her work, and it wouldn't do to bandy about his
real name, for safety's sake. Erik is only twelve years
old. He was born when Willow was already practically
grown, and with some problems that make it hard for
her to keep him with her."

"Problems?" Brandt asked, still trying to absorb the

231

fact that she had a brother much younger than he'd believed.

"Yes. He's slower than other children his age and has certain . . . mental deficiencies. Willow has taken care of him since her parents died several years ago, and although I know she'd much prefer to have him with her, that's just not possible in this line of work. He stays with a pleasant farm family outside Gettysburg, Pennsylvania."

"Then why did Willow take off so suddenly this afternoon?"

"A wire arrived here at the office saying that Erik has fallen ill. It must be serious or the Nelsons wouldn't have felt the need to worry Willow. I sent the telegram over as soon as I saw it, and I assume that's where she's headed."

Brandt leaned forward to slide a blank piece of paper over the desktop toward Robert. "This farm in Pennsylvania . . ." he said in a tone that brooked no arguments. "I'll want directions."

Willow dipped the square of cloth into the bowl of cool water once again and mopped Erik's brow. His fever was coming down, thank God, and he hadn't emptied his stomach since she'd arrived, even though Mrs. Nelson said he'd been vomiting for days.

Everyone's biggest fear was that her brother had contracted cholera, since the nearby town had suffered an outbreak only a month before. But now that it didn't seem he was developing any of the more serious symptoms of that disease, and his fever had begun to lower, they were a little more confident that Erik would recover. Even the doctor, who had left less than half an hour earlier, hadn't seemed terribly worried. He'd given them a list of things to watch for and offered to return if he was needed, but had otherwise felt that Erik's fever would break and he would soon be back to his active, everyday self.

As much as Willow wanted Erik to awaken feeling fit, that prospect was daunting. Her brother, when healthy, was a whir of motion. She didn't know how Mr. and Mrs. Nelson kept up with him, she was only glad they did. They were good to Erik and treated him like one of their own.

She wiped his brow again and silently promised that she would bring him to live with her as soon as she could. It was the same promise she made each time she left after a short visit. And one of these days, she would keep it.

Until she was on the train headed here, frightened beyond reason that she might lose him, she hadn't realized how very much she missed her brother, how much she wanted him to live with her. It stiffened her resolve to build her savings and find a place for the both of them to live. *Soon.*

In fact, directly after she got back to New York, she would talk to Robert. Explain that she needed to establish a permanent residence rather than staying in assorted hotel rooms even when she was back in the city. Ask him to give her more assignments that would keep her close to home. She could hire someone to stay with Erik when she had to be away, but she would much prefer to simply work within the area and never be as far from him as she had been these past several years. She would also ask Robert to give her less risky duties, ones that were unlikely to have dangerous repercussions or lead the criminal element back to her brother.

There were other details to take care of, other things to think through, but Willow knew this was the right move. She and Erik had been apart long enough.

Erik mumbled in his sleep, and she brushed strands of light brown hair off his damp forehead. Then she leaned forward to kiss his brow. "You'll be fine," she whispered. "Just fine."

She was alone in the house, except for Erik, but heard Mrs. Nelson's voice carrying from outside. Mr. Nelson had ridden off for the fields only a few hours ago, so Mrs. Nelson couldn't be talking to him. Unless something was wrong. But in that case, she thought the woman's voice would sound less calm.

Rising from the edge of Erik's small bed, she stretched her stiff spine and moved through the sparse kitchen to the front door. She heard a man's voice now and became even more curious. Not that it was unlikely for neighbors to drop by, but Mrs. Nelson had told her people were keeping their distance because of the cholera scare.

She opened the door and stepped out into the warm afternoon sunshine. And then her feet froze. Her body continued its forward motion, however, and threw her off balance so that she stumbled for a moment before catching herself and drawing to a stop.

"Brandt," she breathed, amazed that she could utter a sound with her lungs totally devoid of oxygen.

He stood beside Mrs. Nelson, his faded carpetbag hanging in one hand. Mrs. Nelson had a smile on her face, while Brandt's seemed curiously blank. She hadn't expected him to be surprised, considering he'd come all this way and had no reason to be here unless he'd followed her.

What she expected, she supposed, was anger. And rightfully so. She'd taken off with no warning, leaving no clue of where she was headed. But even though she'd known he would be upset, she hadn't thought he'd *follow* her.

"Aren't you going to say hello?" he asked. The question sounded simple. It was anything but.

Not sure her vocal chords would comply, she opened her mouth to respond, but before any sound came out, Mrs. Nelson spoke.

"Isn't it nice of your friend, here, to come all the way from New York City to check on you? He says your Robert Pinkerton and some others were concerned about your safety. You know, a woman traveling alone and all."

Willow forced a smile. "Yes, that's very nice of him." Her gaze moved to Brandt, and even though her tongue wanted to trip over the words, she made herself say, "Thank you."

Brandt nodded, but she could tell he wanted to say more, chastise her for her actions. "How's Erik?" he asked instead.

Her mind stuttered to a stop. How did he know Erik's name? How did he know that was why she'd come here? She recalled Mrs. Nelson's earlier words and the answer came to her in a flash of realization: Robert.

"I see Robert told you why I had to leave the city on such short notice." Just how much had Robert divulged?

"Yes." Brandt's eyes fixed on hers, daring her to break the connection. "He told me everything."

Everything. The words fell over her with the impact of a ten-ton weight.

"How is your brother?" he asked again. "Is he all right?"

She inclined her head and swallowed to wet her exceedingly dry mouth and throat. "He's much better," she told him. "We think he's going to be fine."

"We feared at first it was the cholera," Mrs. Nelson added as she retrieved the earlier dropped vegetable basket from the ground at her feet. "But the doc was just here and said it don't look like he's got the cholera after all. His fever's coming down already. 'Course, that's probably because Willow ain't left his side since she got here. She plain dotes on that boy when she's around, and he's plumb crazy 'bout her."

Willow tried to smile, but the expression was grim. She hadn't forgotten that she'd led Brandt to believe her brother's name was Jeremy, that he was grown and had disappeared. She wondered how long Brandt would wait to corner and interrogate her about the lies.

"Would you care to come in and see for yerself?" Mrs. Nelson offered.

And of course he agreed. A pleased grin lifted the sides of his mouth and he gave Willow a smug look as he followed Mrs. Nelson into the small, clapboard house.

Willow clenched her teeth in frustration. She hadn't meant to deceive him by leaving New York that way, but she honestly hadn't given him any thought. From the moment she'd read that telegram, Erik and his uncertain health had been the only thing on her mind. She'd have gladly explained everything—within reason, of course—as soon as she returned.

Except that he'd tracked her down and now she would have to face him much sooner than she'd planned. With a weary sigh, she walked into the house after Brandt and Mrs. Nelson.

They were standing in the threshold of Erik's room, watching the boy as he slept. Pushing past them—because she was just the teeniest bit annoyed—she lowered herself beside her brother and took up bathing his face and neck once again.

She put the back of her hand to his brow and waited for the searing heat to seep through her skin. Instead, there was only a slightly abnormal warmth, a sign that he was getting better by the minute.

Relief washed through her. "He feels cooler," she said aloud, partially to the two people behind her, but mostly to herself.

"Erik'll be hungry when he wakes up. I'll start some of my beef stew and biscuits. That's one of his favorites."

"Good idea," Brandt said, those two simple words filled with meaning. "That will give Willow and me a chance to talk."

When she turned to look, his gaze was determined, his face set in stone, telling her that she was in trouble. He expected answers.

Chapter Twenty-six

"What the hell did you think you were doing?"

Brandt snapped the question the minute Mrs. Nelson was out of earshot. Willow flinched inwardly, but outwardly remained calm by placing the cloth in her hand beside the bowl of tepid water and rising from her post at Erik's bedside.

"My brother was sick," she said simply, facing his accusatory glare head-on. "I had to come. I'm sorry I didn't take the time to tell you before I left, but you found me easily enough."

He strode forward and grabbed her upper arms in his large, callused hands. "Do you think that's why I'm upset?" he spat, giving her a little shake. "Wounded ego?"

Abruptly, he let her go, practically thrusting her away as he turned and stalked across the room. "I'm upset," he grated, "because you could have been hurt."

Willow was completely flustered. What was he talking about? All she'd done was travel by train to visit her sick brother. She'd handled more perilous situations in her sleep.

"Did it occur to you—for even a moment—" Brandt continued, "that we had just finished up a very dangerous case? One in which several young ladies lost their lives? What makes you think you couldn't have been next?"

"Outram Kyne is in police custody," she reminded him. "He can't hurt anyone from a jail cell."

"And what about Virgil Chatham? Have you forgotten about him? Just because his footman was caught dumping the last body, don't think that I've completely dismissed his involvement."

"You think he had something to do with the murders?" she asked eagerly, taking a step toward him. Hearing him give voice to his suspicions validated her own.

"I don't know." His hostility seemed to dissipate a few degrees. "But whether he is or isn't, you still could have been putting your life in jeopardy. The least you could have done was tell me what was going on so I could come with you."

"I didn't think of it," she told him honestly. "And I didn't think visiting my brother was an event that required a chaperone."

"That's not the point." Some of the ire rose in his voice again. "You'd think, after all we've been through, that you would at least have the decency to alert me to your plans."

Willow blinked, not sure she was hearing him correctly. Because suddenly he didn't sound as angry as he did hurt. As though her leaving town without telling him where she was going was a personal affront. "What do you mean 'after all we've been through'?" she asked, feeling a distinct uneasiness settle into her bones.

"We've been together every day for a month, Willow." He lowered his tone to a near whisper. "We've been together every *night* for more than a week. I realize you have no interest in getting married, but I thought we'd established more of a connection than for you to just run off with no hint of where you were headed."

Turning his back to her, he stalked across the room, hands stuffed in his pockets, shoulders sloped in dejection.

My goodness, she'd wounded him, she thought. He was truly hurt that she'd left without him. And she should have realized he'd feel that way, given all his talk about love and marriage.

She simply wasn't used to these expectations. Men tended to try sweet talk and seduction to have their way with her, but none of them would be too fond of finding her still there in the bright light of day. Brandt, however, was the exact opposite. Oh, he'd used sweet talk and seduction, too, but in his case, he not only wanted her to remain in his bed until morning, he wanted her to remain there forever.

The very idea jolted her to the soles of her feet.

Her parents' marriage had more than convinced her that married life was not for her. Her father had beaten her mother whenever he was drunk, which was most of the time. And when he was sober, he'd been just as worthless, unable to hold a job or provide for his family.

Her mother had thought that all Willow's papa needed was a son to mold and nurture. Willow, of course, had been a tremendous failure in that department. And after several miscarriages and stillbirths, so had Erik. Because he wasn't perfect, and though he was a son, he wasn't the son Elmer Hastings had wanted.

Willow didn't for a minute think Brandt would turn out like her father. He drank, certainly, but in moderation. She'd seen him in a fury, yet he'd never raised a hand to her or anyone else. She knew the rage that entered a man's eyes just before he struck out, and she didn't think Brandt was capable of such behavior, especially toward women or children.

She was more afraid that she would turn into her mother. That one day down the road, she would discover that her entire existence depended on a man. She would find herself keeping house for him, bowing to his wishes, providing him with children, most of which they prayed would be sons.

She also had Erik to consider. Most men would have a hard enough time dealing with a woman who already had a child, but for that child—albeit a brother—to be mentally inadequate . . . You could tell just by looking at Erik that he was different. His eyes were a little too large and often held a blank expression, his smile was often too wide and inappropriate to the situation. He had trouble learning, following directions, and speaking in a manner that befit his age.

He was also the sweetest, kindest child she'd ever encountered, and she considered herself lucky to have raised him since their mother died shortly after his birth. It didn't matter to her that he wasn't as smart as other boys his age, that he couldn't attend school and had to be educated at home by Mrs. Nelson and herself, that he would probably never lead a normal life or be able to live on his own. She would care for him until the day she died. And after that, she would be sure he was provided for and well taken care of.

And that, she suspected, was something of which Brandt would want no part. He, like most men, would want a wife who could give him her undivided attention, a brother-in-law who would someday marry and build his own household.

For a moment, she wondered how to explain all of this to Brandt. And then she admitted that it wouldn't be necessary. Once Erik awoke and Brandt got a good look at his face, perhaps heard one of his lengthy recitations on fishing with Mr. Nelson or learning to ride a horse, he would know Erik was far from perfect. After that, Willow wouldn't have to try to convince Brandt of the error of his ways; he would already be racing for the train station and as far from them as he could get.

She should be relieved by the prospect, but she wasn't. If anything, she was beginning to feel heartbroken. And if she had, for even a moment, allowed herself to imagine a future with him, let herself start to fall in love with him, she would be.

Luckily, she hadn't done either.

She hadn't.

Taking a deep breath, she approached his rigid, unyielding form. "I'm sorry," she said quietly. When he didn't move, not so much as an inch, she stepped up behind him and ran her hands over the firm swells of his back. She felt the muscles jump reflexively beneath her touch as the heat of his skin warmed her palms through the soft chambray of his shirt.

"I didn't realize my actions would be so upsetting. When I got that wire, all I could think about was getting to Erik. I grabbed one of the bags I'd already packed and went straight to the depot. I didn't take the time to tell anyone what was wrong. I should have, and I apologize."

A moment passed as she waited for Brandt to respond.

"You know what bothers me most?" he asked softly. For a moment, he didn't say anything. And then he turned to face her. Her hands slipped from his back, but before they could return to her sides, he took them in his own and lifted them so that their arms formed a bridge between their two bodies. "That you never told me about your brother. I understand that it was important to your job to keep up the ruse of looking for your missing brother *Jeremy*. But once we were involved . . . I *don't* understand why you didn't feel you could tell me about your real brother Erik. After all those nights we stayed awake talking. I told you about my five sisters, their five husbands, and all thirteen of my nieces and nephews. You told me about your childhood. Or at least I thought you did. Now I'm beginning to wonder."

He gave her a look that was a cross between disappointment and demand. And he was right. She'd told him parts of her childhood, but they were memories of a childhood that had only existed in her mind. She hadn't even had to lick her lips before recounting the made-up stories because she had blocked out the truth so well that they had almost *become* true to her.

Growing up the way she had, there had been plenty of opportunities to create a detailed imaginary world. One in which her parents were loving and kind, both to her and each other; where they lived in a charming whitewashed, two-story house with a cook and a housekeeper and separate bedrooms so she wouldn't have to sleep on a pallet on the floor.

"The stories about my childhood weren't true," she admitted, only to have him break his hold on her hands and move stiffly away from her. He halted at the foot of Erik's bed, his knuckles turning white as he clutched the rough wood frame.

"They weren't true," she repeated, "but I didn't mean to lie to you."

He whipped around to scoff at her. Not that she blamed him; she'd done nothing *but* lie to him from the beginning.

"What I told you was much . . . prettier than anything

I could have said about my real life. You should know by now that I find fiction much more appealing than reality," she said, with just a hint of defiance.

Rather than satisfying her expectations of an argument, he fixed her with a stare that seemed to freeze her in place, demanding honesty. "Do you think you can tell me now? The truth? About everything," he emphasized. "Your childhood, your brother . . . everything."

"Are you sure you want to hear?" From what he'd told her, Brandt had led a fairly sheltered life. His family wasn't wealthy, but they were well enough off. His parents had been good people; his sisters, though a bit overprotective and supervising of his life even to this day, all sounded delightful, comely, and very loving. She wasn't sure he could handle knowing about her family lineage.

Brandt answered without pause, without reservation. "I'm sure."

Taking a deep breath to not only steel her nerves, but to gather enough air to get through the long account, she began with her earliest memory. She described cowering in a corner of the kitchen with her dirty rag doll, Clementine, while her father bellowed and beat at her mother. For what, she wasn't sure. After so many incidents, over so many things, did it matter?

She told him about all of the times her father had stumbled home in the middle of the night, all of the jobs he'd lost or simply couldn't find because he could never walk a straight line or open his eyes fully before well into the afternoon.

She told him of her mother's numerous pregnancies and equally numerous losses, the pain, the tears, and the final hemorrhaging that took her life. Of little Erik, who was so pink and beautiful . . . and sickly from the very beginning. Not an hour after his birth, the doctor had taken their father aside and told him something was wrong with the boy. From that moment on, her father had never even looked in Erik's direction again.

She told him about raising Erik, even though she herself was only fourteen. About not attending school for a couple of years until Erik was old enough to stay with a kindly widowed neighbor, and then working three times as hard as the other students to not only catch up but to gain enough of an education to build a better life for the two of them.

Her mouth grew dry, but she stopped only a moment to pour an inch of water into the glass beside Erik's bed and swallow it. Then she continued with the details of her early adulthood, her meeting with Allan Pinkerton, and her eventual position with the Agency. Even about her early romance with Robert. She told him everything, up to and including her reasons for turning down his marriage proposal. And then she boldly added that it had nothing to do with her feelings for him because, frankly, he was the nicest, most handsome, and most all-around attractive man she'd ever had the good fortune to threaten with castration. If things were different, she might—just *might*—consider his offer.

"But the circumstances are as they are," she finished. "And perhaps after all of that, you'd prefer to withdraw your suit anyway."

Brandt studied her for several long minutes. So long, in fact, that she began to clench and unclench her fists and shift from foot to foot.

"Since you've kept so much from me," he began slowly, "I think it only fair that I be allowed to have a few secrets of my own. So for a while, I think I'll let you wait and worry and wonder if I still want to marry you."

They heard a strangled gasp from the bed and both whipped their heads around to see a now wide-awake Erik staring at them, eyes round as saucers.

Willow rushed to his side, pouring him a drink and putting the cup to his lips. But he shook his head, pushing the drink away. He coughed, his eyes never leaving Brandt, who stood behind Willow, one hand on her shoulder.

"You . . ." He coughed again and cleared his scratchy throat. "You marry Willow?" he asked, and then the corners of his mouth lifted with a delighted grin.

Chapter Twenty-seven

Brandt nearly choked at the boy's bold question. And worse was the absolutely ecstatic look on his young face. He reached around Willow and took the glass of water from her hand, downing it in one giant gulp.

He didn't know what he'd expected, but it hadn't been Erik's keen observational skills. For a child who was supposed to be mentally deficient, he seemed to grasp the concept of his sister marrying well enough.

For a brief second, Brandt considered denying it. Willow probably expected that response. She certainly expected what she'd told him to repulse him so much, he'd give up any notion of wanting her as his wife.

Nothing could be further from the truth. Knowing about her past only made him love her more, made him realize how strong she really was, made him admire her strength, determination, and tenacity. It also helped him understand why she was so obsessed with her position at Pinkerton and why she took her investigations and fears of being let go from the Agency so seriously.

There was no woman in the world he would ever want more than he wanted Willow Hastings.

So, instead of telling Erik what his sister wanted him to hear, Brandt straightened, put both hands on either side of Willow's neck, and said, "Yes. Yes, I am."

She shot to her feet, hands on hips, glaring at him like he'd just offered to strip her naked and parade her down Main Street. "What are you saying?" she snapped, and her neck actually jolted forward and back with her fury.

"I'm sharing the wonderful news with your brother," he answered, praying she wouldn't be willing to set aside her deep-seated integrity and bludgeon him to death in front of the boy.

"We are *not* getting married," she growled under her breath. She cast a quick glance over her shoulder to see that Erik wasn't catching very much of their conversation. He was sitting up in bed, a pillow propped behind him, still smiling like it was Christmas morning and he was the only child left in the world. "I never said I would marry you."

"You didn't have to," Brandt stated with utter confidence. "I've made up my mind. And even though you'll probably spend several more months denying your feelings, I know you love me. Or at least you'll begin to before long. It's inevitable."

Her lashes fluttered closed, as though she was taking a moment to absorb the meaning of his words. When she opened them, her initial anger had been replaced by amazement. Had she really expected him to withdraw his proposal, to stop loving her simply because he now knew about her less-than-sterling past and her special brother? How shallow did she think he was?

Well, he thought, wincing inwardly at the memory of some of their experiences together, perhaps he hadn't given her reason for a positive opinion of his honor and virtue.

"How do you know it's inevitable?" she asked in a more subdued tone than before. "How can you be so sure?"

For some reason, he knew his answer was very important. His next words could well determine their future. At least the near future, and how smoothly it might run, because he fully intended to have Willow, even if it took an eternity.

"Simple. I love you, and I plan to marry you. And while I suspect you already love me, I'm willing to wait until you feel secure enough to admit it." He paused, letting his words sink in, because he could tell she was considering them. Finally.

"And if you never consent to marry me, then I'll just have to seduce you. I'll keep you so weak from passion, you'll hardly realize I've moved both you and Erik into a brand-new home with me and, for all intents and purposes, set up a household."

"You sound awfully sure of yourself."

He gave her a self-assured smile. "That's because I am."

The muscles in her throat flexed as she swallowed. She didn't argue with him further, but she didn't throw herself into his arms and accept his proposal, either. Instead, she turned stiffly and moved toward the doorway. "I'll go . . . get Erik . . . something to eat." Her words sounded as distracted as he suspected her mind was at the moment.

He waited until she was out of sight before shifting Erik's small legs farther over on the straw mattress and taking a seat beside him. "Is your sister always this stubborn?"

Erik nodded vigorously.

He wasn't sure the boy actually understood the question, but Brandt chuckled and brushed a stray lock of hair away from his face. "I thought as much. How are you feeling?"

"Better. I was *sick,*" he said, his eyes widening dramatically. "I threw up."

Brandt chuckled. Only a twelve-year-old could think vomiting was something to brag about. "I know. Your sister was pretty worried about you."

"My head still hurts, though."

"Do you think some of Mrs. Nelson's beef stew will help with that?" Brandt asked, already smelling the delicious aroma that wafted in from the kitchen.

Erik's face lit up. "Biscuits, too?"

He was learning that Erik's face displayed every emotion the boy was feeling. He suspected that even if the child couldn't always communicate his thoughts clearly with words, one only had to watch his expression to figure out what was going on in his young mind. "I think so."

"Yay!" he cried, clapping.

Resting a hand on Erik's blanketed legs, Brandt decided to get to know the boy a little better. After all, Erik would soon practically be his son. He certainly planned to care for him as he would his own child.

"Tell me what you like to do when you're not lying in bed with a fever." He thought back to when he was Erik's age, trying to recall some of his favorite pastimes. And then he went back even farther to account for Erik's slow development. "Do you like to climb trees, or play with that scruffy mong . . ." He caught himself before he used a word Erik might not know. ". . . dog I saw out front?"

Erik nodded again and sat up even straighter, apparently recognizing a captive audience. "Piddle is *my* dog," he said. "Mr. Nelson brought him home from town for me and all he did was piddle on the floor, Mrs. Nelson said." He giggled and covered his mouth as though *piddle* was a naughty word. And to a twelve-year-old boy, perhaps it was. "Piddle is my favorite thing in the whole world, but Willow says he smells like an outhouse. He doesn't," Erik asserted, his mouth drawn in a firm line.

"You have to admit, Piddle doesn't exactly smell like a field of daisies," Willow said, breezing into the room and meeting Brandt's gaze over the tray she carried. "The name suits him."

"He *does too* smell like a daisy," Erik defended mutinously. "And he *doesn't* smell like an outhouse. Can he come sleep on my bed with me?"

"Definitely not," Willow answered with conviction. A second later, her tone softened. "Not until you've gotten something to eat, at any rate. Are you hungry?"

She settled the tray on his lap and scooted Brandt out of the way to take his place at Erik's side. The stew, Brandt noticed, was mostly broth, which would do the boy's stomach some good. Willow tried to do the motherly thing and feed him bit by bit, but that only lasted half a minute before Erik wrenched the spoon from her hand and began shoveling the soup into his mouth. In his other hand he held a biscuit, and he took big bites between mouthfuls of stew.

"He's feeling better," Brandt told her needlessly. When she turned to face him, he added, "And I like dogs. A lot. In fact, I wouldn't mind having a mutt like Piddle around permanently."

The spoon halted halfway to Erik's mouth as the boy scowled at him. Brandt belatedly realized Erik probably thought he was suggesting he take the dog away, and before Erik became upset, he hurried to clarify the situation. "As long as a boy like Erik was around to take care of him, of course."

Erik smiled and went back to eating.

"I like cats," Willow said.

Of course she did, Brandt thought. Because a cat was the polar opposite of a dog, and if Brandt liked one, Willow would automatically claim to like the other better. It was her way of not only avoiding the subject of matrimony, but of trying to show him how wrong they would be for each other.

Unfortunately for her, he didn't give up so easily.

"I like cats, too. Maybe we can have one of each." He noticed Erik's eyes light up at that suggestion. This was a child who loved animals and would take as many as he could get.

Willow's frown deepened, though she didn't respond.

"Speaking of which, would you prefer to live in New York or Boston?" He knew the question would only irritate her more, but he couldn't seem to help himself. "I make my home in Boston, as you know, since that's where Union Pacific headquarters are located. But they also have an office in New York, and I'm sure I could work out of there. Of course, if you wanted to move to Boston, we could manage that, too. There's no Pinkerton office there, but perhaps Robert could find some local assignments for you, or you could take a different position, if you'd rather. There are also Pinkerton offices in Denver and Chicago, if you prefer. I'm not sure the UP will be able to transfer me to either place, but that's something we can deal with later. Do you have a preference?" he ended casually.

He had the luxury of seeing all the color drain from her face and then flood back directly into her cheeks. "I *told* you we aren't going to be . . ." She glanced at Erik. "Living together, or anything else. I wish you would stop this nonsense and go back to New York or Boston or wherever you plan to live and leave us alone."

"Would it help if I asked Erik what he wanted to do? He could even go back to the city with us, if he'd like."

The minute the words were out of his mouth, he knew he'd made a terrible mistake. Willow blanched and Erik got so excited, he overturned the nearly empty bowl on his lap, spilling brown stew juices all over the quilt.

He should have quit while he was ahead, Brandt chastised himself. He never should have mentioned taking Erik back to New York without first getting Willow's permission. Lesson number one about being a father or big brother-in-law: Never announce an idea in front of the child before clearing it through the mother—or, in this case, sister—beforehand.

"Can I really?" Erik asked, not distracted for a moment by the soup soaking through the bed linens. "Can I meet Robert and see the big eye sign? And will you take me to the big park you talked about? Can I ride on a train and see all the people in the fancy clothes?"

Teeth clamped together so tight Brandt could see the muscle twitching in her jaw, Willow began to strip the bed, collecting the dishes and soiled coverlet. "We'll see. Mr. Donovan and I have a few things to discuss because he shouldn't have said what he did." She flashed a furious glare at him, and he wisely kept quiet.

"Are you going to yell at him?" Erik asked.

"Yes, I believe I will."

Brandt almost chuckled at her calm tone but thought better of it. He was in hot enough water at the moment; no sense increasing the temperature.

She handed Erik a small, well-worn book that looked like a primer or early reader. "You can practice your letters for a while, or take a nap if you're tired. I'll send in Piddle." And then she turned and marched out of the room, obviously expecting Brandt to follow.

Which he did, most obediently.

They were both silent until Willow had deposited the dirty dishes in the cast-iron sink and the soiled quilt in an empty basket by the door and led him outside.

"Piddle," she called, and the big, mangy brown dog lumbered around the corner of the house. His long pink tongue lolled out of his mouth, dripping doggy spittle on her hand and skirt as he bounced around her feet for attention. She laughed at the mutt's antics and held the door open for him. "Go see Erik," she said and snapped her fingers to get the dog into the house.

Still staunchly ignoring Brandt, she closed the door behind them and made her way across the sparse yard with lengthy, determined strides. Pecking chickens cackled and flapped their wings and scrambled to get out of the way.

Willow slid the big barn door open. "In," she ordered with a wave of her hand.

Brandt stepped into the dim interior. The floor was littered with straw, and he saw dust motes dancing in the thin beams of light that peeked through cracks in the walls. All of the stalls were empty, the livestock either being used by Mr. Nelson to plow fields or left out to pasture for the day.

She slid the door closed again, sealing them into even heavier darkness. "If I say I'll marry you, will you stop interfering in my life?"

He drew his head back in surprise, and then his eyes narrowed. "Define interfering."

"Following me, pestering me, telling my brother he and his beloved dog will be coming to live with us. *Interfering*. If I say I'll marry you, will you *stop?*"

The question sounded simple enough.

Nothing with Willow could be so simple.

Still, after a moment of careful consideration, he warily answered, "Yes." It wasn't entirely true; he wouldn't quit meddling in her life if he thought it was in her best interest, but he would stop trying to deliberately provoke her.

"Fine; then I'll marry you."

He blinked. "Really?"

"No, not really," she snapped, her breasts thrusting out over her crossed arms. "But you agreed that if I *said* I'd marry you, you'd leave me alone. So I'm *saying* I'll marry you. Now good-bye."

"Nice try," he muttered, annoyed by her callous tactic.

"What were you *thinking?*" she charged. "Don't you know better than to blurt out something like that in front of a child—especially a child like Erik? All he's ever wanted is to live in New York with me, and now he thinks you've magically appeared to grant his fondest wish. How could you *do* something like that?"

Her body vibrated with tension. Her hands were balled into fists at her sides, buried slightly within the folds of her faded green skirt. He'd never seen her in such plain attire and suspected she kept a change of clothes or two here for when she visited. She would certainly look out of place traipsing around in her New York finery—though she did look delectable in some of those tight, low-cut gowns.

Drawing his mind back to the matter at hand, he immediately apologized. "I'm sorry. I knew I'd made a mistake the moment I opened my mouth. But if Erik has always wanted to go to New York with you, why won't you take him?"

"I can't take him." Turning, she stalked deeper into the shadows of the barn. "Have you forgotten that I'm a Pinkerton agent?" she asked, coming to rest beside an empty wagon bed. "My work is dangerous. I move

255

around a lot, sometimes never knowing where I'll be from day to day. I couldn't drag Erik into that. And I wouldn't feel comfortable leaving him with just anyone while I'm away."

Brandt didn't respond, wanting to hear what she had to say. The truth, for a change, and only the second time she'd opened up to him.

She boosted herself up on the lowered tail end of the wagon and seemed to relax a bit as she rested her hands flat on either side of her hips. "He likes it here," she continued. "The Nelsons are wonderful to him. He has a few friends, and plenty of room to run around and be a little boy. The townspeople have known him since birth and are less inclined to judge him for his inabilities. I'm afraid it wouldn't be that way in New York—or anywhere else I might take him."

Her eyes had a pleading look in them that nearly crushed him.

"Can't you understand that? I'm trying to protect him."

He did understand. Only too well, because he now felt protective of not only her, but of her brother as well. Yet he'd met Erik and taken an instant liking to him, so perhaps others would, too, making that fear unwarranted.

"I do, but you can't protect him forever," he said, careful of both his tone and words, because the last thing he wanted was to upset her again. If he did, he might find himself banished to sleeping outside with Piddle and waking up smelling like an outhouse. It was not a prospect that enraptured him. "You won't always be able to keep him from people you think will be cruel. You won't always be able to hide him away like you're doing now."

"I'm not hiding him away!"

"You are, and we both know it. You're lucky Erik

hasn't figured out what you're doing yet, or I'm guessing he'd have a few things to say about it. He's a wonderful boy, Willow, and he's going to grow into a wonderful man. He's not perfect, though none of us are, so that shouldn't be a vital issue. It's unfortunate that Erik's flaws happen to be physical and therefore more easily visible to those who may not be as accepting of imperfections. Then again, people like that are shallow and vain and will all burn in Hell soon enough, so Erik should be taught not to give a turkey's tail feather about them or the things they might say.

"Are you teaching him that?" Brandt questioned. "Are you teaching him to live in a world where people can be cruel and unfeeling, but where he can thrive all the same? That's what you should be worried about," he said softly, "not about how many people might see him and notice he's different."

He expected her to charge at him, skin him like a buffalo hide. But instead she buried her face in her hands and burst into tears.

Chapter Twenty-eight

Oh, Christ, what have I done?

Brandt stood motionless, his limbs weighed down by fear and uncertainty. What should he do? He'd never seen Willow cry. Except for that time in Robert's office, which didn't count, because they'd all known she was only putting on a show of female hysterics to get out of pretending to be married to him. But she was actually weeping now, her shoulders quaking in misery as tears dripped out from under her palms to darken small spots on the front of her pale blue shirtwaist.

He was an ignoramus. A buffoon. A bumbling idiot. He wanted this woman to marry him. He should be wooing and romancing and bringing her flowers. Instead, what did he do? He criticized her parenting methods and made her cry.

Stepping forward, his hands hovered an inch from her arms before beginning to soothe and caress. He wasn't sure she'd appreciate the gesture; perhaps she didn't want to be touched right now. Perhaps she didn't want to be touched by *him* ever again.

But she didn't pull away, and he took that as a good sign. His thumbs drew circles on her skin through the fabric of her blouse. And then he moved one hand to the base of her neck, enjoying the feel of her silky hair between his fingers. Pulling her downturned head against his chest, he let her cry.

He was beginning to think that he wasn't completely to blame for this outburst, after all. She was probably upset about what he'd said, yes, but he knew Willow well enough to realize that her initial response to being challenged would be to straighten her spine and turn the air blue with indignation.

She was strong and independent and probably never let an emotion through her defenses unless it had a direct bearing on the case she was working. For her to fall apart like this—in front of another person, no less— most likely signaled that she'd been needing a release for quite a while.

So he let her cry it out and did nothing more than hold her, pat her back, and whisper calming words above her temple.

After several long minutes, Willow's tears seemed to subside. She sniffed, wiped her eyes and nose on the front of his shirt, and sat up, avoiding his gaze.

He refused to let her be embarrassed. Being a man, he didn't cry very often himself, but he knew from experience how purging tears could be. He ran his thumbs beneath her eyelids and over her damp cheeks, ran his fingers through her auburn curls.

"Feel better?" he asked softly.

"No." Her voice broke, creating a new wave of misery. "Do you really think I'm too protective of Erik? That I'm smothering him?"

"I don't think you can ever be too protective of a child," Brandt answered honestly, stroking her face and neck. "But I do think you need to begin teaching him how to take care of himself. How to deal with people who may not be as accepting as you and I and the Nelsons. And I don't think bringing him to live with you is such a bad idea. He misses you, he loves you, he wants to be close to you." Brandt put a finger under her chin and forced her to meet his gaze. "Am I wrong to believe you miss him, love him, and want him to be close to you, too?"

He didn't need to hear her answer to know he was right, but her nod pleased him all the same. "Just think," he continued, "you could tuck him into bed every night, read to him, teach him about guns and knives and other assorted weapons from your personal arsenal. Though I'd wait a few years to tell him about his sister's adventures as a songbird in a Jefferson City brothel."

To his great relief, she laughed. The sound was higher pitched than usual and a bit watery. Music to his ears.

"But how am I supposed to take care of him?" she asked in all seriousness. "You know how tenuous my position is at the Agency; even Robert isn't sure how much longer he can keep Superintendent Warner from dismissing me. And I travel so much. I'm not sure I can afford to pay someone to stay with him when I have to be away."

Brandt framed her face in his hands, smiled into her shining violet eyes, and planted a kiss smack on her full, luscious lips. "That's why you have me, sweetheart. I make a good living with the Union Pacific and my job doesn't require me to travel as much as yours might, so I can be with Erik anytime you can't. And most of the times you can. How does that sound?" he asked, still grinning.

A trace of amusement lifted the corners of her mouth. "You're not going to stop pestering me about that, are you?"

He shook his head. "Uh-uh. Are you ever going to stop rejecting me?"

She took a deep breath, wrapped her own arms around his neck, and leaned forward to press a kiss to his mouth. "Uh-huh."

Brandt pulled back, staring at her with what he knew must be a dumbstruck expression. He was hearing things. She'd said *uh-uh*, the same as he had, hadn't she? But his ears were full of wax, or his mind was distracted by her close proximity, and he'd misheard her. "Did you say 'uh-huh' or 'uh-uh'?" he asked to be sure.

"Uh-huh." She kissed his jaw and toyed with the ends of his hair.

He took another step back, breaking all contact with her. Her fingers were beginning to raise his temperature, her lips raising other things, and he wanted to be able to focus his entire attention on her answer to this next question.

"Are you saying . . ." He had to swallow and moisten his dry throat before he could get all the words out. "Do you mean that you *will* marry me? You're not simply telling me that to lull me into a false sense of security?"

She chuckled and slipped her fingers into the waist-band of his trousers to pull him forward, into the crook of her legs. "Yes. I will marry you. No lulling involved." She fumbled with the buckle of his belt while pecking small, closemouthed kisses along his jawline, down his neck, to the throbbing pulse just above the collar of his shirt.

Still awash in disbelief, he put a hand over hers to halt her motions. "Why now?" he wanted to know. A strangled sound moved up from his diaphragm, part laugh, part snort. "After putting me off all this time, why capitulate now, when I've upset you the most about Erik?"

Her eyes grew serious as she held his gaze. "You're the first person who's ever been so accepting of Erik. And even though I was suspicious early on that you were only being nice to him to earn favor with me, I know now that you really do like him. Because you wouldn't be so concerned about his future if you didn't. You'd be trying to convince me to leave him here so you wouldn't have to deal with him, not talking me into bringing him with us. You wouldn't be thinking about how he feels and how he'll develop and who's going to be around to take care of him. I trust you with him," she said simply. And then she tilted her head and gave him a mischievous look. "And you didn't wrinkle your nose when you finally got a good whiff of Piddle."

They both broke into chortles of laughter at that.

"You're wrong about how badly he smells, you know. He doesn't smell like an outhouse. He smells like two outhouses and the East River."

Willow laughed so hard, she fell backwards onto the hard floor of the wagonbed. Chuckling along with her, Brandt climbed in next to her and rolled to one side, propping his head on his bent arm. With the other, he reached out and hauled Willow flush with his long frame.

"You *can* trust me, you know. With Erik, and with yourself."

She touched his face with one fingertip and drew it down to the center of his chin. "I know," she said softly. "If I didn't, I wouldn't be marrying you."

He let out a prolonged breath and touched her forehead with his. "I'm awfully glad we finally got all that worked out. Courting you is damn draining."

She punched him in the gut, just hard enough to elicit a cough of pain. "Don't get cocky, Donovan. I can still back out if your pompousness becomes unbearable."

"You like my pompousness," he teased, giving her a squeeze.

"Hardly," she said with a most unladylike scoff. "Piddle's stench is preferable to your overblown conceit."

"Which reminds me," he whispered in a low voice, "before we got sidetracked by Piddle's differing degrees of malodorousness, I seem to recall your hand being somewhere around the area of my belt buckle. Any chance you planned to continue along those lines?"

Her mouth quirked up in an inviting moue. "I could," she tempted, letting her eyes drift down to his waistband and then back up as she fiddled with the row of buttons on his shirtfront. "Or you could undress me."

That simple suggestion had him hard in an instant. "Are you trying to seduce me?" he asked, surprised the words came out as anything more than a moan.

"Uh-huh."

"God," he groaned, "I love this agreeable, complacent side of you. Tell me what I did to bring this on so I can do it much, much more often."

"Don't get too used to it," she warned him with a laugh, her hands once again working the belt free of his pants.

"Damn," he muttered. His own hands were busy loosing the buttons of her blouse and cupping the lush swells within the lacy confines of her camisole. "Then I guess I'll have to make do with getting used to this." He kissed her with all the love and passion that had been building in him since their last encounter, since he'd begun to know the real person inside the woman who would soon be his wife. "Every night, every day, for the rest of our lives."

"Brandt," she breathed, coming up for air and doing clever things to his heartbeat as her fingers wriggled their way beneath his cotton drawers. "You talk too much. Now shut up and make love to me, or I'll find someone who will."

His grip tightened on her waist. "Snippy, snippy, snippy," he murmured with a tsk of his tongue. "You should have warned me I'd be marrying a fishwife."

"You should have warned *me* that I'd be marrying a man who would rather talk than pleasure his woman."

His woman. Damn, he liked the sound of that. "You're right, I've been remiss." He pulled the tails of her shirt out of the waist of her skirt and then undid the single button at the small of her back. "I hope you'll let me know if I give you *too* much pleasure. I wouldn't want to disappoint my future bride."

"Oh, I'll let you know," she replied dryly.

Sliding the full skirt past her legs and off, he let it fall to the straw-strewn floor of the barn. She wore a pair of frilly white drawers and silky, equally white stockings beneath her lace-up shoes, held to her thighs by light blue garters.

"And were those . . . bells?" He tinkled the tiny silver chimes. "Your garters match your shirt *and* they have bells on them?"

"I like to stay in fashion," she said. "And I just thought the bells were cute."

"Very." He gave them another flick. "But aren't you afraid someone will hear them and get suspicious?"

"The weight of my clothes keeps them quiet. They only jingle when I'm walking around half nude." She chuckled when he waggled a brow. "Shall I take them off?" She asked the question as if she already knew the answer. Because she did.

"No. The shoes can come off, the garters stay. I want to see just what makes them sing."

"I can think of a few things." She bent her knee and placed the sole of her foot flat on his upper thigh, giving him leave to unlace her boots.

He removed one shoe and then the other, letting both drop to the floor. And then he ran his hands along the arches of her delicate feet, over her calves, and up to the edges of the pale stockings.

"The drawers next."

He smiled. "Yes, ma'am." This was one situation where he was more than happy to take her direction. He skimmed the thin material over her hips and off her legs, then paused. "What else?"

Lying there in a pose of delectable perfection, she regarded him with heavy-lidded eyes, her head resting on her bent arms. Her auburn curls ran riot around her face, reminding him of how she usually looked *after* they made love. The thought sent a bolt of desire down through his limbs.

"My shirt and camisole," she instructed, making no move to help him disrobe her.

He ran his hands over the outlines of her garters, tracing her naked torso, until his fingers came to rest under the hem of her top. With his palms against her back beneath the material, he lifted her into a sitting position and watched the shirtwaist fall from her shoulders. Then he lifted the camisole, pushing her arms up over her head until he could remove the garment altogether.

Lowering her back to the wagonbed, he let his gaze absorb every inch of her ravishing beauty. Tousled hair; bare, pouting breasts; smooth belly; tight auburn curls; and long, slim legs encased in fantasy-inspiring garters and hose.

He licked his lips and swallowed hard. "What next, Madame Seductress?"

"Now . . ." she purred slowly, "it's my turn."

Rising to her knees, she hovered above him, pressing on his chest until he leaned back against the side of the wagon. She tugged at his boots first, tossing them to the growing pile of clothes on the barn floor. She lifted herself by placing her hands on his upper thighs, then letting them drift between his legs, practically cupping his rampant desire.

Brandt didn't bother to bite back his groan, which earned him a chuckle from the temptress whose face floated just inches above his throbbing groin.

The most he could see was the top of her head, moving slightly up and down. He didn't know what she was doing, didn't feel anything more than her hands pressing the insides of his thighs. But his shaft seemed to recognize what she *could* be doing and strove to meet her halfway.

And then he felt a wet warmth low on his belly. A second later, he felt the same sensation a fraction higher. Again and again until her head was nearly parallel with his. He looked down to see the front of his shirt lying open, apparently unbuttoned by Willow's teeth and tongue.

"Holy Christ," he breathed. "Why didn't you tell me you could do that?"

A dimple appeared in her cheek as she smiled gamely. "I didn't know until now. You inspired me."

"What else can I inspire you to do?"

She leaned forward, letting her bare breasts rub against his now shirtless chest and whispered wild, hotly erotic suggestions in his ear. And he wanted her to fulfill each and every one of them.

"Which should we start with?" she asked when she raised her voice to a normal level.

"You pick," he said, because he wanted to see what she would do, and he wanted to be surprised.

"All right. But you have to lift up." She undid the front of his trousers and gave them a tug, pulling them down over his raised hips and off his legs.

Now they were both primarily naked, except for her stockings and his drawers. But from the tented front of his underclothes, there was little doubt of how long this covering would remain effective.

Willow noticed the prominence, too, and moved to lie beside him so that her head was level with his groin. She reached out the tip of her index finger and slowly moved it toward the peak of his straining masculinity. The minute she touched him, with just that tiny tip of her tiny finger, Brandt's buttocks shot off the buckboard like a wild mustang being broken to saddle.

Willow laughed in throaty pleasure, running her finger around the crest of his shaft and then down one long side, back up and down the other. "Do you like that?" she asked in a sultry, seductive timbre.

"Do you need to ask?" His own voice was nearly an octave higher than usual, but with Willow doing what she was doing, how could he care? If it would keep her hands and mouth between his legs, he'd don one of her bloody corsets again and sing "Johnny Get Your Gun."

Her head lowered next and he felt the moisture of her tongue through the cotton of his drawers. His hands clutched the sides of the wagon, his nails digging into the rough wood until splinters pierced his skin. Her tongue lolled around the head of his erection, moving lower and lower. She wrapped her fingers into the waistband of his drawers and began tugging the fabric down. They caught on his stiffness and she left the material

267

there for a moment, teasing, taunting, building the sensations her mouth was creating to a fever pitch. And then she lifted her head and removed the garment altogether.

Her lips and tongue continued to torment him as she straddled his legs and his hands tangled in her hair. He let her work her magic for several more minutes, and then he stopped her, pulling her face up to meet his gaze. "Enough," he whispered raggedly. "I want to be inside you. Before it's over too soon and we're both sorry."

She licked her lips as if she'd just dined on a particularly delectable delicacy and knee-walked her way closer to where he was propped against the side of the wagon. Placing her hands on his shoulders, she sat back on her heels so that the springy curls of her mons brushed enticingly along his rigid length.

He wanted to grab her up right then, roll her to her back on the wagonbed, and thrust into her. The only problem with that, he knew, was that he'd climax immediately. He was so close to fulfillment already that one move from the beautiful woman above him and he'd fly over the edge. He needed a second, just a fraction of a minute, to regain his equilibrium and contain his raging emotions.

Willow seemed content to allow him time to regroup. She sat still above him, the tip of her tongue darting out to dampen the corners of her mouth, while her breasts rose and fell with her deep breaths. After a moment, Brandt's own pulse seemed to slow just enough that he thought he could touch her again, have her touch him again, and bring them both to a shattering satisfaction without embarrassing himself. He moved his hands from her waist, where they'd drifted, to her hips, his fingers flexing into her buttocks.

"Ready?" she asked, as though she'd known he

needed a short break and was willing to wait right along with him.

He nodded. "Are you?"

"Oh, yes." Her lips trailed along his jaw. "So are my bells."

With a chuckle at her brazen remark, he lifted her hips and guided her toward his seeking manhood. Her hands slid down his chest, causing his stomach muscles to tighten. And then her fingers closed around his hard length, guiding it into her honeyed warmth.

Brandt sighed in ecstasy. Nothing had ever felt this good, this right. He watched Willow's teeth clamp onto her bottom lip, her head thrown back, her eyes closed. Just as he thought she was getting her bearings, he raised her slightly, then brought her back down, at the same time lifting his hips. The friction wrenched a desperate cry from low in her throat.

This wouldn't last long. He could tell by the quaver in her breathing and the building exhilaration in his blood, all pooling in the part of his body that was so deeply embedded inside the woman he loved. And as much as he wanted to stay inside her forever, keep these heightened sensations on the brink forever, he also wanted to drive into her. A thousand times, her breasts rubbing his chest, her legs wrapped high about his waist.

As though the thought led him directly to the action, he rolled her to her back beneath him, drew her legs around his hips where she crossed her ankles to clasp him tight, and began to thrust into her warm, inviting body.

His movements accelerated, her gasps coming one after another, and the light jingling of bells kept time with them both. Her nails raked long lines into the damp flesh of his back and she screamed as her body tensed and convulsed. At that very moment, his own release hit, and his cries of pleasure mingled with hers.

As their breathing returned to normal and all the muscles in their bodies slackened, her legs slipped from his waist, causing the bells to give one last tinkle of sound. He'd finally discovered exactly what it took to make them sing.

Chapter Twenty-nine

He'd seen her. He'd seen the bitch at the police station where he'd been questioned. She'd been talking with that Pinkerton agent and he'd overheard some officers mention that she, too, was a Pinkerton. Another one, blast it.

The little harlot. She wasn't married to the man she'd been cavorting with, after all. He suspected that her fake husband was also a Pinkerton, and that their imaginary marriage had simply been a ruse set up to track him.

But now it was his turn to track her. Too bad Outram wasn't here. He was so good at following and dispatching with meddlesome individuals. He'd done a fine job with that other Pinkerton agent, who had threatened to ruin the divine plan.

But Outram, the poor sop, had gone and gotten himself caught. That was unfortunate for both of them, but at least Outram wouldn't turn on him; couldn't, thanks to his small impediment.

He chuckled wickedly.

And now he would have to deal with Willow Donovan—or whatever her name really was—himself. Luckily, he was prepared.

Chapter Thirty

Willow and Brandt stepped off the train and onto the wide-planked wooden platform, swinging a giggling Erik between them. She couldn't help but laugh with him. She couldn't remember ever having seen her brother so happy, and she didn't think she'd ever been so happy, either.

Brandt had been right. She'd kept Erik tucked away long enough. From the moment she'd told him of her decision to take him back to New York with her for a short trip, he'd been a nonstop ball of energy. He'd talked the ears off both Nelsons, until Mr. Nelson had hied off to the barn, not to be seen again until he was needed to drive them to the train station.

Erik had worried about Piddle, but the Nelsons assured him they'd look after the dog until he returned. And once he'd felt confident of his pet's safety, he'd turned his entire attention on the trip ahead.

He'd chattered about every aspect of the passenger car

they'd taken from Pennsylvania to New York, and asked so many questions, Willow thought her head might explode. Thankfully, Brandt had been there to answer half of them and take at least a little of the pressure off her.

And even though Erik's presence had garnered several stares and disdainful glares, she had found it quite simple to merely smile at the ignorant people around them, or ignore them completely.

Brandt had been right about that, too. She'd spent years worrying about what others would think of Erik, and now she found that she couldn't care less. Erik certainly didn't seem to notice anything amiss.

In New York, Erik's excitement increased tenfold. He knew all about the city from the stories Willow had told him during her visits, and he now insisted on seeing each and every detail she's spoken of *right this minute*. Even some that she'd heedlessly embellished.

Rather than try to explain why that was not only a daunting prospect but physically impossible, she and Brandt shared a look over Erik's head—one that said they hoped he'd tire soon and be willing to take a nap before they both collapsed of child-induced exhaustion.

When their eyes met again, she smiled. In fact, she'd *been* smiling ever since they'd left the barn after their rather enjoyable tryst. She hadn't thought agreeing to marry him could change her life so much or so rapidly, but it had.

But it wasn't the idea of matrimony—which she still had a fair share of misgivings about—that caused her to feel so content. It was the effect Brandt had on every aspect of her life, from the way he touched her when they made love to the way he made them feel more like a family just by holding one of Erik's hands while she held the other.

"What should we do first?" Brandt asked, and Willow

rolled her eyes at his slow assessment of the situation. One didn't ask such a question of an overly wound-up child. Not when there might be three hundred things on the list. Especially when all she wanted to do was head for the nearest hotel room and sleep for the next two weeks.

Sure enough, Erik began an immediate litany of requests. "I wanna see the river with the big ships, and all the carriages with the horsies, and the eye, and meet Robert, and see the *biiiig* hotel you live in, and . . ."

"I'm sorry I asked," Brandt mumbled, scratching the slight stubble of his jaw.

Willow curled her fingers into her palm to keep from reaching out to touch that stubble herself. With a chuckle, she said, "It might not be a bad idea to drop by the Agency and tell Robert we're back." She turned her attention to Erik. "And you could meet him and see the sign."

"Yay! Yay! Yay! Yay! Yay!" Erik cried, jumping up and down, trusting Willow and Brandt to keep him from falling.

"I think that's a yes," Brandt replied, the smile evident in his voice, even if the words were delivered with dry wit.

Although they probably could have walked several blocks to the Pinkerton offices, they chose to hire a hackney cab as an added excitement for Erik. He insisted on petting the gray sorrel mare before they climbed into the carriage, and then sat on Brandt's lap in order to better see out the small window.

Just as they approached the block where the Pinkerton National Detective Agency was located, they heard music drifting on the air. The telltale music that was sure to change their immediate plans.

"Oh, no," Willow muttered.

"What's that?" Erik asked.

"I'd say the circus is in town," Brandt answered, sounding chipper and eager.

"I wish you hadn't said that." She leaned against the cushioned seat, letting her head fall back and her eyes drift closed. She was too tired for this.

"The circus?" Erik squealed. "The kind with el'phants and tigers and snakes?" His young body vibrated with excitement, and Brandt had to clasp his tiny waist to keep him from toppling off his lap.

Willow was beginning to regret reading so many different books to him and telling him so many fantastical stories. She'd wanted to entertain him with tales of the big, wild world, most of which she'd never expected him to see. Most of which *she* had never seen. But now it seemed the world was living up to Erik's expectations.

"You know about the circus?" Brandt asked.

Erik's head moved back and forth as if it was on strings. "Willow tol' me. There are men who eat fire and fat women with beards." He puffed out his cheeks, then slapped the air out of them with his hands. "And short little people who are full-grown but still not as big as me." He squared his shoulders and stuck out his chest, proud of his size. And then he ruined the grown-up effect by grinning and revealing the gap at the side of his mouth where a tiny tooth was missing.

"You're a pretty smart kid," Brandt told him, ruffling his hair and grinning back with his full set of straight white teeth. "How would you like to go see how many bearded ladies they brought with them?"

Erik's eyes went wide. "Yeah," he said in awe. Then he turned to Willow. "Can we, Willow? Can we, can we, can we?" He bounced with every word, and Brandt let out a deep belly laugh at his antics.

She groaned and ran a hand over her brow. "I just don't know if I can handle the circus."

"Please? Please, can we, Willow? *Please?*"

She opened her mouth to agree—because how could she turn down *that* much eagerness?—when Brandt interrupted.

"You look tired. Why don't you let me take Erik to the circus?" he suggested. "We can drop you at the office and meet you back there when we're through."

"Really?" She sat up a little straighter at the idea. It would be wonderful to spend a few minutes somewhere quiet. Perhaps she could even take a bit of a nap on the sofa in Robert's office and catch her second wind before Erik returned and overwhelmed her with his enthusiasm.

"You don't mind if we go without your sister, do you?" he asked Erik.

Erik shook his head, too wound up at the prospect of seeing someone eat fire to care if she was there or not.

"We'll bring you a candied apple," Brandt offered. And then he leaned out the window and called out directions to the hackney driver.

"This will be fine," Willow said as they approached Exchange Place. "Have him drop me here."

"Are you sure?" Brandt asked.

She nodded. "It will be easier for you to continue on to the circus from here. I don't mind walking the rest of the way." It wasn't far at all, and the streets and sidewalks were pleasantly clear at this hour. Likely everyone was enjoying the traveling circus, the same as Brandt and Erik planned to do.

Brandt told the driver to stop and set Erik aside while he stepped from the carriage and helped her down. "We won't be long," he said, keeping hold of her hand.

"Take your time. I could use the peace and quiet."

He chuckled. "I kind of enjoy his ebullience."

"Good." Her mouth curved up in a knowing half-smile. "Then you stay up with him tonight while he repeats every detail of his trip to the circus a thousand times."

"Gladly. Of course, I'm hoping the tattooed ladies and snake charmers will wear him out. And if that doesn't work, I'm thinking of filling him with sweets so that his mouth is too busy to talk my ear off."

She shook her head, knowing his strategy to be futile. Seeing so many oddities would only increase Erik's storehouse of anecdotes, and feeding him so many sugary concoctions would either increase his energy level or make him sick. Whichever occurred, they would be up all night with him.

Brandt lowered his head to place a soft kiss on her lips. She leaned into him and kissed him back, her fingers curling into the fabric of his jacket.

"We won't be long," he said again, his voice lower this time as the passion in his eyes ignited a similar heat in her own bloodstream.

She nodded, not sure she could speak if she tried.

He kissed her once more, a light peck on her cheek, before bounding back into the carriage, swinging the door closed behind him, and joining Erik to wave good-bye. She raised her own hand to bid them farewell and watched them roll out of sight. Still smiling, she turned and began walking toward the Pinkerton offices.

Chapter Thirty-one

Oh, what luck. What pure, unmitigated joy at happening upon her this day, just as he was about to return home from his solicitor's office—taking a circuitous route, of course, so that he could pass this very location.

He'd been watching for her ever since the night Outram had been caught, driving past the Pinkerton National Detective Agency several times a day, hoping to catch a glimpse of his quarry, but she'd seemed to disappear. He hadn't been able to find her anywhere in the city, even though he'd asked several knowledgeable acquaintances about her possible whereabouts. Discreetly, of course. It wouldn't do to have anyone begin to wonder why he was so curious about the woman.

Everything was so much more complicated without Outram, he thought with a sigh. Here he was, not five yards from his prey, and he had to figure out how to capture her all on his own. Normally, he would simply order Outram to pull the carriage near the sidewalk *where she walked and grab her from the street.*

He only hoped this new driver would turn out to be as biddable as Outram; otherwise he might have to dispose of two bodies this afternoon—the true sinner and the witness. Of course, chances were, Fitch would indeed work out just as well as Outram had. He'd found him in the same rundown part of town, after all, and knew that the salary he paid the frail man would have Fitch looking—or not looking, as the case may be—in any direction his employer required.

Tapping the trap door of the landau with his gold-tipped cane, he ordered the driver to slow and keep the vehicle close to the curb. To his benefit, the sidewalk was far from bustling. This part of town was typically vacant in the middle of the day. And she was headed away from, not toward, the more crowded intersection a block back. He took that as a sign of approval from God.

A man passed her, heading in the opposite direction, and then she was alone. Her heels clicked on the concrete walk, keeping time with her feminine sway. She moved with a purpose he champed at the bit to stifle. Lying little harlot. Hussy. Wanton. He would show her she had no cause for that spring in her gait.

"Gain the young woman's attention," he ordered through the opening in the roof.

The driver, startled by the request, stuttered a moment and then began to call out to her. It took several tries, but finally she paused, turned, and raised her head to address the driver. She lifted a hand to shade her eyes from the blazing sun and listened to the long, convoluted question being asked of her.

He opened the carriage door farthest from her and stepped silently to the street, coming around front of the vehicle in order to approach her from behind. And that's when he pounced. Lifting his cane, he brought it down against her skull with a sharp thud, startling even the horses by the suddenness of his actions.

The woman jolted in shock and the driver jumped to his feet on the raised perch. He shot the man a withering glare, daring him to abandon his post or assist her in any way.

Dazed, she turned, one hand to the back of her head, the other pulling at the strings of her reticule. When she saw him, registered his identity, her eyes widened and she began frantically tearing at her bag with both hands. No doubt for a weapon.

"Hello, my dear," he greeted her politely, as though they were at a crowded luncheon rather than alone on the street, with him trying to knock her unconscious.

Her fingers dove into the bag at her wrist and he realized the urgency of the situation. "Ah, ah, ah," he tutted and once again smashed the cane down on her head.

This time the solid metal came in contact with her temple, and a spot of blood began to ooze at her hairline. For one stunned second, she glared daggers at him. And then her eyes rolled back in her head and she crumpled to the ground.

Opening the door opposite the one from which he had exited and tossing his cane to the floor of the carriage, he grasped her beneath the arms and dragged her up and onto one of the seats. It took some doing and he was puffing with exertion by the time he was finished.

Yes, it had been much easier with Outram around, he thought, as he rapped on the roof and ordered the driver to take them home.

Chapter Thirty-two

"There it is!" Erik all but screeched, pointing and bouncing on the carriage seat.

Brandt shifted to look out the window, following Erik's line of vision to the unblinking eye with the words WE NEVER SLEEP emblazoned above it. Hanging perpendicular to the stone building at 66 Exchange Place, the painted carving clearly marked the Pinkerton Agency.

"Yes, there it is," he agreed. For being mentally challenged, Erik was quite an observant young man. He hadn't missed a trick at the circus—or since Brandt had known him, for that matter. He had trouble with the meaning of some words while speaking and his reading and arithmetic skills were lacking, as Brandt had expected. But even though he was several years behind other children his age, he worked hard and *wanted* to learn.

"It's the eye sign, the eye sign!" Erik sang, still abus-

ing the poor carriage seats by tossing his full weight up
and down like a spring.

Brandt was beginning to understand what Willow
meant when she said the boy never tired. They'd spent
hours at the circus, milling through the crowds, explor-
ing every brightly colored tent and exotic animal cage,
purchasing some small trinket at every booth, and trying
a little of each morsel of food offered.

Erik's hands and face were covered in assorted layers
of red, brown, yellow, and white stickiness. Brandt, himself, felt slightly queasy from all the sweets he'd con-
sumed. Willow should have warned him that, though
Erik would be eager to taste a few bites of each treat he
saw, he rarely finished the entire portion, leaving Brandt
to eat or throw out the rest. By the end of their tour of
the circus grounds, Brandt had begun buying only one
small piece of whatever Erik wanted to try instead of
two and eating or throwing much of it away.

Having seen a multitude of tattoos, three- and five-
legged barnyard animals, as well as such wild beasts as
a giant Python and an agitated lioness, they were now
on their way to Robert's office, where Brandt hoped to
clean the tacky residue from his own face and hands and
turn Erik over to someone else's keeping for just a few
minutes.

He wondered if his impatience to marry Willow and
start a family hadn't been premature. Oh, he still wanted
to marry her; there was no doubt about that. But if one
small boy contained this much energy, he shuddered to
think of having to care for more than one child at a time.

The thought of offspring brought an image of Willow
to his mind, waddling and swollen with his child. To
hell with being tired, he told himself silently, he'd sleep
when he was dead. He wanted to make babies with Wil-

low, to fill their house—wherever they finally decided to settle down—with a dozen little Donovans of all kinds and colorings. Brown-haired and violet-eyed or auburn-haired and green-eyed, whatever combination God decided to produce when they came together to create a new life, he wanted them all.

The carriage drew to a halt in front of the tall building and Brandt stepped out, turning just in time to catch a hurtling Erik as the boy threw himself from the vehicle. The air left Brandt's diaphragm in a grunt of pain as he regained his footing and arranged the child on his hip. Erik was certainly too big to be carried, but it wasn't that far to the door of the office and it was a far cry better than having him race off on his own and possibly having to chase him through the streets of New York.

"Willow here?" the boy asked.

"Yes, Willow is here, waiting for us. Now, Erik, you have to be quiet when we go in, do you understand? There are people working inside and we mustn't disturb them. And your sister may be sleeping, so we wouldn't want to wake her. All right?"

Erik nodded, and then let his body bend all the way backwards over Brandt's arm as they crossed beneath the Pinkerton symbol. Brandt had to tighten his hold and redistribute the boy's weight to keep from dropping him.

Freeing one hand, Brandt opened the front door of the building and stepped into the cool interior. This would be the first time he'd encountered Robert since Willow's confession about their short, long-past affair, and Brandt honestly didn't know what his reaction would be when he once again came face-to-face with the man he now knew to be her first lover. He supposed he felt a niggling of jealousy low in his belly, but he couldn't say he'd honestly been surprised by her revelation. He'd suspected something all along, given their close relationship and the numerous gifts Robert had given Willow over the years.

And yet Brandt felt quite secure in his relationship with Willow, especially now that she'd consented to become his wife. He loved her and knew she loved him. Robert had married since the affair and was apparently quite a devoted husband, so there was really nothing to be concerned about. Brandt might not like the fact that another man had introduced Willow to the intimacies of lovemaking, but he would be the man she spent the rest of her life with, so he counted himself as the lucky one.

Mrs. Girard looked up as the door swung open, startled by their entrance. "Mr. Donovan. What a pleasant surprise." She rose to her feet on the other side of her desk. "And who is this with you?"

"Erik Hastings," Erik replied proudly, in a booming voice. And then, remembering that Brandt had warned him to be quiet, he tucked his chin into his chest and whispered, "Sorry. Erik Hastings."

The secretary's graying brows crossed. "Erik . . . Hastings? Are you any relation to Willow Hastings?" she asked the boy turning her eyes questioningly to Brandt.

"Didn't she tell you we'd brought her brother back with us?" A sickening feeling that had nothing to do with too many sweets seeped into his gut.

"Tell us . . . ?" The woman's hands clenched and unclenched at her breast. "Why, we haven't seen Willow in weeks. Did you expect her to be here?" She tried to keep her tone calm, but Brandt heard the underlying concern in the words.

He dropped Erik, took only a moment to see that the boy had his footing, and then stomped toward Robert's office. Any thoughts of jealousy or male competition fled as fear for Willow replaced every other emotion in his body. "You're damn right I expected her to be here.

We dropped her off outside hours ago. You're telling me she never arrived?"

With his hand already on the knob, he shoved the door open, once again barging into Robert's office unannounced. This time, he was speaking with two men, who whipped around in their chairs at his sudden appearance.

Not sparing a glance for the strangers, Brandt's eyes went directly to Robert, who was shaking his head in displeasure. Throwing his pen to the desktop, he rose and began to speak. "If you break into my office one more time, I swear on all that's holy—"

"We need to talk," Brandt cut in. "Now."

"As you can see, I'm with—"

"*Now*," Brandt said again, the single word sharp and demanding.

Seeming to sense the urgency in his tone, Robert moved around his desk. "I'm sorry, gentleman, but this is important. I'll just be a moment."

Closing the door behind him as he stepped into the outer office, Robert asked in a low voice, "What the bloody hell is going on this time?"

"Willow never showed up here?" Brandt charged.

"Willow?" This time it was Robert's brow that wrinkled. "No. She went to visit Erik, as I told you. I thought she would return with you, if you went to find her."

Brandt swore viciously and spun on his heel to stalk across the carpeted floor, his fists clenching and unclenching with fear and fury. "We arrived in the city hours ago. I took Erik to the traveling circus that's set up only a few blocks away. We dropped Willow at the curb and agreed to meet her here afterwards. Now Mrs. Girard tells me she never arrived."

Robert's eyes darted to Erik, who stood against a far set of oaken file cabinets, sucking nervously on the knuckle of one hand. "No, she never . . . Oh, my God. You don't think . . ."

The men's gazes locked. "Yes, I do think, goddammit. We have to find her."

"I'll assemble as many agents as I can find. Where should we begin looking for her?"

"You know where," Brandt answered, his eyes narrowed, the words lethal.

"Right. Mrs. Girard, watch the boy, if you would, please." Marching down the hall, he knocked on the glass of the nearest door even as he pushed it open. "Jonathan, Gregory, come with me. We have an emergency." Returning to Brandt's side, he lowered his voice and said, "You go find her. We'll be right behind you."

Brandt nodded and stormed into the street. He didn't look in Erik's direction as he passed. He couldn't. Because he didn't know how he would ever explain to the boy that his carelessness had gotten Willow killed.

Willow regained consciousness degree by agonizing degree. Her head throbbed. She groaned, and the sound echoed in her ears. She sniffed and smelled a moldy dampness and melting beeswax. When she tried to stem the pain pounding in her brain with her hand, her arm refused to move. She tried to raise the other and met with the same resistance.

Why couldn't she move? Why did her head hurt without as well as within? A spot at the back of her skull and another at her temple ached, and her hands seemed anchored in place.

That was when she remembered.

Being hit from behind. Turning to see Virgil Chatham bearing down on her, that cane glinting in the sun as he raised it to strike her again.

My God, Virgil Chatham had abducted her. Grabbed

her off the street in the middle of the day.

And Brandt hadn't been there to help her because he'd taken Erik to the circus. She should be glad of that, she supposed. At least they were safe, out of the reach of this madman.

Willow opened her eyes slowly, trying to block out the thudding beat in her brain, not knowing what she might encounter when she looked around. If she was bound, as she suspected by her inability to move her arms, then she was helpless. She'd had a pistol with her, in her reticule, but she imagined the weapon had been discovered by now. And because she'd been with Brandt and Erik, simply traveling back to New York, she hadn't bothered to stick her stiletto into her garter for added protection.

She was doomed.

No. She wasn't dead yet, and that was what it would take to keep her from fighting Virgil Chatham.

Candles burned all around, causing shadows to flicker on the dark, uneven walls surrounding her. Was she in a dungeon? The thought almost tickled a laugh from her throat. Did dungeons even exist anymore? She didn't think so, at least not in America, but she couldn't help noticing the stone confines, the dank odor.

She rolled her head and saw that her wrists were indeed shackled, stretched straight out from her body on the wide platform upon which she'd been laid. Pulling at her legs, she found that they too, were fettered. Although, unlike her arms, they were secured together.

From somewhere, a chill draft blew through the room, causing the candle flames to dance wildly and making her realize that she was not fully clothed. Straining her neck, she looked down the length of her body and saw only pale flesh and a small amount of white material. Her heavy walking dress had been removed, as well as her garters and hose. Only her chemise and drawers remained.

Gooseflesh broke out along her skin. This must be how all those other women had felt; brought here against their will, stripped and tied down. Willow wondered how long Chatham had left them lying helpless. Did he kill them quickly, or had they endured hours of terror and torture, both physically and mentally?

She tried to think back to the condition of the bodies that had been discovered. She didn't recall marks other than the killing wounds to the heart, but she couldn't be sure.

A creak sounded somewhere above her head and she heard footsteps. The blood froze in her veins. He was coming. He was coming to kill her. And even though she knew it was useless, she struggled against the metal bonds that trapped her on the wide table.

"I see you're awake," Virgil Chatham said as he came down a hidden stairwell and moved into view. He wore a long, black cape, clasped at the neck, that covered his entire form.

His voice made her skin crawl, just as it had the first time she'd heard it. She swallowed hard to keep from screaming.

"He brought you back to me, you know. I knew from the moment I saw you that you were not as virtuous as you pretended to be, but I had no idea you were such a transgressor. I realized you had to be dealt with like the others, but you disappeared."

He came to stand at her side, hovering above her. His heavy jowls quivered as he spoke. "You oughtn't have done that, my dear. It only postponed the inescapable. But God's will cannot be averted. He brought you back to me, and now I will carry out His wishes."

Brandt! her mind screamed. And though she knew

there was no way for him to know where she was, no way to realize she was in trouble, she couldn't help being irritated by the fact that after all the times he'd refused to leave her alone when she hadn't wanted him around . . . the one time she needed him, he wasn't there.

Willow wet her dry lips, forcing herself to speak. "You . . . you killed those girls, didn't you?" She asked the question to distract Chatham, to hopefully slow his plans, but also to get him to confess. If a miracle occurred and she did get out of this dungeon alive, she wanted to know every detail of his crimes so there would be no doubt of his guilt. *If* she survived, she would arrest him and testify against him in a court of law, using his own words to convict him.

"Of course I killed them," he answered proudly, turning away from her. "Though it wasn't really murder, as you and those other Pinkertons believe. You can't consider eradicating evil to be murder."

"And you think . . . you're Gideon, don't you?" The flesh of her wrists and ankles burned as she yanked them against the restraints. She felt a stickiness spread over her skin and knew they'd begun to bleed. And still she fought, hoping the added wetness of the blood would help her slip a hand or foot free.

Chatham laughed, a sound that sent chills down her spine. "My dear, you are even worse off than I imagined if you believe I think myself to be the great Gideon. You cannot be someone who existed so long ago. No, I am merely carrying on with his work, his calling. Gideon rid the world of whores and sinners, and I am doing the same. It's God's will."

He turned back to her, a long silver sword glinting in his hands.

"But if you're killing people," she continued, wanting to keep him and that blade as far away as possible, for as long as possible, "doesn't that make you a sinner, too?"

He stopped, his body tensing, the weapon in his hands trembling with rage. "No," he snapped. "You don't understand. You don't see. I'm blessed, sent here on a mission: to cleanse the world of offenders such as yourself."

"What about Charlie? Was he a sinner, too?"

His bushy brows knit and the sword dropped a fraction at his confusion. "Who?"

"Charlie Barker. The Pinkerton agent killed on that passenger train."

"Oh, him."

Chatham said it as though the man had been of no consequence. A man with a wife and three children, who worked hard every day of his life, meant nothing to this maniac.

"I hadn't intended to hurt him. He wasn't a sinner, as far as I could tell. But he was one of you, wasn't he? A Pinkerton agent." He put the point of the blade to the ground and leaned forward, using the length of the weapon to prop up his ample weight. He shrugged a shoulder, indifferent to a man's death. "He knew too much, that's all. He'd found out about my actions because of Yvonne and would have tried to stop me. So I had Outram take care of the problem. I will not be thwarted," he added sharply.

He was insane. He thought he was killing for God and had no compunction over slaughtering anyone who got in his way or threatened to hinder his plans.

She had to keep him talking. Every moment he remained over there was another moment that her heart beat and her lungs were allowed to draw air. Another moment they had to find her—if anyone was even looking.

"Why Yvonne?" she queried. "She wasn't like the other girls."

"Yvonne was a whore," he declared with vehemence. "I thought she was pure, but she was as corrupt as the rest, dallying with that young man outside her parents' home. That's when I realized there were sinners in my own circle. I won't be so shortsighted from now on, I assure you. I'd decided you would be next, even before I realized you weren't who you claimed to be." He raised the sword in both hands, once again aiming it skyward and stalking toward her. "You're just one of many. I intend to continue my duty to God. I will not be stopped."

He stood above her now, the sharpened blade drawing her full attention as she envisioned it plunging into her breast, stealing her life. Oh, God, she didn't want to die. She didn't want to leave Erik and Brandt, not now.

She loved Brandt and she'd never even told him. She'd agreed to marry him, but she'd never actually spoken the words. Possibly because she hadn't realized until just this moment how true they were. She *did* love him, and she *did* want to spend the rest of her life with him, even though he'd badgered her into accepting his proposal.

And now it was too late, because she was going to die. She would never get the chance to tell him how much he meant to her, never get the chance to be the best wife she knew how to be.

"What about Outram? Will you leave him to rot in prison?" Her voice rose in panic.

"Sometimes one must be sacrificed for the benefit of all." His face hardened and he scowled down at her. "No more questions. Let's get on with it."

Willow jerked at the manacles until her joints screamed in agony. It was over. He was going to kill her and there was nothing she could do to stop it. She squeezed her eyes closed and began to pray. Tears slipped down her face and into her hair as he began to chant.

"Asperges me, Domine, hyssopo, et mundabor: lavabis me, et super nivem dealbabor . . ."

Chapter Thirty-three

She wasn't here. He'd searched every inch of Chatham's town house and found not hide nor hair of either of them.

Dammit, where could she be?

She had to be all right. He had to find her, and she had to be safe. He couldn't live with himself if Chatham hurt her, not when Brandt had been the one to leave her open to this threat.

Hell, he couldn't live without her. He *couldn't*. Willow was the only woman he'd ever loved, the only woman he ever *would* love, and he didn't want to think about a single day passing without her in his world.

He *had* to find her.

He started up the wide staircase again, his hand on the newel post, when he felt the wood beneath his fingers give. Moving down a step, he tested the large cherrywood sphere. When pushed in one direction, the piece didn't budge. But when pushed in the other, it slid almost an inch to the side. At the same time, he heard a low squeak.

Rounding the banister, he began looking for the source of that sound. Behind him, the front door sprang open, much the same way it had when he'd kicked it in not ten minutes before. Robert entered, followed by half a dozen armed Pinkertons.

"Where are they?" Robert demanded.

"Damned if I know. I've searched all the rooms; they're nowhere to be found." He indicated the newel post he'd investigated moments earlier. "But I think there is something odd about this staircase."

"Like what?" Robert closed the distance between them and followed Brandt as he continued his search for the origin of the noise he'd heard.

"I don't know, but I'm going to find out." He ran his hands over the polished railing, the progressively increasing height of the wall beneath the stairs, even the floorboards.

He did this for the next few feet of space, and then paused as he sensed a slight protuberance.

"What is it?" Robert queried.

"This part of the wall. It sticks out a bit." He tested every inch of the silk covering and discovered seams at the top and bottom. And on the far left, what appeared to be the opening of a doorway, a fraction of an inch ajar. As though the movement of the newel post had released a hidden latch that kept the secret entrance closed.

As Brandt slid the panel open, he heard voices. Muted and impossible to decipher, but voices all the same. One of which he thought was Chatham's. The other he prayed was Willow's, because that would mean he'd not only found her, but she was still alive.

He inclined his head, signaling Robert, who in turn

gave silent, hand-gestured orders to his men. Even with the flicker of light glowing from below, the decline was dark as a tomb, and it took a moment for their eyes to adjust. With Brandt in the lead, they made their way down the uneven stone steps.

Brandt didn't have a weapon, but he didn't need one when he stepped out of the stairwell and saw Virgil Chatham standing over a tied and defenseless Willow with a downthrust sword aimed directly at her heart.

An animal-like snarl burst from his lips as he hurtled himself into the bastard, grabbing his arms and tackling him to the ground. Brandt tossed the long blade away and began to pummel the soft flesh of Chatham's face. Blood spurted from his nose, split lip, and the slice Brandt's diamond-studded Union Pacific ring made along his cheekbone.

In his peripheral vision, Brandt saw Robert's men surrounding them while Robert released Willow's arms and legs from the iron shackles and drew her into his embrace. Brandt continued to deliver powerful right hooks to the worthless piece of refuse curled into a ball on the floor.

One of the Pinkerton men put a hand on his shoulder. "We've got him, sir. You can stop, we've got him."

His punches slowed. Gasping for breath, Brandt straightened and stared at the man beneath him, fury still washing through him in waves. He wanted to kill him. With his bare hands, he wanted to strangle the life out of Virgil Chatham. For daring to touch Willow, for scaring twenty years off his life, and for murdering all those other women.

Instead, he settled for kicking the bastard straight between the legs and hearing his howl of pain as he writhed on the floor and clutched at his damaged goods.

He left the Pinkerton agents to take Chatham into custody and moved to Willow's side. Shuddering in relief, she lifted her tearstained face from Robert's shoulder and immediately threw herself into Brandt's arms.

"Thank God," he breathed into her hair, squeezing her tight and rocking back and forth as he might with a distraught child. "Thank God you're all right. I'm so sorry I left you. I should have known he would try something like this. I'll never leave you alone again, I swear." He was babbling and he knew it, but he'd never been so frightened—or so relieved—in his life.

Pulling slightly away, Willow framed his face with her hands and held his gaze, her violet eyes burning into his own, which were beginning to feel a little misty.

"I love you." She said the words so softly, he feared he'd heard her wrong. He blinked and leaned close, hoping she would repeat herself so he could be sure.

"I love you," she said once more. "I was so afraid I wouldn't get the chance to tell you that. And I really do want to marry you, for all the right reasons."

Wrapping her arms around his neck, she hugged him again. And this time, neither of them loosened their hold until Robert cleared his throat and told them Virgil Chatham had been taken away.

Brandt shrugged out of his jacket and draped it around Willow's bare shoulders, then scooped her up and carried her out of the dank cellar room. Once they reached the main floor of the house, Brandt settled Willow on the edge of a medallion-backed sofa, found a blanket to cover her with, and then returned her to the cradle of his arms.

"I'm taking her home," he told Robert as he moved toward the door at the front of the house. Their things— or Willow's, at least—should have been transferred back to them Astor House by now.

The vehicles Robert and his men had arrived in stood

at the curb. He opened the door of the nearest and stepped up, Willow still held securely against his chest.

"Where's Erik?" she asked, lifting her face and squinting a bit at the bright light of day after being trapped in the underground prison for so long.

"He's fine," Robert put in, standing in the doorway of the carriage. "He's back at my office with Mrs. Girard."

"I want to see him."

Robert reached in a hand to pat her leg beneath the thick afghan. "You go back to your room with Donovan. I'll fetch Erik and bring him over directly."

She nodded and returned her head to Brandt's shoulder.

"Take care of her," Robert said quietly, reflecting the somberness of Brandt's expression.

"You can count on it."

This time when Willow awoke it was without pain and to the sound of soft voices drifting in from the other room. She stretched languorously and snuggled back into the pillows, listening to Erik regale Brandt with another of his larger-than-life stories. Brandt interrupted to make the occasional comment or remind Erik to keep his voice down so he wouldn't wake his sister, but otherwise feigned interest in every word Erik uttered.

After a few more minutes of just lying there, gathering her strength, Willow sat up and threw her legs over the edge of the bed. She found her robe hanging in the wardrobe and shrugged into it, tucking her hair behind her ears as she entered the adjoining room.

Brandt was sitting on one of the stuffed armchairs before the hearth, watching Erik run from one end of the settee to the other, jumping, twisting, and talking all at once. And in the chair facing away from her sat Robert. Only the back of his head was visible, but she easily recognized him from the color and cut of his hair.

Brandt spotted her first and leapt to his feet. "How are you feeling?" His hands cupped her elbows to avoid her bandaged wrists, and his eyes, dark with worry, examined her for evidence of damage.

"Fine. I'm fine." She squeezed his arm and smiled to reassure him. Truly, she felt wonderful. The time she'd been held captive by Virgil Chatham had been a nightmare, yes, but it was over now. Two murderers had been arrested and would pay for their crimes. She had been frightened but not harmed and was safe now. They were *all* safe.

And though it sounded foolish, she was almost grateful for her experiences this afternoon because they had prompted her to think about her life and make some important decisions and realizations. The most vital being that she loved the man standing in front of her, looking so concerned about her welfare.

She tapped a finger between his eyes, smoothing his wrinkled brow. "Don't look so worried," she told him lightly.

Glancing over his shoulder, she saw Robert waiting a few feet away, seeming equally fretful.

"Will you two please *stop?* Take a lead from Erik," she said, moving to her brother's side. He stopped dancing on the sofa cushions and threw himself into her arms. Willow hugged him tight and sat to arrange his small frame on her lap. "You're not worried about me, are you?"

He shook his head, rubbing the silky material of her robe between his fingers. "Soft," he murmured. And then he lifted his head and focused on the bruised abrasion

299

at her temple. "Does it hurt?" he asked, touching the spot lightly.

"Shh," she whispered, leaning close as though sharing a secret. "We don't want to upset Brandt and Robert again. And it doesn't hurt." She raised her voice for the men's benefit and grinned at Brandt, because she hadn't licked her lips before telling that little white lie.

It *did* hurt, if truth be known. How could it not when she'd been cracked in the skull not once but twice with a rather impressive walking stick? But it wasn't overly painful and would heal soon enough, which made it hardly worth fussing about.

"Is everything all right?" she asked Robert, wondering at his presence.

He nodded but made a motion with his eyes in Erik's direction that made Willow suspect he didn't want to talk in front of the child. It was probably time to put Erik to bed, anyway. According to the mantel clock and the black outside the hotel room windows, it was after nine o'clock.

"Let me just put Erik down for the night," she said, standing and letting Erik slide to his feet on the floor.

"No, I don't want to," he whined. "I don't want to. I want to stay with you." Erik put up a fuss about going to bed, but Willow firmly informed him that he'd had quite enough excitement for one day. And even if *he* wasn't tired, Brandt certainly must be, so they were all retiring for the night just as soon as Robert left in a few more minutes. He huffed, sticking out his lower lip in a pout while she led him into the bedroom and arranged a makeshift bed out of the chaise lounge, but he didn't argue further.

Once he was settled and covered and muttering beneath his breath about not being allowed to stay up longer, Willow turned back to the sitting room, closing the connecting door behind her.

"Chatham has been arrested and will stand trial with his valet for murder," Robert said as soon as she'd returned. "The police have someone working with Kyne to get information about Chatham's crimes and hopefully gain a written confession. We think the servant killed Charlie on Chatham's orders."

"He did," Willow agreed. "Even though Yvonne Xavier wasn't a prostitute, Chatham killed her because he thought she was no better than a whore. He apparently saw her in some man's embrace and decided that was enough of a transgression to require her to die."

She rolled her eyes in disgust. Robert knew all about her and Brandt's theory concerning Chatham's fixation with the biblical figure Gideon and his belief that he was killing sinners in the name of God.

"Charlie must have figured out what was going on," she continued. "He got too close and made Chatham nervous, which is when he ordered Outram to get rid of him."

"You may have to testify," Robert warned her. "And the police will want to question you about what occurred in that cellar, as well as what you learned from Chatham."

Willow inclined her head. She'd known that and was prepared to do whatever was necessary to keep both Chatham and Kyne behind bars for the rest of their lives.

"Other than that," Robert said cheerily, "I only stayed to make sure you were all right, and to keep Donovan, here, from disturbing you." He cast a glance behind him at a scowling Brandt. "He attempted to 'check' on you more than once, as well as threatening to call in another physician, and I was afraid 'checking' would include waking. I thought you needed your rest."

"Thank you, but he's only practicing," she told Robert, grinning at Brandt's deepening frown. "He did tell you we're getting married, didn't he?"

"He mentioned something along those lines, but I didn't believe him," Robert teased. " 'My Willow?' I said. 'Never! She's much too smart to fall for a wastrel like you.' But he insisted, and now that you've supported his story, I guess I have no choice but to accept his word."

With a wide smile, he came forward and put his arms around her waist for a quick hug. "Congratulations. I hope you'll be very happy. All three of you," he added, with a nod at the bedroom where Erik slept.

"Well," he continued, "I'd best be going." Grabbing his hat from the low table before the settee, he twisted the band of the bowler and moved for the door. "If you need anything, be sure to let me know."

"We will, thank you."

As soon as Robert departed, Willow turned and walked straight into Brandt's arms.

"I hope we don't have many more days like this one." Brandt feathered his fingers through her hair, careful to avoid the bump on the side of her head.

"Mmm," she murmured in languid agreement. Her lids felt heavy even though she'd just awakened from a rather lengthy nap.

"I think we need a happy day for a change," he continued, pulling her with him onto the settee. He propped his legs on the low table in front of the sofa and arranged hers over his lap, tucking her head into his shoulder. "So when do you want to marry me?"

She lifted her face and smiled at him. For the first time in as long as she could remember, she was truly, completely content.

Wrapping her arms around his neck and placing a warm, hard kiss on his lips, she curled her fingers into the smooth chambray of his shirt. "Any day you say," she whispered softly. "Any day you say."

Epilogue

Two months later . . .

"I still can't believe you and Brandt are getting married," said Megan McCain, one of Willow's best friends and her matron of honor, as she stood behind Willow at the cheval glass and adjusted the long folds of diaphanous veil covering the auburn waves of her hair. "When Lucas and I asked Brandt to stop in Jefferson City to check up on you, we never expected this."

Willow couldn't quite believe it either. Oh, not the part about falling in love with Brandt. That had been inevitable, even in the beginning, when she'd fought so hard against it. But she couldn't believe she was standing in this opulent hotel room, readying herself to be married. The stiff satin encasing her body from the tips of her toes to just above her breasts should have assured her of the situation, but instead it only made her feel more stupefied.

304

Brandt was downstairs, she knew, waiting for the ceremony to begin. Probably chatting with Lucas and Caleb and his sisters' husbands, and keeping Erik out of trouble, she hoped. Though Erik seemed to have found a kindred spirit in Caleb and Rebecca Adams's son, Zachary. The two boys had been playing together ever since Brandt's friends had arrived in New York three days earlier.

Willow hadn't known the Adamses before now, but from the moment she'd met them, she'd liked them immensely. Megan was Caleb's younger sister, and though she was married now, with a child of her own, they still seemed very close. Having lost out on family ties during her own childhood, kith and kin meant a lot to Willow, and she felt that these people, who weren't actually related by blood, were about to become the next best thing. Brandt had assured her this was so.

Right now, she wished she could imagine her soon-to-be husband pacing and tugging at his collar, as nervous as she. Brandt, however, was the calmest groom she'd ever encountered. And any time she'd mentioned this apparent tranquility of his—in complete contrast to her own belly full of butterflies—he'd simply smiled that sexy, charming smile he reserved only for her and said he had nothing to be anxious about; he was marrying the woman of his dreams.

Well, she was marrying the man of *her* dreams, but that didn't keep her from feeling queasy and clammy and ready to jump out of her skin.

The queasiness, she admitted, could be due to something else entirely. She wasn't positive, since they'd been quite careful about preventing such things, but she had been feeling a touch nauseous in the mornings of late and was a few days overdue for her monthly courses. This wasn't something she wanted to share with

Heidi Betts

Brandt until she was certain, but it was just as well they
were getting married now instead of later.

As though sensing Willow's thoughts about babies, a
low whimper sounded from the bed behind them, and
Megan turned to shush her two-month-old daughter,
Tessa. She had a dark crop of hair just like her mother's,
but Megan insisted she'd inherited her father's stubborn
chin.

The door behind them opened, and Willow whirled
back around to see Rebecca Adams carrying a lovely
bouquet of pink, red, and white roses, with a few bright
yellow daisies added to the mix.

Willow smiled at the woman she'd heard so much
about from not only Brandt but Megan. Rebecca had
light brown hair pulled back in a chignon and a bright,
ready smile. And though she wasn't wearing them now,
a pair of wire-rimmed spectacles had perched on her
nose last evening while she'd helped Willow add one
small adjustment to her otherwise perfect gown.

Willow had also gotten to meet all five of Brandt's
well-meaning but nosy sisters in the past few weeks, and
all she could say was that she was glad they lived a ways
off in Boston.

The only reason she wasn't surrounded by them now
was because she'd asked that they please plan the wedding, from which minister should perform the service
right down to the type of flowers that should be woven
into her veil. After waiting so long for their near-
hopeless brother to finally tie the knot, they had not only
seen to every detail of the ceremony but had talked all
five of their husbands into paying all the expenses—
including a short honeymoon in Paris, of all places.

Erik was to take turns staying with each of them so
he could play with and get to know all of Brandt's nieces
and nephews. This prospect delighted Erik, as he sud-

denly found himself surrounded by more friends and
family than he could count.

When she'd learned of his sisters' machinations, Willow had laughingly told Brandt that their honeymoon
might be the perfect time to brush up on her French.
He'd agreed that would be just fine, as long as she stuck
to her former version of the word *headache* and never
learned the proper translation.

"Everyone's waiting," Rebecca told them, breaking
into Willow's thoughts. She handed Willow the bouquet,
tied with a strip of yellow ribbon that matched the cen-
ters of the daisies, as well as the spring blossoms
threaded through the bride's hair. "Are you ready?"

Willow's heart stuttered in her chest. Why was she so
nervous? It was Brandt, she reminded herself. She loved
him, wanted to spend the rest of her life with him. Of
that she had no doubts whatsoever.

But this was a big step. She'd testified in the cases
against Virgil Chatham and Outram Kyne and seen them
both convicted, so that pressure was out of the way. And
even though she and Brandt were remaining in New
York and she was staying with the Agency, she knew
that their marriage would change things. She would
work and travel less, spend more time at home with Erik
and Brandt. Maybe even with the children she and
Brandt would have together.

She was looking forward to that, she thought, placing
a hand low on her abdomen and wondering if her suspicions were correct. A year ago, she would have
scoffed at the idea of becoming a mother. Now, she almost craved it. Which was why the prospect of cutting
back on her Pinkerton duties didn't bother her as much
as it probably should have.

Willow took a deep breath and let all the tension seep
from her body. Now that she thought through the

changes taking place in her life, she realized she was no longer as anxious as she had been. In fact, she felt quite calm, anticipating the hours to come.

"One thing," she said, and moved to the nightstand beside the bed. Lifting up the hem of her skirt, she slipped the pearl-handled stilleto into her garter. The blue one with the bells that Brandt liked so much.

There. She always felt better when she was armed.

Straightening the folds of her gown, she turned to the other two women. "Do I look all right?"

"You look beautiful." Rebecca gave her a strange look and asked tentatively, "Do you always carry a knife in your garter?"

"Not always," Willow answered, keeping a straight face. "Sometimes I carry a gun."

Megan chuckled. "It's not the weapon that caught my attention. I'm curious about the bells." And then she gave Willow a wink. "Can I borrow those things after you get back? Lucas would love them."

All three women broke out in laughter, and Willow promised to lend her garters to each woman in turn—if she couldn't find new ones in Paris, which she swore to give her very best effort.

"Brandt is going to faint when he sees you in that dress," Megan added, lifting baby Tessa into her arms. "You look amazing."

"Thank you." Flexing and unflexing her fingers around the bouquet in her hand, she said, "I guess I'm ready, then. Lead the way."

She followed Rebecca and Megan into the long hallway and down to the first floor of the luxurious hotel. One of the banquet rooms had been set up with ribbons and flowers and rows of chairs that were now occupied by the hundred or so guests Brandt's sisters had insisted be invited. The equally large room across the hall was filled with tables and attendants waiting to serve the wedding party immediately after the ceremony.

Rebecca passed through the heavy double doors and walked quietly to her husband's side, where he stood talking with Brandt and Lucas in hushed tones. A moment later, Caleb came to the back of the room and offered his arm to Willow. She smiled at her escort and slipped her hand around his elbow.

Balancing little Tessa on one shoulder, Megan propped the doors open and then scuttled ahead to her seat, nodding to the organist and minister as she approached.

The music began, and Caleb gave Willow a reassuring smile as they began slowly walking down the cloth-covered aisle. Brandt stood at the other end, looking as handsome as ever in his charcoal woolen dress suit. When he saw her, all expression washed from his face. His eyes widened and his mouth dropped, and then a smile as wide and charming and sexy as she'd ever seen crossed his face.

He made her feel beautiful and wanted, and she wished they could walk a little faster down this aisle.

Erik sat in the first chair on the bride's side, craning his neck to look back at her and grinning his bright, gap-toothed grin. She was surprised to see that his suit was still in fairly decent condition. He'd pulled the black bow-shaped tie from around his neck, but otherwise he looked like a young gentleman.

When they reached the minister, Caleb kissed her cheek before transferring her hand from his to Brandt's and taking a seat beside his wife and children.

Brandt pulled her close and whispered in her ear, "At least I know you didn't bring a gun to our wedding. There isn't a breath of space to spare in that gown."

She met his eyes and shot him a mischievous grin. "I

wouldn't be so sure about that, Donovan. I may not have brought my gun, but there was just enough room near my thigh for a knife."

He threw back his head and laughed, heedless of the multitude of guests who shot them funny looks. She bit down on a chuckle of her own and gave him a warning cuff to the arm before shifting slightly to face the minister.

They listened as the black-gowned cleric spoke of love and commitment. And then he addressed Brandt as he asked, "Do you, Brandt Maxwell Donovan, take this woman to be your lawfully wedded wife?"

Brandt met her gaze and softly answered, "I do."

Then the reverend repeated the question for her. "And do you, Willow Elizabeth Hastings, take this man to be your lawfully wedded husband?"

She looked into Brandt's green eyes, bright and shining like emeralds, and couldn't keep the happiness from spreading across her face. "Oh, yes," she said in a low voice, never so sure of anything in her life. "I definitely, definitely do."

Before the minister even gave him permission to do so, Brandt leaned forward and kissed her. And for the very first time as Mrs. Willow Donovan . . . she kissed him back.

AUTHOR'S NOTE

I have always been fascinated by the Pinkerton National Detective Agency and enjoyed every minute of the research for *Almost a Lady.* I was even more excited when it seemed that each fact I discovered lent itself to Brandt and Willow's story.

For instance, while Allan Pinkerton (founder of the Pinkerton National Detective Agency) was alive, female operatives were quite common to the organization. He recognized what an asset the fairer sex could be to an investigation, understanding that a woman could not only use her feminine wiles to get information, but that a woman often would not be considered suspect as readily as a man. Unfortunately, his colleagues didn't necessarily agree with him. After Allan's death in 1884, those who took over the Agency began eliminating female operatives from the payroll.

In real life, Robert Pinkerton was Allan's second son and did work under Superintendent Francis Warner at the New York office. Allan's first son, William, remained at the Chicago branch.

Yes, I did take a bit of literary license while creating Robert's character for this story, but I hope that I did his family justice. After all, I have always admired the Pinkertons greatly and like to think that if I'd been born a hundred years earlier, I might have had the chance to be a Pinkerton agent myself.

Fairest of Them All

Josette Browning

A true stoic and a gentleman, Daniel Canty has worked furiously to achieve the high esteem of the English nobility. Therefore, it is more his reputation than the promise of wealth that compels him to accept the ninth earl of Hawkenge's challenge to turn an orphan wild child into a lady. But the girl who's been raised by animals in the African interior is hardly an orphan—and his wildly beautiful charge is hardly a child. Truly, Talitha is a woman—and the most compelling Daniel has ever seen. But the mute firebrand also poses the greatest threat he has ever faced. In the girl's soft kiss is the jeopardy which Daniel has fought all his life to avoid: the danger of losing his heart.

___4513-3 $5.50 US/$6.50 CAN

Always

Lynsay Sands

Bastard daughter to the king, Rosamunde is raised in a convent and wholly prepared to take the veil . . . until good King Henry shows up with a reluctant husband in tow for her. Suddenly, she finds herself promising to love, honor, and obey Aric . . . always. But Rosamunde's education has not covered a wedding night, and the stables are a poor example for an untried girl. Will Aric bite her neck like the animals do their mates? The virile warrior seems capable of such animal passion, but his eyes promise something sweeter. And Rosamunde soon learns that while she may have trouble with obeying him, it will not be hard to love her new husband forever.

___4736-5 $5.50 US/$6.50 CAN

Dorchester Publishing Co., Inc.
P.O. Box 6640
Wayne, PA 19087-8640

Please add $1.75 for shipping and handling for the first book and $.50 for each book thereafter. NY, NYC, and PA residents, please add appropriate sales tax. No cash, stamps, or C.O.D.s. All orders shipped within 6 weeks via postal service book rate. Canadian orders require $2.00 extra postage and must be paid in U.S. dollars through a U.S. banking facility.

Name_____
Address_____
City_____ State_____ Zip_____
I have enclosed $ _____ in payment for the checked book(s).
Payment <u>must</u> accompany all orders. ❏ Please send a free catalog.
       CHECK OUT OUR WEBSITE! www.dorchesterpub.com

Five Gold Rings — Constance O'Banyon, Stobie Piel, Lynsay Sands, Flora Speer

In the Year of Our Lord, 1135, Menton Castle is the same as any other: It has nobles and minstrels, knights and servants. Yet from the great hall to the scullery there are signs that the house is in an uproar. This Yuletide season is to be one of passion and merriment. The master of the keep has returned. With him come several travelers, some weary with laughter, some tired of tears. But in all of their stories—whether lords a'leapin' or maids a'milkin'—there is one gift that their true loves give to them. And in the winter moonlight, each of the castle's inhabitants will soon see the magic of the season and the joy that can come from five gold rings.

___4612-1 $5.50 US/$6.50 CAN

Dorchester Publishing Co., Inc.
P.O. Box 6640
Wayne, PA 19087-8640

Please add $1.75 for shipping and handling for the first book and $.50 for each book thereafter. NY, NYC, and PA residents, please add appropriate sales tax. No cash, stamps, or C.O.D.s. All orders shipped within 6 weeks via postal service book rate. Canadian orders require $2.00 extra postage and must be paid in U.S. dollars through a U.S. banking facility.

Name_____
Address_____
City_____State_____Zip_____
I have enclosed $_____ in payment for the checked book(s).
Payment <u>must</u> accompany all orders. ❑ Please send a free catalog.
        CHECK OUT OUR WEBSITE! www.dorchesterpub.com

Upon A Moon-Dark Moor

Rebecca Brandewyne

From the day Draco sweeps into Highclyffe Hall, Maggie knows he is her soulmate; the two are kindred spirits, both as mysterious and untamable as the wild moors of the rocky Cornish coast. Inexplicably drawn to this son of a Gypsy girl and an English ne'er-do-well, Maggie surrenders herself to his embrace. Hand in hand, they explore the unfathomable depths of their passion. But as the seeds of their desire grow into an irrefutable love, its consequences threaten to destroy their union. Only together can Maggie and Draco overcome the whispered scandals that haunt them and carve a future for their love.

___52336-1 $5.50 US/$6.50 CAN

And Gold Was Ours

Rebecca Brandewyne

In Spain the young Aurora's future is foretold—a long arduous journey, a dark, wild jungle, and a fierce, protective man. Now in the New World, on a plantation haunted by a tale of lost love and hidden gold, the dark-haired beauty wonders if the swordsman and warrior who haunts her dreams truly lived and if he can rescue her from the enemies who seek to destroy her. Together, will they be able to overcome the past and conquer the present to find the greatest treasure on this earth, a treasure that is even more precious than gold. . . .

___52314-0 $5.99 US/$6.99 CAN

Dorchester Publishing Co., Inc.
P.O. Box 6640
Wayne, PA 19087-8640

Please add $1.75 for shipping and handling for the first book and $.50 for each book thereafter. NY, NYC, and PA residents, please add appropriate sales tax. No cash, stamps, or C.O.D.s. All orders shipped within 6 weeks via postal service book rate. Canadian orders require $2.00 extra postage and must be paid in U.S. dollars through a U.S. banking facility.

Name_____
Address_____
City_____State_____Zip_____
I have enclosed $_____ in payment for the checked book(s).
Payment <u>must</u> accompany all orders. ❑ Please send a free catalog.
     CHECK OUT OUR WEBSITE! www.dorchesterpub.com

Savage Devotion
Cassie Edwards

Sailing the deep, clear waters of the Puget Sound, beautiful red-haired Janice Edwards is bound for a new beginning. Leaving behind the wealth and luxury she's known in San Francisco, she hopes to find a simpler, sweeter life in the towering forests of Tacoma . . . and a man who will love her for who she is, not what she has. But when the steamer *Hope* is wrecked by a sudden storm, Janice is rescued by a man like none she's even known. Tall, with muscular limbs and a powerful chest revealed by his buckskin clothing, he is a Skokomish Indian—from all she's heard, a savage to be feared. Yet in his gray eyes she sees tender caring, in his strong arms she discovers untold passion, and in his wild heart she will find . . . savage devotion.

___4735-7 $5.99 US/$6.99 CAN

Cinnamon and Roses
Heidi Betts

A hardworking seamstress, Rebecca has no business being attracted to a man like wealthy, arrogant Caleb Adams. Born fatherless in a brothel, Rebecca knows what males are made of. And Caleb is clearly as faithless as they come, scandalizing their Kansas cowtown with the fancy city women he casually uses and casts aside. Though he tempts innocent Rebecca beyond reason, she can't afford to love a man like Caleb, for the price might be another fatherless babe. What the devil is wrong with him, Caleb muses, that he's drawn to a calico-clad dressmaker when sirens in silk are his for the asking? Still, Rebecca unaccountably stirs him. Caleb vows no woman can be trusted with his heart. But he must sample sweet Rebecca.

Lair of the Wolf

Also includes the second installment of *Lair of the Wolf*, a serialized romance set in medieval Wales. Be sure to look for future chapters of this exciting story featured in Leisure books and written by the industry's top authors.

___4668-7 $4.99 US/$5.99 CAN

A Promise of Roses

Heidi Betts

Spunky Megan Adams will do almost anything to save her struggling stagecoach line—even confront the bandits constantly ambushing the stage for the payrolls it delivers. But what Megan *wouldn't* do is fall headlong for the heartbreakingly handsome outlaw who robs the coach, kidnaps her from his ornery amigos, and drags her half across Kansas—to turn *her* in as an accomplice to the holdup!

Bounty hunter Lucas McCain stops at nothing to get his man. Hired to investigate the pilfered payrolls, he is sure Megan herself is masterminding the heists. And he'll be damned if he'll let this gun-toting spitfire keep him from completing his mission—even if he has to hogtie her to his horse, promise her roses . . . and hijack her heart!

___4738-1 $4.99 US/$5.99 CAN

Dorchester Publishing Co., Inc.
P.O. Box 6640
Wayne, PA 19087-8640

Please add $1.75 for shipping and handling for the first book and $.50 for each book thereafter. NY, NYC, and PA residents, please add appropriate sales tax. No cash, stamps, or C.O.D.s. All orders shipped within 6 weeks via postal service book rate. Canadian orders require $2.00 extra postage and must be paid in U.S. dollars through a U.S. banking facility.

Name_____
Address_____
City_____ State_____ Zip_____
I have enclosed $ _____ in payment for the checked book(s).
Payment <u>must</u> accompany all orders. ❏ Please send a free catalog.
        CHECK OUT OUR WEBSITE! www.dorchesterpub.com